"I want a chance to talk to you alone. No business. Just personal stuff."

"No business? Justin, all we have between us is business." She didn't want to admit to herself or Justin that there was a spark of anything other than business fire between them.

"But we could have so much more. What harm could one drink do?"

"One drink," she repeated. Hell, who was she kidding, she was going to meet him. She wanted to get the measure of the man he was.

"Just one," he said. "I'll do my best to be charming and try to convince you to stay for more."

"I'm a tough cookie," she said.

"I think that's what you want the world to believe, but I bet there's a softer woman underneath all that."

But would she give him a chance to find out?

Dear Reader,

Family is essential to me, and I love writing books that involve a large family. My very first book for Desire™, *The Bachelor Next Door*, was the first time I used alienation from a family as a conflict. In that book my hero's family was all dead and he was the last of his clan. In this book, Selena Gonzalez removed herself from her family because she felt guilty for falling in love with a con man and costing her family everything they owned.

Justin Stern and his brothers are close and have spent most of their lives together, but Justin is a bit of a loner. My sister Donna would say that's because he's the middle child. But I think it's also because of his personality. Justin likes to do things his own way. So falling in lust with his rival doesn't look like anything more than a minor setback to him.

Happy reading!

Katherine

SEDUCING HIS OPPOSITION

BY
KATHERINE GARBERA

Published in Great Britain 2012
by Mills & Boon, an imprint of Harlequin (UK) Limited,
Eton House, 18-24 Paradise Road, Richmond, Surrey TW9 1SR

© Katherine Garbera 2011

ISBN: 978 0 263 89105 8

51-0112

Harlequin (UK) policy is to use papers that are natural, renewable and
recyclable products and made from wood grown in sustainable forests. The
logging and manufacturing processes conform to the legal environmental
regulations of the country of origin.

Printed and bound in Spain
by Blackprint CPI, Barcelona

Katherine Garbera is the *USA TODAY* bestselling author of more than forty books. She's always believed in happy endings and lives in Southern California with her husband, children and their pampered pet, Godiva. Visit Katherine on the web at www.katherinegarbera.com, or catch up with her on Facebook and Twitter.

One

Justin Stern pulled his Porsche 911 to a stop in the parking lot of the Miami-Dade County Zoning Offices. As the corporate attorney and co-owner of Luna Azul he was always busy and he liked that. Unlike his younger brother Nate, who was out partying every night and keeping the nightclub in the public eye, Justin preferred the quiet comfort of his office. He had worked hard to make sure that Luna Azul was where it was today from a financial perspective and he was determined to see it continue to grow.

That's what he was doing here today—ensuring that the future of the club didn't just rely on the nightclub crowd. He had negotiated the purchase of a strip mall that was run-down and in desperate need of repair. He'd researched the deed and found that it had changed hands about ten years ago and that had been the start of the disrepair of the buildings.

He envisioned an outdoor plaza with restaurants and shops that would help revitalize the area and bring a new revenue stream into the Luna Azul Company.

All he needed to do was file the final paperwork here today, and they could proceed with the expansion plans.

It was a beautiful spring morning, but he took no notice of it as he walked to the building. He took the stairs to the eleventh floor instead of the elevator because elevators really weren't an efficient use of time. He was happy to see there were only two other people in the waiting room. He took a number from the reception desk and then took a seat next to a very pretty Latina woman.

She had thick hair that curled around her face and shoulders in soft waves. Her skin was flawless, her olive complexion making her brown eyes seem even bigger. Her lips were full and pouty; he found he couldn't tear his eyes from her face until she raised one eyebrow at him.

"I'm not a creep," he said with a self-effacing grin. "You're just breathtaking."

She flushed and rolled her eyes. "As if I'd believe that line."

"Why wouldn't you?" he asked, turning to face her.

"I'm used to smooth-talking men," she said. "I can spot one a mile away."

"Just because I'm complimenting you doesn't mean that I'm BSing you," he said. She was really lovely and he liked the soft sound of her voice. She was well put together. He had no idea of designers or fashion but her clothes looked nice—feminine. For the first time in a very long time he didn't mind having to wait.

"I suspect you can be very charming when you put your mind to it," she said.

"Perhaps," he said. "Not really. I'm usually straight to the point."

"You don't strike me as blunt," she said.

"I am," he said. He wasn't giving her a line—she really was gorgeous. She had caught his eye and distracted him. And he didn't mind at all. That was the surprising part for him. "Your eyes…are so big, I could get lost in them."

"Your eyes are so blue that they look like the waters in Fiji."

He laughed out loud. "Is that what I sound like to you?"

"Yes," she said with a smile. "Honestly, I'm not all that."

She was all that and a lot more, but he wasn't the best when it came to talking to women. In a corporate boardroom or at a negotiating table he was the best but one-on-one when he was interested in a girl…well that was when he got caught up.

"What brings you here?" he asked, then shook his head. "Zoning."

"Zoning," she said at the same time. "I'm here to file an injunction.

"Is it for your own company or a client?" he asked, wanting to know more.

"My grandparents think that an outside company is trying to buy their property and turn it into some big commercial club. So I'm checking it out for them."

"Do you live here in Miami then? Or just your grandparents?"

"My entire family lives here," she said. "But I live in New York."

"Oh. So ours will have to be a long-distance relationship," he said.

She raised her eyebrow at him. "This relationship might not make it out of the waiting room."

"I'm not giving up on us so easily," he said.

"Good. One of us should fight for this," she said, deadpan.

"I guess it will be me," he said with a grin. He couldn't help it. Something about this woman just made him smile.

A nattily dressed man came to the counter. "Number fifteen."

She glanced at the paper in her hand. "That's me."

"Just my luck. Any chance you'll give me your number?"

She tucked a thick strand of her hair behind her ear and reached into her handbag. "Here's my card. My cell number is on the bottom."

"I will call you," he said.

"I hope so…what's your name?"

"Justin," he said standing up and taking the card from her, but he didn't look at it. "Justin Stern. And what should I call you other than beautiful?"

She was quiet a moment as she looked him over, a light going on in her eyes. "Selena," she said. "Selena Gonzalez."

She walked away and he watched every sway of her hips. Then her name registered. Gonzalez was the last name of Tomas's big-gun lawyer and granddaughter. Selena Gonzalez…wait a minute; he was lusting after the corporate lawyer Tomas Gonzalez had called in from New York to stop his plans for the strip mall.

That wasn't cool.

Dammit, he wanted to call her. It wasn't very often

he met a woman who got his rather odd sense of humor and could banter with him. But now...

Then again, she didn't live here. She was in town for a few weeks at most, he thought. That made her the perfect woman for him.

Was he out of his mind? She was gumming up the plans he'd worked hard for. And if she was anything like her grandfather, she'd be stubborn and unwilling to realize that change was necessary if they were going to keep their section of Calle Ocho alive and kicking.

Selena Gonzalez left the zoning board with the information she needed and an injunction in hand. The emergency call from her grandfather three days ago made it sound like there was going to be a big bad company trying to take away her grandparents' market. From the information she just received...well, she still wasn't sure.

Justin Stern had intrigued her and made her wish that he was a stranger. But she'd heard enough about the smooth-talking rich boy who was trying to muscle out her grandparents to know that Justin wasn't the Mr. Congenial he had portrayed in the waiting room.

If the Luna Azul Company did succeed in developing the old strip mall that housed her grandparents' business now she had a feeling their neighborhood would change. She'd seen the plans that had been submitted by the company—they showed an upscale shopping area designed to bring tourists into the neighborhood. That wasn't what her grandparents' Latin American grocery store was about, but it wasn't the nightclub they feared would be built, either.

As she drove home, she took in the lush, tropical sights of Miami. Her family had wanted her home for a long time. She acknowledged to herself that if it hadn't been for this legal emergency she'd still be ignoring their pleas.

This area made her…it made her all the things that she didn't like about herself. When she was home she was impulsive and passionate. And made stupid decisions—like giving her number to a handsome stranger in a waiting room.

And after all that had happened with Raul ten years ago, she'd been afraid to come back home. She hadn't wanted to face her past or the memories that lingered everywhere she went in her old home and her old neighborhood. As she parked in front of her grandparents' house, she drew a deep breath.

"Did you get the injunction?" her grandfather asked, the minute she stepped through the door.

He wasn't an overly tall man—probably no more than five-eleven. Life had been good to Tomas Gonzalez and he wore his success with a gently rounded stomach. He could be tough as nails in business but he always had a smile for his family and a hug and kiss for her. One of fifteen grandchildren that lived in a three-block radius of his house, Selena had always felt well loved in this home. Especially after her parents' death eleven years ago. A drunk driver had taken both of her parents from her in one accident, leaving her little brother and her alone to face the world. Her grandparents had stepped in but it hadn't been the same.

"I did, *abuelito,*" she said. "And tomorrow I will go down to the Luna Azul Company offices and talk to them about our terms if they still want to go ahead with their plans."

She sat down at the large butcher-block table in the kitchen. The kitchen was the one room where they spent most of their time at her grandparents' house. Her grandmother was in the other room watching her shows.

"Very good, *tata.* I told you we needed you," he said. *Tata* was his nickname for her—just a sweet little endearment that made her feel loved every time he used it. "Those Stern brothers think they can come in and buy up all our property but they aren't part of our community."

"*Abuelito,* the Luna Azul Company has been a part of the community for ten years. From what they told me in the zoning office, they've done a lot for our community."

Her grandfather threw his hands up in the air. "Nothing, *tata,* that's what they have done for our community."

She laughed at him. She was used to his being passionate, even melodramatic about Little Havana. Her grandfather was part of the pre-communist Cuba—an energetic and creative environment—and he'd brought that with him to Miami when he'd become an exile. He still talked about Cuba with fond memories. It was a Cuba that no longer existed, but his stories were always enjoyable.

"What are you two laughing at?" her grandmother asked, coming in to refill her espresso cup with sugar and coffee.

"Those Stern brothers," her grandfather said. "I think Selena is just what we need to keep them in their place."

Her grandmother sat down beside her. She smelled of coffee and the gardenia perfume she'd always worn. She wrapped her arm around Selena's shoulder. "You promised to stay until summer, *tata*. Will you be able to take care of all this by then?"

She hugged her grandmother back. "Definitely. I want to make sure that you get the most out of this new development."

"Good. We want to own our market…the way we used to," Grandfather said.

Selena felt a pang around her heart as she realized that the reason they didn't own their own market was because of her. They were mere renters in the market the Sterns planned to develop, but once they had owned the place. Until Selena messed everything up. She had to make this right for them. "I met Justin Stern at the zoning office. So I will set up a meeting with him," Selena assured her grandparents.

"Good," her grandmother said. "I am going back to my shows. Are you staying at your house?"

"I haven't decided yet," she said. She still owned a house here. She didn't know if she wanted to go back and stay in it all alone. But staying here wasn't a solution; after living alone for so long, she needed her space.

She shrugged. "What's the use of owning a house if you never use it."

"I will send Maria over to make sure it's clean and ready for you," her grandmother said.

"That's not necessary," Selena said. Her grandparents were the caretakers of the old Florida house while she was in New York. It was the house she'd lived in with Raul while they'd both been in school at the University of Miami. There were a lot of memories in that place.

"I can clean it out if I need to," Selena said.

"No. We will make it ready for you. You concentrate on Luna Azul and Justin Stern," Grandfather said.

She shook her head. "He's a very charming man, *abuelita*. Have you met him?"

"No, but *abuelito* has, several times. You find him shrewd, right?" her grandmother said, turning to her husband.

"*Si*. Very shrewd and very…he watches people and then he makes an offer that is exactly right for you. He's like the devil."

Selena laughed, thinking that her grandfather's observation was spot on. "He is silver-tongued."

"*Si*. Watch yourself, *tata*. You don't want to fall for another man like that," her grandfather said.

She wrapped an arm around her own waist as her grandmother got to her feet and yelled at her grandfather in Spanish, telling him to let sleeping dogs lie. Selena quietly left the kitchen, going into the backyard and finding a seat on the bench nestled between blooming hibiscus plants underneath a large tree covered with orchids.

She'd stayed away for so long because of Raul and everything that had happened between them. But now that she was back she was going to have to face her past and really move on from it. Not run away as she'd done before. And she liked the thought of focusing on Justin Stern. He was just the man she needed to forget the past and start to live again here.

Justin signed a few papers that were waiting for his signature and then sent his administrative assistant out for lunch. *An injunction*. Selena Gonzalez with her sexy body and big eyes had filed an injunction against the company to keep them from beginning with their construction work until they proved that they were using local vendors. Now their plans for a ground-breaking in conjunction with the tenth anniversary gala was going to be slowed down if not halted.

"Got a minute?"

Justin glanced up to see his older brother Cameron standing in the doorway. Cam was dressed in business casual, as was his way. He was the one who ran the club and made sure the business there was on track. Unlike Justin, who always wore a suit and spent the majority of his time at his office here in the downtown high-rise complex.

"Sure. What's up?"

"How'd things go at the zoning office?" Cam asked, coming inside and sitting down in one of the leather armchairs in front of his desk.

"Not so good. The Gonzalez family filed an injunction against the building. I'm going to spend the afternoon working on the paperwork we need to file in response. I'm hoping to speak with their lawyer later and see if we can negotiate some kind of deal."

"Damn. I wanted to have the ground-breaking at the tenth anniversary celebration. I was also hoping we could maybe sign up some new, high-profile tenants, but this could put a damper on things."

"I will do what I can to make it happen. Don't get your hopes up, the neighbors and existing tenants in that market don't like us."

"Use your charm to convince them otherwise," Cam said.

"I'm not charming."

"Hell, I know that. You should send Myra."

"My assistant?"

"Yes, she's friendly and everyone likes her."

She was nice, but she didn't have the right kind of

experience to talk to the current occupants of the strip mall and make them understand what was needed.

"I'll head over there after I talk to Selena."

"Who is Selena?"

"Tomas Gonzalez's lawyer."

"Sounds like all the opening you need to get them on our team."

"Stop trying to manipulate me into doing what you want," he warned his brother.

"Why? I'm good at it."

Justin threw a mock punch at Cam who pretended to take the hit.

"Go. I have real work to do," Justin said.

"I will."

Cam left and Justin leaned back in his chair. He had plenty of business to keep him occupied but instead he was thinking of Selena Gonzalez—the lawyer and the woman.

His intercom buzzed. "There's a Ms. Gonzalez on line one."

Speak of the devil. He clicked over to the correct line. "This is Justin," he said.

"Hello, there."

"Hi. I must be remembering our conversation wrong," he said.

"I know I said I'd let you call but I've never been one of those women who waits for a man." Her voice was just as lovely over the phone as it had been in person. He closed his eyes and let the sound of it wash over him. She was distracting. And he needed to keep her from shaking him from his target.

"I'm glad to hear that. I thought you might be difficult given that you filed an injunction against me."

"That wasn't personal, Justin," she said. And he liked the way his name sounded on her lips.

"Yes, it was, Selena. What can I do for you?"

"I didn't realize we had mutual interests," she said. "When we met, I mean."

"I know what you meant…by mutual interests do you mean we both want to ensure that the Latin market is a vibrant part of the community?

"I want to make sure that some big-deal club owner doesn't take the community heritage and bastardize it for his own good."

"I guess you're not coming in here with any pre-conceived notions," he said wryly.

"No, I'm not, I know exactly what kind of man I'm up against. My *abuelito* said you are a silver-tongued devil and I should watch myself around you."

"Selena, you have nothing to fear from me," he said. "I'm a very fair businessman. In fact, I think your *abuelito* will be very happy with my latest offer."

"Send it to me and I will let you know."

"Come down to my office so we can talk in person. I prefer that to emails and faxes."

He leaned back in his chair. He knew how to nego-tiate, and having Selena here on his own turf was the way for him to get what he wanted. No one could turn him down once he started talking. To be honest, he'd never had a deal go south once he got the other party in the same room with him.

"Okay, when?"

"Today if you have time."

"Can you hold on?"

"Sure," he said. The line went silent and he turned to look out his plate-glass windows. The skyline of downtown Miami was gorgeous and he appreciated how lucky he was to live in paradise.

"Okay, we can do it today."

"We?"

"My *abuelito* and I."

"Great. I look forward to seeing Tomas again."

"And what about me?" she asked.

"I've thought of little else but seeing you again."

She laughed. "I'm tempted to believe you, but I know you are a businessman and business must always come first."

She was right. He wanted her to be different but the truth of the matter was that he was almost thirty-five and set in his ways. There was little doubt that someday he might want to settle down but it wasn't today.

And it wouldn't be with Selena.

"Good girl," he said.

"Girl?"

"I didn't mean that in a condescending way."

"How did you mean it?" she asked.

He had no idea if he'd offended her or not. "Just teasingly. Maybe I should stick to business. I'm much better at knowing what not to say."

She laughed again and he realized how much he liked the sound of that. He thought it prudent to get off the phone with her before he said something else that could put the entire outdoor plaza project at risk.

"I'll see you then. How does two o'clock sound?" he said.

"We'll be there," she agreed and hung up.

Two

As Selena and her grandfather left for their meeting, her other relatives were arriving to start cooking the dinner. Since she hadn't been home in almost ten years, the entire Gonzalez clan was getting together for a big feast.

To some people coming home might mean revisiting the place they had grown up, for her coming home meant a barbeque in the backyard of her grandparents' house and enough relatives to maybe require an occupancy permit.

Being a Gonzalez was overwhelming. She had forgotten how much she enjoyed the quiet of her life in Manhattan until this moment. This was part of what she'd run from. In Miami everyone knew her, in Manhattan she was just another person on the street.

She had the top down on her rental Audi convertible and the Florida sunshine warmed her head and the breeze stirred her hair as they drove to Justin Stern's office.

Having the top down did something else. It made conversation with her *abuelito* nearly impossible and right now she needed some quiet time to think. Though Justin Stern had flirted with her, she knew he was one sharp attorney and she'd need to have her wits about her when they talked.

"Selena?"

"Si?"

"You missed the turnoff," her grandfather said.

"I…dang it, I wasn't paying attention."

"What's on your mind?"

"This meeting. I want to make sure you and *abuelita* are treated fairly."

"You will, *tata*."

She made a U-turn at the next intersection and soon they were in the parking lot of Luna Azul Company's corporate headquarters. The building was large and modern but fit the neighborhood, and as she walked closer, Selena noticed that it wasn't new construction but had been a remodel. She made a mental note to check on this building and to investigate if having the Stern brothers here had enhanced this area.

"You ready, *abuelito?*"

"For what?"

"To take on Justin."

"Hell, yes. I've been doing it the best I can, but…we needed you," her grandfather said.

They entered the air-conditioned building. The receptionist greeted them and directed them to the fifth floor executive offices.

"Hello, Mr. Gonzalez."

"Hello, Myra. How are you today?" her grandfather

asked the pretty young woman who greeted them there.

"Not bad. Hear you've brought a big-gun lawyer to town," she said.

"I brought our attorney. Figured it was about time I had someone who could argue on Mr. Stern's level."

Myra laughed and even Selena smiled. She could tell that her grandfather had been doing okay negotiating for himself. Why had he called her?

"I'm Selena Gonzalez," Selena said stepping forward and holding out her hand.

"Myra Temple," the other woman said. "It's nice to meet you. You will be meeting in the conference room at the end of the hall. Can I get either of you something to drink?"

"I'll have a sparkling water," her grandfather said.

"Me, too," Selena said and followed her grandfather down the hall to the conference room.

The walls were richly paneled and there was a portrait of Justin and two other men who had to be his brothers. There was a strong resemblance in the stubborn jawline of all the men. She recognized Nate Stern, Justin's younger brother and a former New York Yankees baseball player.

Her *abuelito* sat down but she walked around the room, and checked out the view from the fifth floor and then the model for the Calle Ocho market center.

"Have you seen this, *abuelito*?"

He shook his head and came over to stand next to her. The Cuban American market that her grandparents owned was now replaced with a chain grocery store. She was outraged and angry.

"I can't believe this," Selena said.

"You can't believe what?" Justin asked as he entered

the conference room. Myra was right behind him with a tray of Perrier and glasses filled with ice cubes.

"That you think replacing the Cuban American market with a chain grocery store would be acceptable."

"To be honest we haven't got an agreement with them yet," Justin said. "This is just an artist's concept of how the Market will look."

"Well the injunction I filed today is going to hamper your agreement with them."

"It will indeed. That's why I invited you here to talk."

She was disgusted that she had fallen for his sexy smile and self-deprecating charm at the zoning office because she saw now that he was a smooth operator. And she'd had her fill of them when she was younger. It made her angry to think that in ten years she hadn't learned not to fall for that kind of guy.

"Then let's get to work," she said. "I've drawn up a list of concerns."

"I look forward to seeing them," Justin said. "And Tomas, it's nice to see you again," he said, shaking the older man's hand.

"I'd prefer it if we could stop meeting," Tomas said.

"To be fair I'd like that, too. I want to move this project forward," Justin said.

She bet he did, he was probably losing money with each day that they waited to break ground on their new market. But she was here to make sure that he realized that he couldn't come in and replace traditional markets with a shiny upscale shopping area with no ties to the community.

"What is your largest concern?" he asked. "This was a Publix supermarket strip mall before you first came to it, Tomas. So you have had chain grocers in the neighborhood before. We can invite another retailer if you'd prefer that."

Selena realized that Justin didn't necessarily understand what their objection to his building in the community truly was.

"Justin, this strip mall is part of the Cuban American community. Our family's store isn't just a place for people to pick up groceries, it's where the old men come in the morning for their coffee and then sit around and discuss the business of the day. It's a place where young mothers bring their kids to play in the back and have great Cuban food.

"This is the heart of the neighborhood. You can't just rip it out."

Justin knew this meeting wasn't going to be easy. He'd figured that out the moment he met Selena. She was the kind of woman that made a man work for it. And he knew that she was looking out for the interests of her community and to be fair he needed that community to want to shop there. Even though they'd do a good crossover business from the club and he had an arrangement with some local tour companies to add the new Luna Azul Market to their tourist stops once it opened, it would be the neighborhood residents that would make or break this endeavor.

"I'm open to your suggestions. So far Tomas has only demanded that we leave the strip mall the way it is and I think that we both know that isn't a solution."

"We both don't know that," she said.

"Have you been down to the property lately?" he asked her. "The mall is old and run-down. The families that you speak of are dwindling, isn't that right, Tomas?"

Tomas shrugged but then glanced over at Selena.

"The buildings need repairs and the landlord…you, Justin, should be making them."

"I want to make more than repairs. I'm not even sure if they meet the new hurricane wind resistance standards."

Selena pulled out a notebook and started writing on it. "We will check into it. Have you considered forming a committee with the community leaders and your company?"

"We've had a few informal discussions."

"You need to do a lot more than that. Because if you want the neighborhood support you are going to have to open a dialogue with them."

"Okay," Justin said. "But only if you serve on the committee."

She blinked up and then tipped her head to the side. "I don't think that I need to be on there."

"I do," Justin said. "You grew up there, and are also familiar with the legal and zoning issues. You will be able to see the bigger picture."

"I don't think—"

"I agree with him, *tata,* you should be on there," Tomas said.

"Tata?" Justin asked, smiling.

She glared at her grandfather. "It's a nickname."

She blushed, and it was the first crack he'd seen in her all-business, tough-as-nails shell.

The business deal was going to go through whether Tomas and his allies wanted it to or not. Justin had already scheduled a round of golf with the zoning commissioner, Maxwell Strong, at the exclusive club he belonged to to get him to change his mind. And over the next week he'd work on finding a way out of the legal hole that Selena had dug for him. But he wanted to see more of her.

And this committee thing would be perfect. Plus, he did actually want the community behind the project. "Myra, will you set up a meeting time for us...I think we should use Luna Azul. Tomas and Selena will send you a list of people to invite."

"I'd like to take a closer look at the plans for the market," Selena said.

"I'll leave you two to discuss that," Tomas said. "I need to call around and see when everyone will be available to meet."

"Myra will show you to an office you can use," Justin said.

After Tomas and Myra left the room, Justin studied Selena for a minute. Her head was bent and she was making notes on her legal pad. He noticed that her handwriting was very neat and very feminine.

"Why are you staring at me?"

"I thought I already told you that I like the way you look."

"That wasn't just you trying to...I don't know what you were up to. Did you know who I was in that lobby of the zoning office?"

He shook his head. "No. I wish I had known."

"Why?"

"Maybe I could have talked you out of filing that injunction," he said with a laugh.

She chuckled at that. "Wow, that's putting a lot of pressure on your supposed charm."

He grabbed his side pretending she'd wounded him. "Good thing I'm tough-skinned."

"You'd have to be in order to work in the neighborhood you do. How did you and your brothers manage to make

Luna Azul a success without getting the community behind you?" she asked him.

"Some locals do frequent the club but we rely on the celebs for business. They bring in their own crowd of followers. We book first-rate bands and we have salsa lessons in the rooftop club…so we do okay. Have you ever been there?"

She shook her head. "I left Miami before you opened your doors."

"Why did you leave?" he asked.

"None of your business," she replied with a tight look that told him he'd somehow gone too far.

"My apologies. I expected you to say you needed some freedom…would you have dinner with me tonight?"

"Why?"

"I believe in keeping my enemies close."

"Me, too," she said.

"I'll take that as a yes."

"It is a yes. But I'll pick the place." She wrote an address at the bottom of her legal pad and then tore the paper off and handed it to him. "Be there at seven. Dress casual."

"Do I need to bring anything?"

"Just your appetite."

She gathered her things and then stood up and walked out of the conference room. He watched her leave.

Inviting Justin to her family get-together was inspired. He wanted to do business in this community but he didn't understand it. This would be his lesson.

On her way home, she'd driven down to the strip mall to see her grandfather's store, and it had been run-down more than she expected.

Something was needed, but an outlet mall or a high-end shopping plaza wasn't it. The Calle Ocho neighborhood leaders wouldn't stand for. Plus, she wanted to ensure that her grandparents got the best deal possible.

They had always been at the center of things in Little Havana and she wasn't about to let Justin Stern take that away from them.

She also stopped by her house. When she entered, she was swamped with memories but managed to brush them aside as she freshened up and got ready to walk back over to her grandparents'. The last thing she wanted was to be here, she realized. She packed a bag with some clothes she found in the closet, locked the house and pointed her rented convertible toward the beach.

Her New York law practice had made her a wealthy woman. And considering this was the first real break she'd taken from work in the last eight years she thought she deserved a treat. All she did was work and save her money. Well that wasn't completely true—she did have an addiction to La Perla lingerie that wouldn't stop. But for the most part all she did was work.

So as she pulled up at the Ritz and asked for a suite for the next month, Selena knew she was doing the right thing. She was in luck and was soon ensconced in memory-free luxury. Just what she needed.

As she was settling in, her cell phone rang and she glanced at the number. It was a local number but not one she recognized. She answered it anyway. "This is Selena."

"This is Justin. How about if we have drinks at Luna Azul first so you can see the club?"

"No."

"Just a flat-out no, you aren't going to even pretend to think it over," he said.

"That's right. I am not staying near there, anyway. I'm at the Ritz," she said. She was kicked back on the love seat in her living room reading up on Justin on her laptop.

"How about a drink in the lobby bar?" he suggested. His voice was deep over the phone—very sexy.

"Why?" she asked. She wasn't sure spending any time alone with him was the right thing. She wanted to keep it all business between them. That was the only way she was going to keep herself from acting on the attraction she felt for him.

"I want a chance to talk to you alone. No business—just personal stuff."

"No business? Justin, all we have between us is business." She hoped that making that statement out loud would somehow make it true. She didn't want to admit to herself or Justin that there was a spark.

"But we could have so much more."

"Ha! You don't even know me," she said.

"That's exactly what I'm hoping to change. What harm could one drink do?"

"One drink," she repeated. Hell, who was she kidding? She was going to meet him. She'd invited him to her welcome-home party so he could get to know her family and not only because of business. She wanted to see how he was with them to get the measure of the man he was.

"Just one," he said. "I'll do my best to be charming and try to convince you to stay for more."

"I'm a tough cookie," she said.

"I think that's what you want the world to believe but I bet there's a softer woman underneath all that."

She hoped he never found out. She had tried so hard to bury the woman—*girl*—she'd been when she'd graduated from the University of Miami and left her hometown behind. Were there still any vestiges of that passionate side of her left after Raul had broken her heart?

Sure she dated, but she was careful that it was just casual, never letting her emotions get involved. Raul had taught her that the price to be paid for loving foolishly wasn't one that only she paid. Her grandparents had almost lost their business because of her poor judgment in men, and Selena had vowed to never be that weak again.

"Pretty much what you see is what you get with me," she said, uncomfortable talking about herself. "What about you? Are you all awkward charm and sleek business acumen?"

He laughed. "I guess so. It's hard when you grow up with a charismatic brother—everyone just expects you to be the same."

"How many brothers do you have?" she asked. Though she'd spent the afternoon reading about them on the internet she wanted to hear how he described his family. She had no idea what it had been like to grow up the son of a wealthy, semi-famous pro golfer or to have a brother who played for the Yankees. "I know your dad played pro golf."

"Yes, he did. I have two brothers…"

"That's right. And you're the middle one?"

"Yes, ma'am. The quiet one."

"I haven't seen you quiet yet."

He laughed again and she liked the sound of it—a little too much. No matter how charming he was she wasn't going to let him past her guard. She had to take control and remind him that they were doing things on her terms. "Okay, so one drink. Why don't you come by around—"

"Five. We can have hors d'oeuvres, too."

"Five? That's two hours before our date. How are you going to make one drink last that long?" she asked, but she was already getting up and starting to ready herself to meet him. It was only forty minutes until five.

"If things go well I don't want to cheat you out of spending time alone with me."

"You are so thoughtful," she said.

"I am. It's one of my many gifts."

"I'll remember that when we are doing our negotiations for the marketplace," she said with a laugh. "Five o'clock in the Ritz lobby bar."

"See you there," he said and hung up.

She went into the bedroom and looked at herself in the mirror. She looked like she'd just come from work. She opened her closet and realized she had a closet full of casual and work clothes. Not exactly the sexiest clothing in the world.

Did she want to look sexy for her date with Justin?

"Yes," she said, looking at herself in the mirror. If she was going to get the upper hand on Justin she was going to need to pull out all the stops.

It sure was going to be fun to go head-to-head with Mr. Know-Your-Enemies.

Three

Justin valet-parked his car and walked into the lobby of the Ritz on South Beach. The view from the restaurant here was breathtaking and easily one of the best in this area. He glanced at his watch. He was a few minutes early and as he scanned the lobby he didn't see Selena.

He walked to the lobby bar and found seating for two in a relatively quiet area. He knew that he had to get to know Selena better for business reasons. He had to know how she thought so he could make sure he made the right offer—one she'd accept so that he could get the market back on track. He hadn't gotten the Luna Azul Company to where it was today by not knowing how to read people.

But he wasn't going to deny that he wanted Selena. There had been a moment in the conference room this afternoon when he'd wished they were alone so he could pull her into his arms and see if he could crack her reserve with passion.

"Justin?"

He glanced over his shoulder and felt like he'd been sucker punched. The prim, reserved woman he'd flirted with was gone and in her place was a bombshell. Maybe it was just her thick ebony hair hanging in waves around her shoulders, or the red lipstick that drew his eyes to her full mouth. But his gut insisted that it was the curve-hugging black dress she wore that ended midthigh. He skimmed his gaze down to her dainty-looking ankles and those high-heeled strappy sandals that made him almost groan out loud.

"Selena," he said, but his voice sounded husky and almost choked to him.

She arched one eyebrow and smiled. "Happy to see me?"

"That is an understatement. Let me get us a drink. What's your poison?"

"Mojito, I think. I need something to cool me down."

He signaled the cocktail waitress and placed their drink order before diving right in. "Tell me about yourself, Selena. Why are you living in New York when your family is still here?"

"No small talk?" she asked, turning her attention away from him and skimming the room.

"Why bother with that?" he asked. "We both want to know as much about each other as we can, right?"

"Definitely. I just didn't plan on going first," she said with a smile as she turned back to face him again.

Every time she talked he tried to concentrate on her words but he couldn't take his eyes from her lips. He wanted to know how they would feel under his own.

What kind of kisser would she be? Would she taste as good as he imagined?

"I'm a gentleman," he said. And he didn't want to show her any weakness.

"So it's ladies first?" she asked.

"In all things, especially pleasure," he said.

She blushed as their waitress arrived with the drinks. She started to take a sip but he stopped her.

"A toast to new relationships."

"And a quick resolution to our business problems," she said.

He clinked his glass to hers and watched as she took a swallow of her cocktail. When she took the glass from her mouth she licked her lips and he felt his blood begin to flow a little heavier in his veins as his groin stirred.

He wanted her.

That wasn't news. But sitting here with her in the bar was starting to seem like a really dumb idea. He needed all his wits about him because it was apparent that Selena was playing with her A-game and he needed to as well.

"You were going to tell me all your secrets," he said.

She laughed. "I was going to tell you the official version of my life."

"I'll take whatever you offer," he said.

"I bet you will. Okay, where to start?"

"The beginning," he suggested, shifting his legs to make room in his pants for his growing erection.

"Birth?"

"Nah, skip to college. I did a little internet research on you and saw that you graduated from the University of Miami. What made you choose to go to Fordham Law

School instead of choosing something closer to home?" he asked.

"I needed a change of scene. I was pretty sure that I wanted to practice corporate law and I had done an internship for one summer with the firm that I work for now. So it made sense to go there."

"That's about the same time your grandparents sold the marketplace and switched over to being renters in the space. Did they do that to pay for your education?" he asked.

Her face got very tight and she shook her head. "I had a scholarship."

"I did a deed search to see who had owned the property before the previous owner and it was your grandfather. I can't understand why he sold," Justin continued. He really wanted to know why ten years ago, Tomas had made the decision to sell the marketplace property and become a rental tenant instead. That made no sense to Justin as a businessman. But it also made no sense based on what he knew of Tomas. Tomas liked being his own boss.

"What about you? Harvard law graduates can usually write their own ticket to any law firm but you came back home and worked with your brothers instead, why?"

Justin stretched back and looked at her for a minute. That was complicated. He couldn't tell her that coming back was the hardest decision he'd ever made because even his brothers didn't know that.

"They needed me," he said. It was close to the truth. He didn't hold with outright lies.

He took another sip of his drink and then leaned forward. "Why are you here now?"

"My grandfather said you were too slick and he couldn't trust you."

"That's hardly true. Tomas is very shrewd. And don't change the subject. Why did he sell the marketplace if not for your education?"

She flushed and her hand trembled for a minute and then she took a sip of her drink.

He waited for her to answer but she didn't say anything.

"Selena?"

"That is a private matter and I won't discuss it with you."

Selena was surprised that he'd dug back on the deed. But she shouldn't have been. She may have momentarily distracted Justin with her clothing and changed appearance but he'd adjusted quickly by pulling the rug out from under her with that question.

"Okay. I can respect that. I was just thinking that if they hadn't sold the property perhaps it wouldn't be so derelict now," Justin said.

He was right. Selling that property had been a mistake and that was why she was here. To right the wrong she'd caused when she'd allowed herself to get suckered by a smooth-talking con man ten years ago.

She'd never seen him coming, Raul had swept her off her feet, and then once she'd fallen for his sweet talk, he'd used that love she had for him against her. The con he'd run on her had been simple enough. He was starting his own company, a luxury yacht business, and needed some initial investors. She'd put all of the inheritance she'd gotten from her parents into it, and in a calculated move on Raul's part she'd convinced her grandparents to mortgage the market and invest, as well. Raul took all the money and disappeared overnight.

The ensuing investigation into Raul's disappearance

had been an upheaval in their lives. It had taken almost two years to get it sorted out and at the end with lawyers' fees and private investigator charges her grandparents had no money left. They were forced to sell the marketplace and become renters. Raul was eventually caught and brought to justice, but their money was never repaid.

It had been one of the most humiliating times of her life and she'd been very glad to escape Miami to Fordham where she knew no one. She'd started over and been very careful since then not to let her emotions get the better of her.

"You are very right," she said. She took another sip of her mojito. The smooth rum and mint drink was soothing. Justin watched her each time she swallowed and she knew she'd been distracting him all evening.

She liked the feeling of power it gave her to know that she could manipulate him. She wondered if that was what Raul had felt as he'd slowly drawn her into his web. Had it been the power? She hadn't thought of that in years, but her experiences with men had taught her that in all relationships—personal and business—it all came down to who had something the other wanted. And right now, she had something that Justin wanted a lot.

"I know," he said. He was cocky and she had to admit that it was a trait she was beginning to enjoy in him.

He seemed so in control. She'd been told she gave that impression, as well, but she knew underneath her professional persona she was usually a mess. Was it the same for him? But she couldn't detect any chinks in his armor. She was starting to realize that even distracted he was going to be a tough opponent.

She leaned forward to place her drink on the table

and noticed his eyes tracked down toward her breasts. She shifted her shoulders so the fabric of her dress drew the material taut over her curves and then sat back.

"Have you thought of selling the property back to my grandparents? I think that would be the easiest solution." Then she could conclude this business in Miami and take the first flight back to New York and her nice, safe, regular life. A place where the businessmen she encountered looked dull and gray like a Manhattan winter instead of like Justin, who was tan, vibrant and hot…just like Miami.

"I don't think so," he said, looking back up at her eyes. "Your grandparents don't…"

"What?"

"They don't have the resources to make the property profitable the way that the Luna Azul Company does. I mean, they would probably fix up their market but it is going to take a lot of capital to revamp the entire area. And that is the only way you are going to keep your current clientele and get new customers."

He had a point but she didn't like the thought of an outsider owning the market. It also irked her that this situation was entirely her fault. If she hadn't fallen for Raul so many years ago, her beloved *abuelito* wouldn't have to deal with the Stern brothers on their terms.

"Granted but if you take away the local feel of the marketplace, you will lose money."

"That's where you come in. I liked your idea of forming a committee. I wish I'd thought of it sooner," Justin said. "But enough business. I want to know the woman behind the suit. I like your dress by the way."

She tossed her hair and made herself let go of the work part of being with Justin. There was nothing to be accomplished tonight. He'd either come around to her way of thinking or he'd find out how many complications she could put in the way of his business deals.

"I noticed you liking it."

"Good. Are you finished with your drink?"

"Why?"

"I want to take you for a walk along the beach."

"I'd like that," she said, getting to her feet. "I miss the beach."

"I live right on it. That was one thing that motivated me to come back home after Harvard. I like living some-where so temperate."

"What else?" she asked. She suspected that family must be important to him. That was at odds with what she usually encountered in type-A, driven business executives, but then Justin didn't exactly fit the mold of what she expected from guys to begin with.

"Why are you really here?" she asked as they stepped out into the warm early-evening.

"I told you I like to know my opponents," he said.

"I can see that," she said. She did as well. Normally when she was negotiating something for her company she spent a lot of time researching the players involved in the deal. Winning almost always came down to who had the most information. "You were trying to throw me off my game a little, right?"

"In part," he admitted. "But honestly, you aren't what I was expecting from the Gonzalezes' lawyer."

"Because I'm a girl?" she asked using his term. "You know that calling me a girl wasn't exactly flattering?"

"I didn't mean it that way," he said. "It's because you're so sexy. I can handle going up against a girl but when she is making me think of long, hot nights instead of business—well I figured turnabout was fair play and I should do something unexpected like ask you out."

She bit her lower lip. He was a very frank man, which shouldn't surprise her. From the moment they'd met he'd been that way. He was the kind of man who shot from the hip and didn't worry about the consequences.

And she was a woman who'd been damned by the consequences of her reckless heart before. She had to remember that her grandparents were in this situation with the Luna Azul Company specifically because she'd followed her heart and they had paid the price.

"I'm not looking for a relationship," she said. "I am focused on my career."

"I can see that," he said. "But unless you're into lying to yourself, you'll admit that there is something between us."

She could admit that. There was a powerful attraction between them. Something that was more intense than anything she'd ever experienced before. She wanted to blame it on Miami and her old self, but she knew that it was Justin. If she'd been here with any other man she wouldn't have felt like this.

That was enough to make her pause. Justin was different and that very difference was enough to make him dangerous.

"Lust," she said. "And that is nothing more than a chimera."

"An illusion? I don't think so. Lust is our primal instincts telling us to pay attention. You could be a potential mate for me," he said.

She stopped walking on the wooden boardwalk and turned to face him. He'd put on a pair of aviator-style sunglasses and with his jacket slung over his shoulder he looked like he'd stepped off a yacht. He seemed like a man who was used to getting everything he wanted.

"What?" she asked. "There is no way you and I could

ever be mates. I just don't know if I should believe you or not. You're not really looking for a mate for more than one night, right?"

"Usually, I'd say so, but the way I am reacting to you throws my normal playbook out the window."

She shook her head. "Your playbook? Any guy who has one of those isn't someone I'm interested in."

"That sounded worse than I meant it to. I was trying to say that this attraction I feel for you is making me forget every rule I have about mixing business and pleasure."

"I can't afford to take a chance like that with you, Justin."

"Because of Tomas?"

She wished it were that simple. "If it didn't involve my grandparents…"

"What do you mean?" he asked.

She had no idea. She wished she had some answers. "Say I met you on vacation, I'd jump into a fling with you. But this is my home and my family and I can't afford to compromise anything."

"There is no need to compromise anything," Justin said, putting his hand in the center of her back and urging her to start walking again.

She shook her head and the scent of gardenias surrounded him. He closed his eyes and breathed deeply. Why was it that everything about Selena was a turn-on for him? "I'm not going to take no for an answer. We are both good at negotiating."

"This isn't easy for me. My grandparents deserve my undivided attention, I owe them," she said.

"Why do you owe them?" he asked. He wanted to know more about what had happened ten years ago and he was determined to get some answers, but not right now.

"I just do."

He nodded. "Well, I owe my brothers, and my company deserves my undivided attention, but I can't think of business when I'm with you. Right now all I can think of is your mouth and how it will feel under mine."

"Saying things like that is not helping me," she said, closing her eyes and wrapping her arms around her own waist.

If he pushed a little bit harder he could have her. He knew that. But he didn't want to crumble her defenses. He pulled her closer to him and moved them off the path out of the way of other walkers. "Have you thought about it?"

She nibbled on her full lower lip as she looked up at him. "I have, but I'm not about to play into your hands so easily."

He lowered his head, wanting to kiss her but at the same time wanting—no needing—her to want it too. He wanted her to be so attracted to him that she forgot her rules and her fears and everything else just faded away.

"Justin, stop manipulating me."

"I'm not," he said. "I want to see what it will take for you to forget about business and just see me as a man."

"Stop trying to play me," she said. "Just be yourself."

"I don't think you'd trust me," he said.

"I don't trust you now," she said. "And that feeling that you are toying with me is never going to help your case. I do want you but I don't want to be your pawn."

Her honesty cut straight through him. He really didn't

want her to be his pawn. He wanted her to be his woman. That was it.

He needed Selena no matter what the circumstances. And he was going to do whatever he had to to make that happen. He couldn't just walk away.

"I'm sorry. I was trying—"

"I know what you were trying to do," she said, lifting one hand and tracing the line of his lips. "I can understand it because I don't want to end up the weak one either."

He could hardly think when she touched him. He slid his hands together at her waist and pulled her more closely into his body.

He rubbed his lips against hers briefly and then stepped back before he gave in to temptation and ravished her mouth.

"We need…to walk," he said.

He took her hand with his and led her down the path. She laughed softly and he knew she was very aware of his desire. That didn't bother him at all. He wanted her to be very aware of him as a man and he knew that he'd accomplished that.

"We can't walk away from this," he said.

"I know," she admitted. "But I won't let this kind of attraction take control of my life."

He understood that. As a man, part of him was glad to hear that she wanted him that powerfully. The other part, the businessman who never took a day off, was glad to hear it, too, because it meant that he had the potential to use that attraction to get what he wanted.

Walking took the edge off her and allowed him to start thinking of something other than lifting her skirt and finding the sweetness between her legs. "What if we pretend you are on vacation?"

"Why?"

"Then it's like you said, we're just two people who are attracted to each other."

"Like a vacation fling?" she asked.

"Exactly like that. No talking about our families and their business interests. Just two people who've met and started an affair," he said.

"So it ends when I go back home?" she asked.

His gut said no. He didn't want to think about Selena leaving but he put that down to the fact that she was new to him. "If that is what we both decide, then yes."

She pulled her hand from his, stopped walking and turned to look out at the ocean. She wrapped one arm around her waist and he wondered if he'd ever know her well enough to know what she was thinking.

"I wish it could be that simple," she said, "But we both know there is no way we're going to be able—"

"I'm not someone who takes no for an answer," he said.

She glanced over her shoulder at him and he saw that fiery spark was back in her eyes. This couldn't be more than a fling and he wanted to keep it light. But the only way he was going to be able to deal with her in the boardroom was if he had her in his bedroom.

"I'm not going to let you bully me into making a decision like this."

"Is that what I'm doing or is that what you are telling yourself?"

She turned to face him full-on and walked over to him, hips swaying with each step. His mind went blank and suddenly he didn't care why she agreed but only that she did. He needed her to be one hundred percent his. And nothing was going to stand in the way of that. Not business and not even the lady herself. He knew that Selena Gonzalez wanted him and now he just had to find the right button to push, to convince her that she was willing to take a chance on him.

"I know my own mind, Justin Stern," she said as she closed the gap between them. She put her hands on his shoulders and tipped her head back to look up at him. "And I know exactly what I want."

She went up on her tiptoes, tunneled her fingers into his hair and planted a kiss on him that made him forget everything else. All he did was feel.

Her breasts cushioned against his chest. Her supple hips under his hands as he rested them there. Her soft hair brushing his cheek as she turned her head to angle her mouth better over his.

And then the thrust of her warm tongue into his mouth. How she slowly rubbed hers over his and then lifted her hands to his face to hold him right above the jaw. She kept his head steady as she tasted him and he let her.

Hell, there was no stopping this woman. She had turned his own game back on him and left him standing still. He drew his own hands up to her tiny waist and pulled her off balance into his body.

He sucked on her tongue when she would have pulled it back. Her hands slid down his neck to his shoulders and she moved her head again and a tiny moan escaped her.

His erection nudged the top of her thighs and he shifted his hips against hers and heard her moan again. This was more like it, he thought. This was the kind of negotiation he wanted. Both of them alone together.

Just man versus woman and let the winner take all.

Four

Selena had forgotten what it was like to turn the tables on a man sexually. She did it all the time at work but this was personal and she liked it. A heady mix of passion and power consumed her and she knew that it was well past time she got back in touch with this side of herself.

She'd given in to Justin not just because of the lust that was flowing between them but also because she needed to reclaim her femininity.

She took Justin's hand and led him back to the hotel. "Why are we wasting our time out here when we could be up in my room?"

"Your room? I thought you weren't sure about my proposition."

"I guess you think too much." Turning the tables on Justin had knocked him off balance and she knew he would be easier to deal with now. "I like the idea of a vacation fling. It's been too long for me and being with you…well let's just say you are the perfect distraction."

He frowned at her, but she didn't care. She wasn't stupid. She knew that even though Justin wanted her—she knew he wasn't faking his attraction to her—a part of him was focused on how to use the lust they both felt to his own advantage.

And she wasn't going to let him do that. She wanted him. She needed a distraction from being back here in Miami. She was thinking too much about the girl she had been and Justin was the distraction she needed.

"Come back to my room," she said, leaning closer and kissing his neck right under his ear. "That's what we'd do if we were on vacation."

Justin nodded. "But we aren't on vacation."

"Have you changed your mind?" she asked.

"No. But I don't like the way you changed yours. What's going on behind those beautiful brown eyes?" he asked.

She pulled back. She couldn't do this. It wasn't like her to just impulsively invite a man back to her room. He was right, what was she thinking?

"Nothing. Nothing is going on," she said. "I think I had a momentary fever but it is passing now."

She felt small and a bit rejected. She'd actually never been that bold with a man before. The dress and the way that Justin treated her had made her feel like she was sexy, an enchantress, and now she was realizing she was still just Selena.

"I think we should head back to the hotel. I need to freshen up before heading to dinner. I will meet you there."

She turned to walk away needing to get back to her

room. She needed to find someplace private to sit down and regroup.

"No."

She glanced over her shoulder at him.

"No?"

"That's what I said. I am not letting you run away," he said, taking her hand in his. "What's going on with you?"

She shook her head and swallowed hard. "I'm sorry. You are making me a little…crazy."

"That's good. That's what I was going for…trying to distract you," he admitted.

"Well, you did a good job tonight. But that won't affect me in the boardroom when we are meeting with your group and the community leaders."

"I didn't think it would. To be honest I'm trying to even the scales. You have me thinking about your curvy body and kissing you instead of business and I wanted you to think of me."

"Does that mean you don't really want a vacation fling with me?"

"Hell, no. I want you more than I want my next breath. But I want you to want it for the right reasons—not because you think it will help you in the boardroom. I do believe we can keep this attraction between us private and explore it."

She thought about what he was saying. She wanted him and she wasn't going to deny it. "I'm not—Miami is more than just my home. It's the place that shaped me into the woman I am today and coming back here is stirring up all kinds of things in me I didn't expect."

"Like what?" he asked.

Justin was dangerous, she thought. He made her feel

so comfortable and safe that she would tell him almost anything. "This dress for one thing. I bought this for you."

"I like it."

"That was my intention, but at home…in Manhattan I'd never wear this."

"Good," he said, leading them back toward the hotel. "Be yourself with me, Selena. I want to see that woman you keep tucked away from the rest of the world. I don't want to be like every other guy to you."

"There is no way you could be. My family told me you're the devil."

He laughed. It was a strong masculine sound and it made her smile. "I haven't been called the devil before."

"To your face," she said.

"Touché," he said as they reached the hotel and stepped into the air-conditioned lobby.

Chills spread down her arms and she shivered just a bit. "Are we okay now?" he asked.

"I think so," she said. "I will meet you—"

"Get whatever you need. I want to take you to Luna Azul."

"Why?"

"I want to show you my family," he said.

"After," she said. "I need some time to myself before we go to dinner at my grandparents."

"Really? I was hoping you'd go with me. I don't want to walk in there by myself."

"Since when does the devil show fear?" she asked.

"I have no idea, since I'm not the devil," he said.

"What are you?" she asked.

"Just a man who likes a pretty girl and doesn't want to screw up again."

Selena watched him walk away, wondering if she'd underestimated him and if that would be at her own peril.

Justin sat quietly in his car parked on the street in front of the Gonzalez home. Selena had withdrawn into herself and there had been no drawing her out. He had a feeling that Selena's attitude was the least of his problems as he got out and walked up the driveway to the house.

There was music coming from the backyard and the delicious smells of charcoal and roasting meat wafted around him. This was a cozy neighborhood, the kind of place where he could buy two or three houses and not feel the sting in his checkbook, but a place where he'd never fit in.

Was this what Selena had been talking about when she said Luna Azul didn't belong in Little Havana?

"*Amigo,* you coming?"

The guy who walked by him was in his early twenties with close-cut dark hair and warm olive-colored skin. He wasn't as tall as Justin and his face was friendly.

"I am indeed," Justin said. He had a six-pack of Landshark beer in one hand and some flowers for Selena's grandmother.

"How do you know Tomas?" the young man asked.

"We're in business together." Justin wasn't about to pretend he had any other reason to be here. In fact, in light of his drinks with Selena he thought wooing her was going about as smoothly as the entire buying-the-marketplace deal. What was it with the Gonzalez family? Was it impossible to find a common path with them?

"Truly? My *abuelito* usually doesn't do business with...wait a minute, are you Justin Stern?"

"That's me," he said. Great, nice to know that he already had a reputation here and he hadn't even arrived yet.

"Oh, ho, you have some guts showing up here," the kid said.

"I was invited, and I'm not a bad guy," Justin told him. "I am trying to find a way to make that market viable, not to run your grandparents out."

The kid tipped his head to the side, studying him. "I'm watching you."

"I'm glad. Family should look out for one another. And I'm not going to take advantage of your grandparents or your family. My main concern is making money from the property we bought."

"Is money all you care about?"

Justin shook his head. He saw Selena walking up toward the house from where they stood in the shade of a large palm tree. She'd changed from the sexy dress she had worn earlier into a pair of khaki walking shorts and a sleeveless wraparound top. She was enchanting, he thought.

He forgot about how unwelcome this guy was making him feel and focused on Selena.

"Leave him alone, Enrique. He's not a bad guy," Selena said as she came up to them.

"He told me the same thing," Enrique said. "Are you sure about him?"

Selena shrugged. "Not one hundred percent but I'm getting there."

"If we do business with your family," Enrique said, turning to Justin, "I want to talk to you about deejaying at Luna Azul. Why do you only hire New York and LA deejays?"

Justin had very little to do with the everyday running

of the nightclub he owned with his brothers. "I don't have an answer for that but I can find out. If you send me a demo tape—"

"I don't think Enrique wants to work for you," Selena said.

"I'll make my own decisions, *tata*," Enrique said. He reached around Justin and hugged her. She hugged him back.

"Enrique is my little brother," she said.

"I'm taller than you now, sis. I think that makes me your 'big' little brother," Enrique said with a grin that was familiar to Justin. He'd seen it on Selena's face a few times.

"You'll always be my baby brother," she said, looping her arm through Enrique's and Justin was relegated to following the two siblings up the walk to the house.

Justin had the feeling he'd always be an outsider. Too bad his little brother wasn't here tonight. This was exactly the type of party that Nate was better at than he was.

But he was here to achieve two things: first, to have Tomas lift the injunction against Luna Azul and second, to get Selena to be that warm, seductive woman she'd been on the beach again.

He'd pulled back for her sake, had instinctively known that she wasn't the kind of woman who could start an affair, even a short-term one, with a man she barely knew.

But tonight he'd change all of that. He slipped his arm through Selena's free one and she hesitated and lost her footing, glancing up at him.

"What are you doing?"

"Just making sure everyone knows who invited me to the party."

Enrique laughed. "No one's going to doubt that, bro. This is Selena's welcome-home party. Did you know she hasn't been back here since my tenth birthday?"

Why not? "No, I didn't know that. I'm honored to have been invited to this party then."

"Don't forget that," Enrique said. He dropped Selena's arm to open the front door of the house. The air-conditioned coolness rushed out and the sounds of the party filled the lanai.

"Enrique's in the house," Enrique yelled and there was a round of applause.

Selena took a deep breath. "I am not sure this was my best idea."

"I am. I want to get to know your family."

She paused there on the step so that they were almost eye level. "Why? So you can use it to your advantage?"

"No, so I can start to understand you."

He put his hand on the small of her back and directed her into the living room. Everyone surrounded her and welcomed her home. But standing to the side, Justin realized that Selena hesitated to be a part of them. She held a part of herself back and he wanted to know why.

Selena was amazed to see Justin actually fitting in with her family. He was standing by the grill talking to the men about baseball of all things. But then she guessed he would know a little bit about the sport thanks to his brother, the former ball player.

"What's the matter, *tata?* Aren't you enjoying your party?"

Her grandmother sat down beside her and put her arm around Selena's shoulders. For just a minute she felt like she was twelve again and a hug from this woman could solve all of her problems. She put her head on her grandmother's shoulder and just sat there enjoying the scent of gardenia perfume and how safe she felt at this moment.

"No, I'm not. I feel like everyone is watching me," Selena said.

"They are. We have missed you so much since you left."

"I don't want everyone to remember what happened. I'm sorry, *abuelita*. Did I ever tell you how sorry I was?"

Her grandmother tucked a strand of Selena's hair behind her ear and kissed her lightly on the cheek. "You did. Stop living in the past, that's all done and we are better for it."

"Better? If it wasn't for me you wouldn't be in this position with Justin Stern."

"And you wouldn't have met him. I've noticed you watching Mr. Stern."

Selena blushed. "Given my track record with men, that should alarm you, *abuelita*, not make you smile."

Her grandmother laughed. "The heart doesn't care about the same things as the brain. My own sister Dona was in love with a gringo and our papa forbid her from seeing him and do you know what she did?"

"She ran away and married him and they lived happily ever after. Even reconciling with the family eventually," Selena said. She'd heard this story many times but for the first time she understood what her grandmother had been trying to say to her. "Why would Aunt Dona do that? I mean living away from the family is hard."

"She wasn't on her own, *tata*, not like you in New York. That's why I think everything has happened for a reason. A man drove you away from your family and this man," she said, gesturing to Justin, "has brought you back to us regardless of his intention."

"I'm not sure I'm ready to see Justin as a white knight."

"He is cute, though."

"*Abuelita,* I'm not sure you should be noticing that."

"Why not? It's not like I said he has a nice butt," she added with a wink.

"But he does have one, doesn't he?" Selena agreed and then blushed, remembering the way the rest of his body had felt pressed to hers.

"He sure does."

"*Abuelita,* what would *abuelito* say if he heard you talking like that?"

"He knows where my heart lies," she said. "Can I say something to you, *tata?*"

"Of course."

"You have never known where your heart lies," she said. "You were always fixated on getting out of here and doing bigger and better things, but I don't think you understood the true cost."

There was truth there. Truth that Selena had never wanted to acknowledge before and she knew that it was time to. Maybe it was because she was thirty now and had made enough mistakes in her life to have really experienced the ups and downs in life. "I think you are right."

"I know I am," her grandmother said with a laugh. "Are you thirsty? I need another mojito."

"Did I hear my lady ask for a mojito?" Tomas asked coming over to them.

Her grandmother stood up and kissed her grandfather. "Yes, you did."

Selena watched them together and felt a pang in her heart. Her own parents had married young and filled their house with love and laughter and a few tears when it took so long for her mother to have a second child. She wanted what those couples had. That was her destiny. Though she loved her job and her apartment in Manhattan.

"Come and dance with your grandfather," Tomas said, drawing her to her feet.

"Wouldn't you rather dance with *abuelita?*"

"I will dance with her later. Right now I want to dance with my beautiful granddaughter. I'm so happy you've come home, *tata.*"

Enrique was playing music with a strong Latin beat, mixing the contemporary artists with the old ones her grandfather and his brothers liked. The song playing was a samba and she danced with her grandfather, forgetting all of her troubles and her worries. Laughing with her cousins and aunts and uncles over missteps and bumping hips.

She closed her eyes and for a second allowed herself some self-forgiveness and enjoyed being back in the best home she'd ever found. She enjoyed the smile on her grandfather's face and the way her little brother looked as he spun the music and watched their family.

Her family.

Her eyes met Justin's and she felt a pulsing start in the very core of her body and move up and over her. She wanted that man. But she could never have Justin and have her family, too. Because no matter what he might say, his objective was always going to be money and hers had to be the heart of this family and the community they lived in.

She turned away from him. She wished she were the big-city woman she'd thought she was. Someone who could have a short-term affair that was about nothing but sex. But a big part of her wasn't sure that she could. She was still the sheltered Latina she'd always been. And being back here she felt more that woman than ever before.

She wanted more from Justin Stern than just sex. And he could never give her that.

Five

Justin liked Selena's cousins, Paulo and Jorge. They made him laugh and he understood them because they were both successful businessmen who were used to doing what they had to to get the job done. If only Tomas were a little more like his grandsons, then Justin had the feeling he wouldn't be facing an injunction.

"I'd love to have you on a committee I'm putting together to make sure that the renovation of the Cuban American marketplace is both profitable and a benefit to Little Havana."

"I'll think about it. But my plate is pretty full," Jorge said.

"I'll do it," Paulo said. "We need new investors to come here and I really like what you've done with Luna Azul. That's the kind of club we need down here. And it drives business to my restaurant."

"That's the kind of synergy I think we can have at the marketplace."

"You should call it a Mercado instead of marketplace," Selena said coming over to join them.

"She's right," Jorge said. "I think you should have a Latin music store there. My boys have to drive across town to find the music and instruments they need. And you could tie it to the bands that play at Luna Azul... have them stop in there for a release party or a little concert."

"I like that idea," Justin said. But discussing business while Selena was standing so close that she was pressed against his arm wasn't conducive. He could barely think since all of the blood in his body was racing to his groin and not his brain.

"Did you invite them to be on the community committee?"

"I did," he said.

"Good, so you are done talking business?"

"No," Justin said.

"He's like us, *tata,* he'll be dead and buried before he stops trying to make a deal," Paulo said.

Justin laughed and Selena smiled but he could tell that her cousin's words disturbed her. A few minutes later the food was ready and the other men moved to prepare the platters for everyone to eat. He took Selena's arm and drew her away from the crowd.

"Why does what Paulo said bother you?" he asked her.

"It just reaffirmed my fears that you are attracted to me because it might make dealing with my family easier," she said.

That was blunt and honest and he shouldn't have been

surprised, since Selena wasn't the kind of woman who was tentative about anything.

"I want you," he said. "That's it, end of story. If you said to me right now that you were going to keep that injunction in place against my company until we both died, it wouldn't change a thing. I still want you naked and writhing against me."

"Lust."

"We discussed that."

"I know. And I thought I'd found a solution."

"Vacation fling," he said.

"It's the only way to keep this in perspective," she said.

He understood where she was coming from. He'd watched his own father love a woman who didn't want him. Not the way he wanted her. It had always been Justin's fear in relationships. He knew that if he ever fell in love it would dull his razor-sharp edge when it came to business. And he'd been careful to make lust his criterion for a relationship. Never really getting to know the family or friends of the women he slept with.

"I'm not going to lie to you, Selena. I will use whatever means necessary to make that marketplace successful, but that will not change how I feel about you. And I always go after what I want."

"I bet you get it, too," she said.

"Yes, I do. Today has been eye-opening for me."

"Because of that dress I wore earlier?" she asked.

"Partly. I don't think I've recovered full brain function since then."

She laughed. "It's nice to know I have a little power over you."

"You have more than you know. Inviting me here was

a very well-played move on your part. Talking to your cousins made me realize that we should be reaching out here more than we do. Luna Azul is successful in this location without community support. Imagine what we could do with support."

"I have imagined it. That's why it is important that my grandparents are in on the ground level."

"I see that. I can't wait to have the first committee meeting."

"Me, too," she said.

"Now about us," he said after a few minutes of silence had fallen between them.

"There isn't any *us*."

"Not yet," he said. "But we both want it, so it's silly to pretend that we don't."

"Vacation fling, right?"

"I'm open to suggestions," he said. "I don't want to forget that you have a life in another part of the country and that you will be going back there."

"That was a surprisingly honest thing for you to admit," she said.

"There is no reason for me to pretend that you don't have the potential to be a heartbreaker. I've never met another woman like you, Selena."

He was a shoot-from-the-hip kind of guy and he wasn't going to change at this late date. Especially where Selena was concerned. She needed to know that even though he was suggesting a vacation fling, he wanted it as badly as she did. He couldn't get her out of his mind and until he did he had the feeling he was going to be operating on backup power instead of at full strength.

Everyone filled their plates and sat down to eat, and though he knew these people thought he was their enemy, he felt like he could be part of this family. He wanted to be here not as a business rival, but as Selena's date.

After dinner was over, Selena mingled for the rest of the evening trying to stay as far from Justin as she could.

He'd waved at her earlier and said goodbye, but that was it. She tried not to be disappointed. After all that had been her one desire, right? She'd been tired of trying to avoid him and the attraction she felt for him. Now she could just be a granddaughter and a niece and a cousin and not have to answer uncomfortable questions about a man who was too good-looking and a point of conflict with her family.

"Why are you hiding out over here?" Enrique asked as he sat down next to her on the wrought-iron bench nestled between the hibiscus trees.

"I'm not hiding out," she said. "I'm just taking a break."

"From the family?" he asked. "I guess when you aren't used to it our kin can be a little overwhelming."

She had to agree. It had been so long since she'd been to a family gathering that she found it tiring and loud. And she wasn't sure she fit in here anymore.

"Are you used to it?" she asked him.

He shrugged. "It's all I know."

"Have you thought any more about coming to New York and living with me for a while?"

She wanted her baby brother to see more of the world than just this slice of it but so far he'd resisted her efforts to bring him up north to the city.

"I have, *tata,* but I don't think I will do it. I like Miami and the family and everything. And I don't want to move away from here."

She nodded. She understood where Enrique was coming from. When she'd left home, she'd felt she had to and those first few years had been terrifying. She'd hated being away from everything familiar. That first October had felt so cold and she'd almost come back home; only shame had kept her in New York. Only slowly had she shed the girl she'd once been and become the woman she was today.

"It's an open invitation."

"I know it is, sis. How'd you like my music?"

"I loved it. You are a talented deejay."

"I know," he said with an arrogant grin. "I'm going to use Justin Stern to get a gig at Luna Azul."

"How is that going to work? He's not an easy man to use," she said. She didn't want her brother and Justin spending too much time together.

"He wants something from us and I will offer to help him get it if he helps me."

Her brother was always working an angle. "Be careful. Justin isn't the kind of guy who gives up things easily."

"I can tell that. But I think with the right manipulation it could work."

"Let me know if I can help. He's putting together a committee to discuss his marketplace. Perhaps you can get a gig at the ground-breaking if we reach an arrangement with his company."

"Great! I like that idea, *tata*."

She hugged him close. "I knew you would."

She missed Enrique probably the most of all the people she'd left behind. He'd only been ten when she'd left. It had been just a year after their parents had died and she knew she should have stayed to help in raising him but she'd been too young to do that. And after Raul and the con he'd run on her family, she'd had to get away and prove herself.

"I wish you'd move back here, *tata*."

"I can't."

He nodded. "A group of us are going clubbing, you want to join?"

"Who?"

"The cousins. Some of them are older than you."

"Geez, thanks."

"You know what I mean," Enrique said. "It will be fun. And it's not like you have to be at work tomorrow."

"That's true. I'm on vacation—sort of," she said, thinking back to earlier when Justin had offered to be her vacation fling. Was she overthinking this?

"You are on vacation. Come on, live a little."

She nodded. "I'd like that. Am I dressed okay?"

"You're perfect," Enrique said. "Hey, guys, Selena is coming with us."

"Great, let's go."

She followed Enrique over to Jorge and Paulo and a group of her other cousins. The tiki torches that had been placed around the edge of the yard still burned and there were plates and cups littering every surface.

"I have to help clean up first," she said. Her grandparents didn't need to be doing all this work by themselves.

"No, you don't," her grandmother said as she came up behind her and wrapped an arm around her waist. "Go and have some fun with your cousins. Remember what it's like to have family around you."

"*Abuelita,* I always remember that."

"Then I hope you also know that we love you. I will call you in the morning," her grandmother said.

"I'm not staying at my house, *abuelita*."

"Where are you staying then?"

"At the Ritz. Call me on my cell phone, okay?"

"Tata…"

"I just couldn't stay there. I hope you aren't upset."

"I'm not upset, but I worry about you."

"The hotel is nice and I can relax there," Selena said.

Her grandmother hugged her. "Then that is all that matters."

"Whatever you do, don't call too early, *abuelita*," Jorge said. "We are going to be partying all night. It's not too often the prodigal daughter returns home."

Selena shook her head. "I'm not the prodigal anything."

Jorge put his arm around her as they walked through the house. He and she had been so close growing up. Their mothers were twins and the two of them had been born only eight days apart. Jorge was more than a cousin to her. He was her big brother and her childhood twin.

"That's the sad part, *tata,* you don't even realize how important you are to us all and how much we've all missed you."

"But I am responsible for ruining—"

"You aren't responsible for anything but the actions you took to make things right. And you did make up for everything that happened long ago. Stop punishing yourself for it," Jorge said.

"I'm not punishing myself."

"Yes, you are. And it's time you stopped."

* * *

Nate and Cam weren't pleased with the news that they'd have to wait on the ground-breaking. Actually, Nate didn't seem to care too much but Cam was ready to use every contact he had to make the Gonzalez family suffer.

"We can't do that," Justin said as he sipped his Land-shark beer and relaxed in the VIP area of the rooftop club at Luna Azul.

"I know but it would make me feel good. Tell me what you have planned."

"I'm taking the zoning commissioner out for some golf, which should help to speed up the review process. We haven't broken any laws and I've reviewed the in-junction they filed against us."

"Are we in the right?"

"We haven't done anything yet so technically we're fine. There is a zoning provision to keep the marketplace as part of the community. I think this committee will satisfy that."

"Good. Then there's no problem?"

"Cam, bureaucracy runs slowly. And you want every-thing finished yesterday. We are going to be lucky to have a ground-breaking at the tenth anniversary party."

Nate shook his head. "Cam, are you going to stand for that defeatist attitude?"

"Shut up, little bro," Justin said. "We have to be realistic."

"I don't have to be," Cam said. "I have you to do that. I think I will be on the committee with you and we will get as many local business owners involved with the anniversary celebration as we can. Once they have a vested interest in the celebration they will help make things happen."

"I agree," Justin said. "I have a young deejay who I can get to play at the marketplace ground-breaking—he is Tomas Gonzalez's grandson."

Cam nodded over at him. "You're already taking steps to make this happen. Keep us updated on your progress."

"I will. How's everything else going at the club? Do you need anything from me?" Justin asked.

"Just get the approvals for that ground-breaking taken care of, we can handle the rest," Nate said.

"I will. I'm going to take a few days for a staycation," Justin said.

"What? You can't take any time off," Cam said. "Not now."

"I guess I'm explaining this wrong. I'll be working every day but at night I'm going to be staying at the Ritz," Justin said.

"Why?" Nate asked. "I mean the Ritz is nice but why not stay at your home?"

There was no way he was going to tell his brothers that this move involved a woman. "I just haven't had a break lately and staying at the Ritz will give me one."

"As long as you are still working, it doesn't matter to me," Cam said.

"I might have you check in on some friends who are staying down there," Nate said.

"I don't want to have to check in on your celebs."

Nate ran with the celebrity crowd—all friends he'd made back when he'd been a major league baseball player. And Nate still used these connections for the club, even though he was recently engaged to Jen Miller, a dance instructor at Luna Azul. They were a cute couple and very happy together. Justin was surprised that his playboy brother had fallen for the pretty dancer and her quiet lifestyle.

While Justin was glad his younger brother had kept in contact with the glitter set, the last thing he wanted was to have to socialize with them.

For the most part he had nothing in common with people who traded on their looks or talent to get by in the world. He'd always used hard work and determination.

"Fine. We can have drinks tomorrow night when I'm down there."

"Why do we have to?" Justin asked just to needle his brother.

"Because you are making me drive down there. And you're buying!" Nate said as his cell phone rang. He glanced at the screen and then excused himself.

Warm breezes blew across the rooftop patio. "I like this place," Justin said.

Cam arched one eyebrow at him. "I'm glad to hear it, considering you helped me build it."

Justin nodded. "I know. I wonder how different it could have been if we had real community support?"

Cam took a sip of his whiskey and then rubbed the back of his neck. "In the early days it would have made a big difference. I hate to think of what it was like before Nate got injured and came home…do you remember that first summer when he just sat in the back of the club and his baseball playing friends visited?"

"Yes. You wanted to turn the club that we'd invested every last penny in, into a sports bar."

"Hey, it seemed like a good idea at the time," Cam said.

"It was a good idea, I'm just glad we didn't have to do

it. By the way, Selena suggested calling the marketplace the Mercado. I like it."

"Yes, I like it, too. Who is Selena?"

Justin took a deep breath. It didn't matter that he and Cam held equal positions of authority in the company; Cam was always going to be Justin's big brother. "She's the lawyer the Gonzalezes hired. She's also their grand-daughter."

"Pretty?"

"Breathtakingly beautiful," Justin admitted.

"Can you still be objective? If not, we can use one of your junior managers to take the lead on this."

"No," Justin said. "I've got this under control."

"Is she staying at the Ritz?"

Justin just nodded.

"I'm not sure how under control you have this," Cam said.

"I'm not going to let you down or do anything to hurt the Luna Azul."

"I know that," Cam said. "What about yourself? Are you going to do anything to harm *you?*"

Justin finished his drink with a long, hard swallow and then got to his feet. "I'm the Tin Man, Cam. No heart. So nothing to be hurt by Selena."

Justin walked away from his brother and wished that it wasn't true. But he had learned a long time ago that women and love never really touched him on a deep level. True, this attraction to Selena was intense but it would burn out like all things did.

Six

Justin walked through his house, pausing beneath the portrait of his family that had been done when Cam graduated high school. They looked like the perfect family. Picture-perfect, he thought. On the outside they'd always made sure to present a front that others would envy.

And what a front it was. His father, the pro golfer, who traveled to tournaments in his private jet, and their socialite mother, who moved in all the right circles and made sure that her sons were successful and dated the right kind of girls.

He glanced up at his mother, really staring at the blonde woman with her perfectly coiffed hair, and wondered why she'd never been happy with their family. No matter how well he did in school or how well Nate had played baseball, she'd never been pleased with them.

KATHERINE GARBERA   71

She'd never smiled or shown them any real signs of love or affection.

He'd often thought that all women were that way but he'd seen his brother fall in love with Jen and therefore got to see a different side to women. Jen had cracked through Nate's doubts. Justin was still a bit cynical but seeing how Jen and Nate had worked together to make their relationship successful...well, it made him wonder why his mom hadn't tried just a little bit harder to make it work with his dad.

"Mr. Stern?"

He glanced over his shoulder and saw his butler standing there. "Yes, Frank?"

"I have your bags ready. Do you want me to drive you to the Ritz?"

"No. I'm going to take the Porsche."

"I will park it in the circle drive. Do you need anything from me?"

"No. You can take the next two weeks off."

"Thank you, sir, but I don't have anywhere to go," Frank said.

Justin knew that Frank was always at work and he appreciated it. "Don't you have any family?"

"Not really. I left them behind a long time ago. I could go to Vegas but I really don't like to go more than once a year."

Justin smiled at his butler. Frank was a very carefully measured man. He didn't want to give in to his enjoyment of gambling and let it become an addiction. Frank would only go to Vegas and only once a year.

"I get that."

"Can I ask you a question, sir?"

"Go ahead."

"Why are you going to the Ritz? You have a better place here."

Frank was making perfect sense, logically speaking. "I am…let's just say there is a woman at the Ritz."

"And you want to be closer to her? I think you should invite her here," Frank said.

"That would make things a lot more complicated."

"I guess it would," Frank said.

It probably still didn't make sense, but Frank was his employee and was never going to tell him he was barking mad, even if that was what he thought. Frank was good at holding his tongue. "Frank, sometimes I think I don't pay you enough!"

"I agree, sir," Frank said. "I'll bring the car and get your bags in it."

"Thank you, Frank."

"Just doing my job, sir."

"I appreciate it," Justin said. Frank left and Justin moved away from the portrait.

Was he making the right decision or was he just going to come off as a stalker? If he and Selena were going to have a vacation fling it would make sense for them to both be at the hotel. That's how vacation flings happened.

He knew from experience. He liked the anonymity that being at the hotel would afford them. If he brought her to his home, she'd see his family and his neighbors and it would make their fling seem more real.

And when she left to go back to New York he'd have memories of her in his space. He didn't want that. He wanted their relationship to be uncomplicated. To be a true fling. One where neither of them got hurt.

He wasn't going to pretend that she didn't have the potential to hurt him. He had no idea what the outcome would be of an affair with her but he couldn't resist the thought of having her in his arms.

He wanted her.

That was the bottom line and he was going to do whatever he had to in order to get her. He didn't care if he had to pay the cost later.

All around him were the trappings of success and that made him even more determined to ensure that this thing with Selena worked out. He wasn't used to failing and he wouldn't this time. Selena was the first thing he wanted just for himself.

Selena was buzzed and hot and had forgotten the last time she'd had this much fun. Clubbing wasn't her thing. To be honest it never had been. She'd always been a very studious girl and when she'd met Raul he'd kept her isolated from others. Part of the reason his con had worked so well.

But tonight she didn't want to think about any of that. Jorge came out of the club and sat down next to her on the bench. "Are you hiding out?"

"No. Cooling down. I haven't danced that much in years," she admitted.

"What do you do for fun in New York?" he asked.

"Nothing. I don't have fun. I just work and go home."

"All work and no play makes for one big boring life, *tata*."

"It didn't seem so bad until tonight," she admitted. "It's a quiet life but also an uncomplicated one."

Jorge put his arm along the back of the bench and hugged her to his side. "You need to relax."

"I think you are right. Tonight was a lot of fun. I

never guessed that just dancing would be so liberating. I forgot about everything when I was out there."

Jorge smiled at her. His grin reminded her of her father's and she felt a pang in her heart. She missed her parents so much.

"That's the point of clubbing. I think we will have to take you out again."

"I might let you," she said. "But I'm worn out now. I am going to call a cab to take me back to my hotel."

"Hotel? Why aren't you staying at your old house?" Jorge asked.

"Too many memories," she said.

He nodded. "Why haven't you sold that place?"

She shrugged. "I sometimes get income from renting it and I give that money to *abuelito*. It's the least I can do."

"*Tata,* you have to let go of the past or you are always going to be stuck in it," Jorge said.

"I did let go, remember? I live in New York," she said.

"That wasn't letting go, that was running away," Jorge said. "You are punishing yourself by staying away. No one in the family blames you for what happened. You need to forgive yourself."

"That is easier said than done," she said.

"Don't I know it," he said.

"How do you know that?" she asked.

"I had an affair last year. Carina took me back and she says she's forgiven me, but I don't think I will ever feel worthy of her again."

"Carina is a nicer person than I am," Selena said. "I would never…"

"I thought so, too. But what I have with her is worth

fighting for. I had no idea how much I loved that woman until I thought I'd lost her forever."

"Love is so complicated," Selena said. Raul had been able to manipulate her because she'd been totally in love with him. Other people had told her he wasn't the perfect angel she'd believed him to be but that hadn't mattered. In her mind and in her heart she'd made excuses for him. She didn't want to do the same with Justin.

"Yes it is," Jorge said. "But there is nothing else like it on earth. I wouldn't trade my feelings for Carina for anything."

"Did I hear my name?" Carina asked, coming out to join them. "I wondered where you got to."

"Just visiting with Selena. I don't think she knows how much we all miss her."

"We do all miss you," Carina said. She looked over at Jorge, and Selena had the impression that Carina still wasn't sure of her man. She might have forgiven her husband, but it was clear that she hadn't relearned how to trust him.

"I'm calling a cab," Selena said.

"No, don't," Jorge said. "We will take you home. I'm ready to be alone with my woman."

Carina closed her eyes as Jorge hugged her close and it was almost painful to watch them together now that Selena knew their secret. She wondered if all couples had a secret. Something that bound them together and made them stronger. And she did believe her cousin and his wife would be stronger once Carina knew that Jorge was sincere. But that would take some time.

Jorge went in to tell the rest of her cousins that they were leaving.

"Tonight was fun," Selena said.

"Yes, it was. It's not really my scene—I like to stay

at home, but Jorge likes to hit the clubs and we have worked out a compromise where we will do it once a month," Carina said.

"Does that work?" Selena asked.

"It does. I actually like going out with him. It's not the way I thought it would be. And Jorge has agreed to take ballroom dancing classes with me."

Selena couldn't see her cousin doing ballroom dancing, but if it made Carina happy, she guessed that he would do it. "Where do you take lessons?"

"At Luna Azul. Jen Miller, who teaches their Latin dance classes, also knows ballroom and she is showing us a few moves."

"Do you think Luna Azul has been good for the neighborhood?" Selena asked her, her head clearing from the mojitos she'd been drinking all night.

"I do. They have captured the feel of old Havana in the club. My papa won't admit it to his friends but he likes going there because it reminds him of the stories his *abuelito* used to tell of pre-Castro Havana."

"I need to check it out and learn a bit about the enemy."

"I think you will be surprised by how much it fits given that they are outsiders."

Jorge came out of the club and they left. During the ride, Selena sat quietly in the backseat of the Dodge Charger. She thought about Justin Stern and dancing with him. She had a feeling that he'd claim to be an awkward dancer, but prove to be very efficient at it.

She closed her eyes and thought about the night and what she'd learned. She'd almost made a costly emotional mistake when she'd asked Justin up to her room. But living at the hotel was giving her the distance she needed from her family and tomorrow she'd figure out how to start a fling with Justin. Flirting with him earlier and dancing tonight had stirred her blood. She wanted Justin Stern and she wasn't going to deny herself.

Justin checked in and got settled in his hotel room. He'd left a voice mail for Selena. He was surprised she was out so late. It was almost midnight. Where was she?

He didn't like the tight feeling in his chest or the anger he felt at not knowing where she was. They were nothing but business rivals to each other. Nothing more than that. He'd have to remember that fact.

He paced around his room like a caged tiger. She was probably with another man. Why shouldn't she be? There wasn't another man in this city who was bringing as many complications to the table as he was. Not one. And he knew it.

She was the last woman he should be this obsessed with but the truth was he did want her. And he should never have let her go when he'd had her in his arms earlier.

The only time they were going to be this unaware of the complications of hooking up was right now. Before they got to know each other better. That was how things like this worked.

He didn't think about it anymore but just walked out of his room. He needed a walk to clear his head.

The elevator opened as he was standing there and Selena got off the car.

"What are you doing here?" they said at the same time.

"I'm staying here," she said.

"So am I."

"Why?" she asked. "And how did you get on my floor. That is almost stalkerish."

"I'm not stalking you. I had no idea this was the floor you were on. I asked for a suite."

"Okay, fine. But why are you here?"

"If we are going to have a vacation affair, we both should be on vacation."

She tipped her head to the side. "I guess that makes a little sense. But...I liked staying here where no one knew me."

"We just met," he pointed out.

"That's true but you are already trying to worm your way under my defenses."

"Worm? That isn't exactly flattering."

She smiled. "Good, it wasn't meant to be."

"Where have you been tonight?" he asked.

"Clubbing with my cousins. I've never been clubbing before," she said. "Have you ever gone?"

"Yes. I'm co-owner of a nightclub, remember?"

"That's right. You probably write it off on your taxes as research."

He did, but he didn't say so. "Did you dance with a lot of men?"

"Jealous?"

"Incredibly," he said, moving closer to her. She was leaning against the wall next to the elevator and he put his hands on either side of her head.

He leaned in closer until his lips brushed against hers. "Who did you dance with?"

"My cousins, my brother, but I dreamed it was you," she said with her eyes half-closed. "I don't think I should have told you that."

He felt that tight ball in his stomach relax. "You definitely should have told me."

He kissed her softly on the lips and she wrapped her arms around his neck.

"Are you a good dancer?" she asked as he broke the kiss.

"I don't know. No one has ever complained," he said.

"I knew you'd say something like that. Do you like holding me?" she asked.

He realized she was a little tipsy and saying things that she probably wouldn't have otherwise.

"I do. Do you like being in my arms?"

"Definitely. But you are just my vacation stud, remember that," she said to him.

"I won't forget it. Which room is yours?"

"Number 3106," she said. "Why?"

"I think we should get you to your room and out of the hallway."

"Good idea. I'm tired, Justin."

"I know, sweetie."

"Sweetie? Did you call me sweetie?"

"I did. Any objections?"

"No. I think I like it, but we're really not close enough for you to call me that."

"I wish we were," he said.

"Do you?"

"I wouldn't have said it if it weren't true."

"Are you a straight talker?" she asked.

"Sometimes. With you I am more than I want to be. You seem to bring out the awkward truth in me."

She giggled, and the sound enchanted him. She was such a sweet girl when her defenses were down. He helped her open her door and saw that her suite was laid out the reverse of his.

"I wanted you in my room earlier," she said.

"Not really," he said. "I think you were trying to throw me."

"I was," she admitted. "But a part of me did want you here. It's so much easier to start an affair before you have time to think of the risks involved."

"Yes, it is. But we aren't going to start one tonight," he said.

"We aren't? Why not?" she asked.

He leaned down and kissed her because he was human and a man who wanted her very much. The kiss was passionate and intense, all the things he'd known it would be, but at the same time the taste of those minty mojitos she'd been drinking all night lingered on her tongue. She wasn't herself tonight. And he wanted her to be fully aware of what she was doing when they did become lovers.

She wrapped her arms around his neck and tipped her head back to look up at him. "I like the way you feel in my arms."

"I do, too. I've never had a woman fit so well in my arms before. Your head nestles just right on my shoulder, your breasts are cushioned perfectly on my chest," he said, and he slid his hands down her back to her hips, "and your hips feel just right against mine."

She swiveled her hips against his. "Yes, they do. Are you sure you don't want to stay with me tonight?"

"No, I'm not sure," he said, but he wasn't going to. He wanted Selena but he wanted her on his terms. And that meant having her respect. She was going to be a vacation fling, not a one-night stand. So he slowly drew

her arms down from his shoulders and gave her a kiss
that almost killed him when he pulled away.

"Good night, Selena," he said and then walked out
of her suite and went down the hall to his.

Vacation affair be damned, he already cared about
her more than he wanted to admit.

Seven

Two days later, Selena wasn't too sure how she found herself on Justin's yacht sailing around Biscayne Bay.

True, he hadn't given up his pursuit of her at all. She'd been surprised when he'd taken a suite on the same floor as her at the Ritz but she shouldn't have been. He was a very thorough man.

"I forgot how much I like Miami," she said.

"And the nights here?" he asked. She stood next to him in the cockpit while he piloted the boat. He'd told her when they arrived that he had a staff of three, but most of the time preferred to do short trips by himself.

"Definitely. I love the nights," she said, putting her hand on his shoulder and rubbing it. She liked the way his hard muscles felt under the cloth of his dress shirt.

"I thought the committee meeting went well today," he said.

She shook her head. "We're on vacation, so we can't talk business."

He arched one eyebrow at her. "Are you sure?"

She nodded. She'd had fevered dreams of Justin for the last two nights. Since she'd met him he was someone she just couldn't turn her back on, and tonight with the sea breeze in her hair and the smell of the ocean surrounding her, she realized she wasn't going to just walk away from Justin Stern. It might not be the smartest thing she ever did but she knew she was going to have an affair with this man.

She wanted to know the man beneath the clothes. The one that few others had seen and that would belong to only her.

Belong to her? she wondered. Did she really want him to be hers? She wanted him in her bed taking care of her sexual needs, but for anything else?

"Very sure. But it's a fling, Justin, it can't be more than that."

"I agree. Do you mind helping me out with dinner?"

"Uh, I guess not. I should tell you my culinary skills are limited," she said. "I live on takeout and microwave dinners."

"They must agree with you," he said, skimming his gaze over her body, lingering at her curves.

"They do. What do you need from me?" she asked.

"I have a picnic basket on the table in the galley and a bottle of pinot grigio chilling in the wine refrigerator. Will you bring them up?"

"Yes, are we dining on the deck?"

"Yes, aft…you'll see where the cushions are set up. I'm going to find a safe place to drop anchor and then I'll meet you down there," he said.

She moved to go past him down the short flight of stairs but he stopped her with a hand on her waist.

"Yes?"

"I'm very glad we have this time together," he said. It was one of those awkward things that he sometimes said that made her heart skip a beat. He was sweet when he wasn't so arrogant and cocky.

"Me, too," she said.

He leaned down and rubbed his lips over hers. His breath was minty but when he opened his mouth and his tongue swept into hers she tasted *him*. She held on to his shoulders; he deepened the kiss and she realized this was what she'd been craving. This was what she needed.

She'd been alone too long. Working to forget the pain she'd run from and afraid to take a chance on being with another man. Now Justin seemed like he was the remedy.

They hit a wave and it jarred them off balance. She fell into Justin, who was careful to keep them both on their feet.

"I better pay attention to where we are going," he said.

"Yes, you better. I have plans for you," she said.

He wriggled his eyebrows at her. "You do?"

"Indeed…you mentioned a bottle of wine and I might need a big strong man to open it for me."

He threw his head back and laughed. She smiled at him. This was what she needed. A nice break from a long day of negotiating. And it didn't matter that she was with the man who'd been arguing with her all day.

She climbed down the steps and went into the galley. She'd been on yachts before and though there was luxury in every inch of the boat it didn't make her feel uncomfortable. Justin had made this place homey. Selena's favorite touch was a picture on the galley wall of Justin and his brothers, all shirtless and looking yummy, playing a beach volleyball game.

She leaned in closer for a better look at the photo and realized that Justin had a scar on his sternum. Reaching out she traced the line and wondered how he got it. There was so much more to him than what she knew from the boardroom, but she knew she had to be cautious with him on their personal time.

If this was going to be a fling, then she shouldn't know too much about him. How was that going to work? She wanted to know everything about Justin. She needed to figure out what made him tick so she could make sure he didn't get the upper hand on her.

Could she do it?

Hell, she knew she was going to try. She wasn't about to walk away from him whether that was wise or not.

She heard the engine stop and the whir as he dropped anchor and realized she was staring at his photo instead of doing what he'd asked of her.

She opened the wine refrigerator and grabbed a bottle of Coppola Pinot Grigio and then picked up the picnic basket, which was heavy.

She emerged from the galley just as he came down from the pilot deck.

"Let me get the basket," he said.

She handed it over to him and followed him to the back of the boat where he'd already arranged some cushions. With a flick of a button, music started playing. She shivered a little as she realized that this evening was part of a fantasy she'd always harbored. Not one she'd ever told another soul about but somehow Justin had gleaned enough from her to know that this was what she'd always wanted.

Justin had always loved the water. It was the one place where he and his brothers had been alone with their father. Since his mother got seasick she never came out on the boat with them.

His dad had taught all three of the boys everything they needed to know about sailing—and navigating the waters around *her*. But that was it. He didn't have any useful lessons when it came to women. As Justin and his brothers had gotten older, their father merely warned them not to fall in love.

Love is a sweet trap, my boys, Justin remembered his father saying.

Sitting on the deck in the moonlight, listening to the soft voice of Selena, Justin couldn't see what his father had meant. Not with this woman.

"Dinner was very nice," she said. "Though I don't know that your culinary skills are any better than mine."

"Just because I had a little help from Publix?" he asked.

"Yes. And I am going to treat you to dinner tomorrow night."

"You are?" he asked. Perfect, he already planned for the two of them to spend every night together. It would be difficult later in the month as he started to have commitments with the tenth anniversary celebration. He knew he needed to make every minute with her count.

"Definitely. I will even cook for you. The one dish I know how to make."

"What is it?" he asked, suspecting that she must be

able to cook even though she said she mostly had others cooking for her. He did the same thing because when you only cooked for one it wasn't that much fun.

"A traditional Cuban one. I'm not going to say any more. I want you to be surprised."

"I already am. I thought you were never going to ask me out," he said with a mock frown.

"I haven't had a chance. You've been hitting on me since we met. I couldn't get a word in edgewise."

"It's your fault."

"How do you figure?" she asked.

"You are one hot mama! I knew I couldn't let the chance to get to know you pass me by."

She put her wineglass down and moved over so she was sitting next to him. She had her legs curved under her body and as she leaned forward her blouse shifted, and he glimpsed the curve of her breasts encased in a pretty pink bra.

"I am so glad you didn't," she said in a soft, seductive voice.

Everything masculine in him went on point and he knew that he was tired of waiting. Tired of playing it safe with her. Life seldom offered him a chance like Selena represented. She was everything he wanted in a woman.

He reached out and touched her, tracing the line of her shirt and the soft skin underneath. She shifted her shoulders as she reached for him.

"Unbutton your shirt," she said. "I want to see your chest."

"You do?" he asked.

She nibbled on her lower lip as she nodded at him.

"You do it," he said.

She arched one eyebrow at him. "I should have guessed you'd want to be in charge here."

"I am always in charge," he said, bringing her hands to his mouth and placing a wet, hot kiss in the center of her palms before putting her hands on his chest.

She took her time toying with the buttons, caressing his chest as she undid each one. She paused at the scar on his sternum; she traced the edges of it with her forefinger.

"How did you get this?"

"I wish I had some glamorous tale to tell you but it happened when I was in college—young and a little bit reckless, I'm afraid."

"How?"

"It's not sexy, let's not talk about it," he said.

"I want to know. I have a long scar on my thigh which I might show you if you tell me how you got this," she said, running the edge of her nail over the line of the scar.

He shuddered in reaction, loving her hands on his body. He was intrigued, too, wanted to see her thighs and what she was talking about.

He took her hand in his and rubbed it on his chest where she'd been stroking him. "Frat party plus pretty girls plus impulsive need to show off equaled this scar."

She started laughing. "I wouldn't have pegged you for the show-off type."

"I guess I'm not trying hard enough if you can't see me strutting my stuff to get your attention."

She leaned in close, coming up on her knees and putting both hands on his shoulders. "You have my attention, Mr. Stern. What are you going to do with it?"

He put his hands on her waist and drew her even

closer to him until she was straddling his hips and her skirt fell over his lap. When she shifted, he felt the core of her body brush over his erection.

"I guess I have your attention," she said.

"You do. Now about that scar on your thigh," he said.

"I haven't decided if you've told me enough to get to see it."

"I am going to see it," he said, sliding his hands up under her skirt and caressing every inch of her thigh. He couldn't feel anything on her left thigh but on her right one there was a slight abrasion. "I think I've found it."

"You have," she confirmed. Then she leaned down to kiss him and he let her take control of this moment.

Justin's hands slid up and down her back and she forgot everything but the sensations he evoked in her. She put her mind on hold and just reveled in the sensation of being on the sea on this beautiful warm night with this man who wanted nothing but her body.

There was a freedom in this that she had never experienced before. A freedom to be here with him. It didn't matter that later she might regret this. Right now it was exactly what she needed.

"Why did you stop kissing me?" he asked.

"I'm trying not to think," she said. "It's not working."

"Then I'm not doing my job," he said. "I should be sweeping you away from your worries."

"You should be…I think talking isn't going to help. Why don't you put your mouth on me and make me forget."

He arched one eyebrow at her. "Do I have that power over you?"

"You have no idea," she admitted.

She had tried to justify this attraction, to blame it on the fact that she was back in Miami. But that wasn't it—she knew it was Justin, pure and simple.

She wanted his mouth on hers. She needed his hands sliding over her body, and she had to touch him. She was tired of being good and living an honest life. Not that there was anything dishonest about this, but she just needed a chance to let loose and Justin had offered her that.

"Kiss me."

"Yes," he said. His mouth found hers. He sucked her lower lip between his teeth and held it gently there while he suckled.

She swept her hands under his shirt enjoying the warmth of his skin and the strength of his muscles under her fingers. She liked the light dusting of hair on his chest and how it felt as she ran her hands over him. She lingered at his scar, tracing the outside edges of it and then followed the trail of hair as it narrowed on his chest and dipped into his waistband.

She pulled back so she could see him. He lounged back against the pillows and cushions with his shirt open. He looked like a pasha of old and she felt like a willing sex slave sent to please him.

She shifted back so her thighs rested on her heels. She pushed his shirt off his shoulders and he pulled his arms out of it.

He reached for the sash on the left side of her blouse and undid it. As the fabric fell open he put his hands on her waist and drew her up and back over his thighs. He reached under her shirt, his large hands rubbing over her bare midriff and then spanning her waist.

"You are so tiny," he said.

"I'm not," she said. She was an average-size girl; it was just that Justin was a big man with big hands.

He pushed her blouse off her shoulders and it fell off her arms behind her. He brought his hand up and slowly traced the pattern of her bra. Traced it from her clavicle down her chest to the curve of her breast.

He ran his finger down the edge where the cup met the other and then back up. She had goose bumps on her chest and her nipples stirred inside the cups of her bra. Wanting to feel that firm finger of his on them.

He reached behind her and undid the clasp and then carefully peeled the cups away until her breasts were revealed to him. He dropped the bra on the deck where her blouse was.

He cupped both breasts in his hands, letting his big palms rub both of her nipples in a circular motion. The sensation started a chain reaction in her. She loved the feeling and shifted her hips against his erection to satisfy the ache that started at the apex of her thighs.

He spread his fingers out, caressing the full globes of her breasts, and then slowly drew his right hand up to the tip of her nipple. But he didn't linger there.

He circled her areola with his forefinger and then bent forward, holding her back with one hand. She felt the brush of his breath against her nipple as it tightened and then a tiny lick of his tongue.

"More," she said. She was desperate to feel his entire mouth on her nipple. "Suckle me."

He shook his head and she felt his silky hair against her breast as he continued to trace over her breast and nipple with his tongue.

The crotch of her panties was moist and she felt almost desperate to feel more of his mouth against her.

She tried to shift her shoulders and force him to take more of her nipple but he just pulled his head back.

"Not until I'm ready," he said.

"Be ready," she ordered him.

He gave her a purely sexual smile. "Not yet."

He treated her other breast to the same delicate teasing and she was squirming on his lap when he lifted his head. But when she put her hands on his chest and saw him shiver, she knew she had her own power over him.

And it was intoxicating. Leaning forward she tunneled her fingers through his hair and let the tips of her breasts brush against this chest.

He moaned, the sound low and husky.

"Do you like that?" she asked, whispering into his ear.

"Very much," he said. Using his grip on her waist he pushed her back into the cushions and came over her.

His hips were cradled between her thighs and his arms braced his weight above her. He rotated his hips and his erection pressed against the very center of her.

She moaned softly and he leaned down over her.

"Do you like that?"

"Yesss."

He smiled down at her and lowered his head to her body. He used his mouth at her neck and nibbled his way down to her breasts.

He cupped them in his hands as she undulated under him, trying to get closer to what she needed. And what she needed was this man. She needed to feel him naked above her and hot and hard inside her.

She shifted her legs, curving her thigh up around his hips. The position shifted him against her and he said her name in a low, feral tone of voice.

He didn't stop in his slow seduction but his hands swept down her body and she felt her skirt slowly lifted until the juncture of their bodies wouldn't allow it to come any farther up. She lifted her hips and moaned as the tip of his shaft rubbed her.

He pushed her skirt higher and then she felt his hands on her butt. He rubbed his palm over her and then pulled her skimpy bikini panties down. He leaned up over her, kneeling between her legs as he stripped them off.

He tossed them aside and looked down at her. His chest rose and fell with each breath he took and his skin was flushed.

His erection was visible behind the zipper of his pants and she felt another surge of power that she affected him so visibly.

She lifted her arms behind her head and twined her fingers together, the movement forcing her breasts forward.

He watched each move she made. She brought her left leg up and then slowly let it fall wide, exposing her very center to him. He put his hand on her ankles and drew her legs open even farther and then leaned forward.

"You are truly the most beautiful woman I've ever seen," he said. "I want to take my time and explore every inch of you, but my body wants something else."

"What do you want, Justin?"

"To hear you moaning my name while I'm buried inside of your silky hot body."

"Me, too," she said. This wasn't about power but about pleasure. And it had been too long since she'd enjoyed a man just for the pure thrill of it.

"Come to me," she said.

He shook his head. "No. I want to make this last. I

want to make you come so much that you forget every other man but me."

She tipped her head to the side studying him. He'd already wiped every man from her mind. She only saw him. She'd dreamed of him before this...was this a mistake?

She shook her head as she felt his hands on her again. She didn't care if this wasn't smart. She wanted Justin and she was going to have him. Tomorrow she'd sort out the problems this brought to her. This night was hers.

She felt the warmth of his breath on her stomach and his finger caressing the outer edge of her belly button. He drew his hands down her hips, then down farther until he found that scar on her thigh. He traced it with his finger, then lightly with his tongue.

His mouth on her sent pulses of warmth through her core and she knew she was close to orgasm. Every pleasure point she had was pulsing.

He parted her thighs and dropped nibbling kisses up their length. His fingers skimmed over her feminine secrets and then came back. He rubbed his palm over her center and her hips jerked upward.

She felt the cool night air on her most private flesh before his breath bathed her. His tongue danced over her flesh and she clenched her thighs around his head. He put one of his hands on her stomach and shifted between her legs, lying down there.

He lifted his head and looked up the length of her body. Their eyes met and something passed between them. She didn't know what but she felt like he'd found a secret she'd kept hidden even from herself.

He lowered his head again and when he sucked on her intimate flesh everything inside of her clenched. Her breasts felt too full, her nipples were tight little points and she was wet and dripping. She wanted him inside of her and she grabbed at his shoulders hoping to hurry him. To make him come up over her. But he stayed where he was.

His tongue and teeth were driving her toward a climax, which felt too intense. She lifted her thighs and held his head to her body with her hands in his thick silky hair. She arched her hips as she came in a blinding rush.

"Justin, yes, keep doing that," she cried out. She couldn't stop the sensations rushing through her. They were intense and almost scary in the pleasure they created.

He kept his mouth on her until she stopped trembling in his arms. She tugged at his shoulders, wanting him to come up over her. But he sat back on his heels between her legs and watched her.

She wanted to give him the same pleasure he'd given her. She sat up and pushed him back against the pillows and reached for his zipper, carefully lowering it and freeing his erection from his boxers. There was a tip of moisture at the tip and he shuddered when she wiped it off with her finger and brought it to her mouth to lick it.

He tasted salty and vaguely like his kisses. She stroked his shaft from the root to the tip, swiping her finger over the tip each time. With her other hand she cupped him and squeezed gently.

His breath sawed from his body as he grew even harder in her hand. She leaned forward and let her hair brush over his erection. He shuddered again and his hands burrowed into her hair as his hips came forward and the tip of his erection touched her lips.

She licked the tip and then took him into her mouth.

He moaned that deep guttural sound of his again. She loved the feeling of him in her mouth. He was too big for her to take his entire length but she stroked her hand on him and drew her mouth up and over him, sweeping her tongue over the tip.

His hands tightened in her hair and he drew her off his body. "No more. I need to be inside you."

"Now?" she asked. It was what she was craving, too.

"Now," he said, pushing her onto her back and coming down between her legs. He found her opening with the tip of his erection and it was the naked flesh-on-flesh moment that jarred her.

"You feel so good," he said. "Should I get a condom?"

"I'm on the Pill," she said.

"Good," he said and thrust into her.

She came in that instant, just a tiny fluttering of a climax as he filled her all the way to her womb. His abdomen hit her in the right spot and he drew back and entered her again. Slow, long thrusts that made her moan and writhe beneath him.

His chest and shoulders were above her and she held him tight, lifted herself closer to him. "You feel so good."

"So do you," he said. His hips moved with surety between her legs until she was overwhelmed with the feel of him.

The hair on his chest abraded her aroused nipples and she shuddered again as she felt everything inside of her building to another climax. And this one felt even more intense than the other two he'd given her.

He put his hands under her, cupping her buttocks in his hands and lifting her hips higher so that he could get deeper on each thrust. He leaned over her, whispering dark sex words into her ear and she felt the first fingers of her orgasm teasing her. Making her shiver under him. Then he drew back and thrust heavily into her, his hips moving faster and faster until she screamed with her climax.

She felt his hips continue to jerk forward and the warmth of his seed spilling inside of her. He thrust two more times before collapsing on her. He breathed heavily and his body was bathed in sweat. She wrapped her arms and legs around him and held him to her like she'd never have to let go.

She looked up at the night sky and realized that she really didn't want to have to let him go.

Eight

The last thing that Justin wanted to do was get up and move away from Selena. Holding her in his arms was the most addicting thing he'd ever done. But the sea breezes were getting stronger and he knew they couldn't stay on the deck all night. He slipped out of her and rolled to his side, coming up on his elbow.

Her lips were swollen from his kisses and her eyes sleepy as she looked up at him. He drew one finger over her lips and then realized that he was never going to get enough of her. He was spent from making love but he still wanted to lie next to her and hold her in his arms.

That was dangerous stuff.

Tomas Gonzalez may have found the one weakness that Justin had. One he himself hadn't realized until this very second.

"I guess we have to get up," she said.

"I was thinking about carrying you down to the bedroom."

"What are you waiting for?"

He scooped her up in his arms and then stood up. He liked the feel of her there. She wrapped one arm around his shoulders and her long, silky hair rubbed against his arm as he carried her down the stairs.

The stairs were narrow but he turned to enable them both to fit. She felt right here—in his arms and on his yacht.

He glanced down, noticing she stared up at him. "What are you thinking?"

"That this was exactly what I needed," she said.

He felt the same way but he'd never admit that out loud. Already he knew that if he was going to continue to keep control over this affair he needed to play his cards close to his chest. Make love to her—he knew he had to keep doing that. There was no way this one time had satiated him. He was satisfied but he still craved more.

He laid her on the center of his bed with the navy blue comforter and stood next to her. He wanted this to be more than he knew it could be. More than she wanted from him. But it wasn't.

"I have to wash up," he said. It wasn't romantic but then sex technically wasn't supposed to be about romance. It was dirty, hot and sweaty and it made him feel very primitive and possessive. Especially with her.

He padded in his bare feet to the head and washed up quickly, bringing a warm washcloth back to the bed to gently wash between her legs. She was still where he'd left her and when he pulled the covers back and laid down, she curled onto her side and put her arm around his waist.

He put his arm around her and drew her closer to him. The soft exhalation of her breath stirred the hair on his chest. And it was only as the moonlight trickled through the porthole window that he realized she hadn't said anything since he'd carried her downstairs.

"Are you okay?" he asked, rubbing his arm up and down hers.

She shrugged.

"Selena?"

"Yes?"

"Talk to me," he said. He wanted to know her secrets and this moment was as close as they were going to get to really seeing the truth in each other. They were both vulnerable.

Yes, he realized, she was vulnerable. That wasn't what he intended to make her feel but he was very glad that what they'd shared had affected her.

"I'm not sure what to say. I thought that I'd have an affair with you and still be able to keep you off your toes in the boardroom but now I'm second-guessing that. I'm not sure that this was wise," she said.

He tipped her head up to him so that their eyes met. "I'm not sure it was, either, but I don't think we could have waited much longer for this."

"Why?"

He needed her but he wasn't going to admit it. "The attraction between us is very strong."

"Yes, it is."

"I for one was distracted all day today by the small glimpses I got of your cleavage each time you leaned forward to gesture to something on the map."

She laughed, and it was a sweet sound. "I will have to remember that."

"I have no doubt that you will. Let's not overthink this," he said. "We are two people out of time here. Our ordinary worlds are far away and for now there is only the two of us."

"You make it sound so simple and so appealing. But I know that every action has a reaction."

"And every reaction is bad?" he asked.

"Not at all. But every reaction causes ripples and I don't want to hurt my grandparents...not again."

He shifted them on the bed so she was lying on her back and he was next to her propped up on his elbow.

"Tell me about it," he invited. "Whatever it is that you did to hurt them before."

She brought her arms up to her waist and hugged herself and he didn't like that. He was here with her now; she should turn to him for comfort.

He stroked her arm and she patted his hand.

"I don't think it's the right story for tonight but I will tell you about it sometime."

"Tomorrow?" he asked. "After you cook me dinner."

"Stop being so bossy," she said, but she smiled when she said that, so he suspected she didn't really mind.

"It's part of my charm."

"You always put such a heavy burden on your charm."

"And it doesn't measure up?"

"You measure up just fine," she said, sweeping her hands down his chest and cupping him in her hand.

He was no longer interested in talking and instead made love to her in his bed, then held her quietly in his arms afterward as they both drifted to sleep.

* * *

The next morning, Justin showered in the guest room while Selena used the master bathroom. He gathered her clothing first and left it lying on the bed so she'd find it when she came out.

He hadn't planned on making love to her last night, but then he hadn't planned on much when it came to Selena Gonzalez.

She totally knocked him for a loop. Since the first time he'd laid eyes on her he'd been lost. That wasn't right, he was a very successful businessman and he didn't get lost. He always had a motivation for everything he did. He had to remember that Selena wasn't only an attractive woman, she was also a powerful adversary.

That's right, he was doing what he had to in order to ensure that Luna Azul continued to prosper. And no matter that he was determined to keep the personal and business parts of their lives separate, he knew something had changed between them last night.

His BlackBerry pinged and he glanced at the screen to see the reminder of his 10:00 a.m. tee time with Maxwell Strong. He still had an hour but getting the boat back to the marina and then dropping Selena at the Ritz was going to eat into his time.

He got dressed and checked the master bedroom. Selena's clothes were gone. When he got upstairs, he found her sitting on the bench at the stern of the boat. She had on a pair of huge sunglasses that covered not only her eyes but also most of her face.

She might be wearing yesterday's clothing but she didn't seem unkempt. In fact she looked cool and remote—untouchable.

He paused and studied her, realizing that just because he'd had her body last night didn't mean he'd come close to unraveling all the secrets that made Selena who she was.

"Ready to head back to the real world?" he asked.

She tipped her head to the side and studied him. "I guess we have to. I have a meeting this morning that I'm going to be late for unless we get moving."

"I have one as well," he said. "I have a Keurig machine in the galley if you want some coffee."

"No thanks. I'm a tea drinker," she said.

"I wouldn't have pegged you for one," he said, climbing the stairs to the pilot house.

He glanced over his shoulder and saw that she'd followed him.

"Why not?"

"You just don't look the type."

"There's a tea type?" she asked.

A part of him knew it was time to let this conversation drop but another part was just dying to see how she'd react. "Yes, I'm thinking white-haired old ladies sitting around in homemade sweaters, having little cakes and drinking tea out of pots covered in quilted cozies."

She punched him in the arm. "Not only old ladies drink tea. And those cozies can be very nicely made."

"I told you I didn't see you as a tea drinker."

"You aren't winning any points for that," she said.

He pushed the button to turn on the engines and the boat roared to life. But he didn't really want to head back to the port. He wanted to stay out here on the sea with just Selena. If he were a different man he'd ask her to run away with him or maybe just kidnap her and sail off for some exotic port of call, but he wasn't.

And they both had family to think of. The Gonzalez family would probably crucify him if he tried to abduct their prodigal daughter.

"Why are you looking at me like that?"

"I'm contemplating kidnapping you and keeping you naked in my bed."

She shook her head. "You'd never do it. You'd never let your brothers down like that."

"You wouldn't go for it either. I bet you'd jump overboard and swim back to Miami if I tried it."

She shrugged. "Maybe."

He steered them to the harbor, the engines and the sea wind whipping around them. "No maybe about it. You feel guilty where your grandparents are concerned and you'll do whatever you have to in order to make them proud this time."

She wrapped an arm around her waist and turned away from him, staring out over the horizon. He wondered if she'd really be happy running away with him. Lord knew he was tempted, but she had been right. He would never do that until he had everything settled for Luna Azul. It wasn't just a company he worked for, it was his family legacy, and he wasn't about to lose it.

"When are you going to trust me with your past?" he asked her.

"Tonight," she said. "I want you to come to my house. It will be easier to talk about the past if you are there. But if we do this…we won't be a vacation fling anymore."

"Are you sure you want to chance it?"

She studied him for a long minute and he had the feeling that she was searching for answers in his face. He wanted her to find what she was looking for but this morning he didn't have any notion of what she needed from him. After making love to her last night he'd thought he'd know her better but instead he found she was still a mystery to him.

"Yes. I think that we have to keep moving forward. I don't want to walk away...not yet."

He knew that the end was possible—even probable given the way they'd come together—and he was bracing himself for it. Still, starting a relationship and expecting it to end wasn't the best idea.

"We're like a short-term partnership," he said.

"Trust you to put it in terms that would be better suited to the boardroom, but yes, that's exactly what we are. It will be mutually advantageous to both of us while it lasts."

"And pleasurable," he added. He slowed the boat as they reached the marina and he maneuvered his yacht into its slip before turning off the engine.

"What time tonight?" he asked her.

"Seven? Is that too early?"

He took her hand and led her down the gangway to the deck. "No, it sounds just right. Do you want me to drop you at the Ritz?"

"Yes, please," she said.

He drove her to the hotel and let her off, then watched her walk away. He pulled back out into traffic before she was inside the hotel because he didn't want to sit there and think about how hard it was to let her go.

Nine

Selena drove through Miami like the devil himself was chasing her. She wanted to escape her thoughts. It wasn't that she was afraid of Justin; it was simply that he represented a part of her that she wanted to pretend didn't exist anymore. She wanted to drive away from the area and never look back. But running away wasn't her style any more, either.

She pulled into the parking lot of Luna Azul. At a little after ten on Tuesday morning there wasn't much action here. She had an appointment with Justin's older brother, Cam. Through the grapevine she'd heard that he had been the one to raise his younger brothers after both parents were killed. Cam had been twenty at the time.

She pushed her sunglasses up on her head as she entered the cool dark interior of Luna Azul. The club was gorgeous with a huge Chihuly installation in the foyer. The building had once been a cigar factory back in the early 1900s. It was inspired by the success of Ybor Haya's factories in Key West and Ybor City near Tampa Bay.

The Miami factory had been started by the Jimenez brothers and prospered for several years until cigarettes became more popular and eventually the company went out of business. When Selena had been growing up this factory was a derelict building that was a breeding ground for gang-related trouble.

Seeing it today, she had to admit that the Stern brothers had improved this corner of their neighborhood.

"You must be Selena."

She glanced up as Cam Stern walked toward her. He was the same height as Justin and they both had the same stubborn-looking jaw, but there the resemblance ended. Justin was simply a better-looking man. Where Justin's eyes were blue, Cam's were dark obsidian, and Cam wore his hair long enough to brush his shoulders.

"I am indeed. You must be Cam," she said, holding out her hand.

He shook her hand firmly and then let it drop. "I'm glad you could come down here. I wanted you to see what we've been doing here in the last ten years and why it's important that we get the Mercado project going so we can revitalize the area the way we did with the club."

"No one doubts you can pour money into a project and make it successful. I've said as much to Justin. The Gonzalez family is concerned that you are going to take away a vital community shopping center and make it an upscale shopping area of no use to the local residents. We aren't interested in having more of the celebrities you bring down here socializing while families are trying to buy their groceries."

Cam tilted his head to the side. "I can see that you have inherited your grandfather's fire."

"I'm flattered you think so, but I'm not half as obstinate as he is."

Cam laughed as she'd hoped he would. And she realized that Cam was a nice guy. Not because of the laughter but because he'd asked for this meeting. She suspected that he was trying to help her and the rest of the committee understand and see the human face of Luna Azul.

"I grew up here on Fisher Island, Selena—is it okay to call you by your first name?" he asked.

"Of course, I'm planning to call you Cam."

He smiled at her. "Let's go up to the rooftop. I want to show you our club up there."

"I want to see it. My younger brother has told me that he is interested in deejaying here and he has heard that the rooftop club is all Latin music."

"That's right. We start each evening with a couple of professional dancers teaching our guests how to salsa. Then we have a conga line to get them out there onto the dance floor."

"Sounds fun. One thing that Enrique also mentioned is that most of the staff isn't from our neighborhood."

"That's true. We had so much resistance from the local leaders when we bought the club that I didn't get any local talent auditioning for the roles we had. I had to look beyond Little Havana to find the people I needed," he said. "But that's beginning to change."

For the first time she truly understood how hard it must have been for the Sterns to come in here and try to open this place up. And when they got off the elevator at the rooftop club she was astounded by the feel and look of it. To be honest she felt like she was stepping into one of her grandfather's pictures of old Havana.

"This is perfect," she said. "My *abuelito* would love this. It looks like the patio where he and my grandmother met."

"Thank you," Cam said. "We spent a lot of time trying to capture the feeling of Cuba pre-Castro."

"You did it. But why did you choose to build here? You could have chosen downtown Miami or South Beach and not encountered any resistance."

He glanced out in the distance where the skyline of Miami was visible. "I wanted to be a part of this community. When I was a boy we had a nanny from Little Havana and Maria used to tell me stories of Cuba when she'd put us to bed each night."

"That's sweet. So you did it for her?"

He arched one eyebrow at her in a way that reminded her of his brother. Justin was in her mind today. No matter what she tried, he wasn't going to be easy to relegate out of her head.

"I did it because this building came on the market—it had been foreclosed on. It was a bargain. Justin was still in college and it was before Nate made it big in baseball. I had Maria's stories and a building I could afford and I thought I might have a chance at making this work—about as much a chance as a blue moon."

"A slim one," she said.

He nodded and despite the fact that he was supposed to be the big bad corporate enemy of her grandparents she understood that he and his family had come to this neighborhood the same way her family had. Looking for a chance to put down roots and make their fortune.

* * *

The Florida sun was bright and hot as Justin drove his golf cart over the course. Next to him Maxwell talked about his daughter's impending high school graduation and the fact that she was making him nuts.

"I thought kids were easier once they were no longer toddlers," Justin said.

"That's a lie parents try to spread around to convince other adults to join their club of misery," Maxwell said with a laugh.

"I know you'd do it again," Justin said.

"I would. She's a great kid. It's just since January she's been like a crazy person. Her moods swing and she goes from being so mature I can see the woman she's become to being more irrational that she was when she was six. It's crazy. But I know you don't want to hear about that."

"Nah, I don't mind hearing about your family. You give me a little insight into how the other half lives."

"Ever think of joining the married ranks?" Maxwell asked.

"Haven't found the right girl yet," Justin said, but that was his standard line. The truth was that he was married to his work. But he wouldn't mind making a little more time for Selena. That thought slipped through without him realizing it.

He wondered what their children would look like—what?! Hell, no he didn't wonder about that. He was focused on the Mercado and making that successful. "It'd be hard to have a wife when I have to spend all my hours at the office trying to figure out things like this zoning hiccup."

Maxwell laughed. "I knew that was the real reason you invited me out here today."

"Hey, I listened to your kid's stories," Justin said with a grin. He and Maxwell were friends; they'd played together on the same beach volleyball team a few summers ago.

Maxwell had also been very helpful when Cam had wanted to add the rooftop club to Luna Azul. There had been an issue with the noise and it had taken some careful negotiating with Maxwell and the zoning office to get that taken care of.

"That you did. Well near as I can tell you aren't in any direct violation of zoning laws with your proposed marketplace. There is an ordinance in that area that specifies we have to bid the work out to local craftsmen before giving you the go ahead. So if you told me you were getting bids from all Little Havana companies I'd see no reason to deny you the building permits you need."

Justin nodded. That made sense. He pulled to a stop at the seventh hole and Maxwell got out and set up his shot. He had the committee to think about and knowing them as he was coming to, he thought he could get them to recommend the construction companies he used for bids.

"What about the vendors?"

"You have to use a local vendor to replace an existing local vendor. So in your plaza, you have a Cuban American grocery store. If you want to get rid of the one there you have to go with a local chain. You might be able to get a Publix in there but nothing national. I think I saw Whole Foods on your specs, that won't be possible."

Justin wasn't surprised. "Is that legal?"

"Pretty much. You can file a lawsuit if you want but it will take you years to get it through the court system.

It's easier to just work with the local business owners and get them on your team."

"That's what you think," Justin said.

Maxwell laughed. "Your problem is that you are used to being the boss. You might have to compromise."

"No way," Justin said with a pretend frown. "Seriously, I have a committee that has local business owners on it so I think we should be able to get some movement on this soon. What do you need from me?"

"Some quiet so I can take my stroke," Maxwell said.

Justin was quiet as Maxwell took his shot and got close to the hole. Justin had played this course a million times since he was a boy. His father had taught him to play here at the country club and he was normally able to make a hole-in-one on this green.

He lined up and took his shot landing it in the hole. Maxwell whistled but they had played together before and pretending he couldn't do something when he could went against Justin's grain.

"I need to see three bids from the construction companies you are using, making sure at least one is local to Little Havana and then you are good to go. Don't forget what I said about the tenants because they won't."

"I hear that. You know when Cam first bought the club they wanted nothing to do with him so we never considered that they'd want to be part of the marketplace," Justin said.

"You are in a different place than you were then. I'm just guessing here but seeing the success you guys have made of Luna Azul probably has a lot of business owners at that strip mall hoping that you can do the same thing to their businesses, which is why they don't want you to use outside vendors this time."

"It's nice to see how much ten years has changed things," Justin said.

"It is. Sitting in my office it's hard to remember ten years ago, I mean I'm looking at changes in some areas that we thought we'd never see. Swampy area that is now being zoned commercial. That's crazy, man."

"It is," Justin said. The conversation turned to the Miami Heat's chances of making the finals this year and they finished their round of golf. Justin knew that he'd learned nothing that he couldn't have found out from talking to Maxwell on the phone but this had been nicer and for a few hours he'd been able to stop thinking of Selena and how she'd felt in his arms last night.

The committee meeting was scheduled for five o'clock that evening and Selena arrived ten minutes late because her grandmother had found out she wasn't staying in her house and had wanted to talk. Luckily Selena's brother had stepped in and gotten their grandmother off her back so that she didn't have to delve into why she owned a home and didn't want to stay there.

Selena thought a woman as superstitious as her *abuelita* would just understand about ghosts from the past and memories that lingered in a place.

She also thought her reasons would be obvious to anyone who'd known what she'd been through with Raul. She thought a bit more about how she'd let him steal so much from her. Not just her grandparents' money but also the home she'd inherited from her great aunt. It wasn't full of childhood memories but it had been a place that Selena had made into a home and Raul had stolen the safety of that home from her.

Tonight she realized was her chance to return and maybe reclaim it. It wasn't lost on her that she was invit-

ing a man she wasn't sure she could trust to help her
do that.

She walked into the downtown offices of the Luna
Azul Company fully expecting to see Justin in the conference room but instead Cam was there. She frowned
but then told herself that didn't matter. This was the
business side of their relationship.

Did they have a personal side? She felt like they were
lovers and that was it. She had to remember there was
no relationship. It didn't matter that she had slept in his
arms, there wasn't anything permanent between them.

The room was filled with her friends and cousins.
The community leaders were her family. Everyone with
a stake in the Mercado was here.

"Justin is running late today. And now that Selena
is here we can get started. I'm happy to say that after
meeting with Selena and talking to Justin, I think we can
come up with a solution that will work for all of us."

"We will see," her grandfather said.

"I think you'll be pleased, Tomas," Cam said. "I feel
like I should apologize for not coming to the community
leaders before you went to the zoning commission. It is
just that ten years ago when we opened the club no one
wanted us to be a part of the community."

"Times have changed," Selena said. "Now what is it
you have to offer us?"

"First off we would like to hire a local construction
company to do the renovations and Justin is going to
bring the solicitation for bids. Can you recommend some
companies to us?"

Selena liked the sound of this. She wondered if last
night was the reason why Justin had changed his mind.
"We can forward you a list. Pedro, you have just added
on to your bookstore."

"Yes, I did and I'm very pleased with the work I had done. That is great for the construction companies, Cam, but what about the business owners who are already in the marketplace?" Pedro asked.

"We will be using the existing vendors for the most part but we will be redesigning the stores," Justin said entering the room.

He had been outside today—his tan was deeper. He was dressed the same way he'd been when he left her this morning and it felt like it had been longer than eight hours since she'd seen him.

"We don't want slick-looking new stores," Tomas said.

"I will be consulting with each of you individually. I'd like to schedule meetings over the next few days to figure out what you think will work and for us to consult with you. Then hopefully you will lift your protest and we can get to work."

"We'll see," Selena said. "Justin, do you have the requests for bid?"

"I do," he said, handing them to her.

She glanced down at the forms and skimmed them. "Can I have a few minutes to meet with the committee without you guys?"

"Sure," Cam said.

The two men left the boardroom and Selena stood up and looked at her grandfather and the other men and women she'd grown up with. "I think we are in a position to get what we want if we handle this carefully. No one can be thrown out of their business due to the constraint that another local must be brought in if they don't renew your lease."

"That's good news. Now how do we keep the Cuban American feel in this new development?" Tomas asked.

"How many of you have been to Luna Azul?"

A few hands were raised but not enough. "Tonight's assignment, folks, is to go check out your enemy. I want you to visit the downstairs club to see the kind of effort they have put into redoing the building, but I think you will all be impressed by what they've created on their rooftop club. That's the kind of ambiance and feeling I want to see them bring to the Mercado."

"What do you mean by that? I can't take your *abuelita* to a night club."

"It's not a night club like you are thinking, *abuelito*. And you have to do it. Then we will all meet tomorrow… can we use your bookstore again, Pedro?"

"*Si,* that sounds good to me."

"They are going to build their marketplace no matter how many obstacles we put up. We just have to ensure they build it the way we want it," Selena said.

There were a chorus of murmurs around the table but everyone agreed to go to Luna Azul that night. "Will you be there?" Tomas asked.

"I checked out the club earlier. And I have plans tonight," she said.

"With who?" her grandfather asked.

"None of your business," she said.

"It must be a man," Pedro said.

"Never you mind," Pedro's wife Luz said. "She told you to keep your nose out of it."

"I am. It's just not like our Selena to have a date."

And this was why she lived several states away from these people. She knew they loved her and cared about her but she didn't like having her entire life discussed in a committee meeting.

"Okay, that's it. I'm going to go and get the Stern

brothers and tell them we should be ready to meet with them again early next week."

"That works for me," Pedro said and soon everyone else agreed. The other business owners left and Selena's grandfather kissed her before following them out.

He paused on the threshold of the conference room. "Come for breakfast tomorrow so we can talk."

"*Abuelito*—"

"No arguments, *tata*. I want to know about this man you are seeing."

"You don't have to worry about him being like Raul."

"I'm not, *tata*. The fact that you are being so secretive tells me that you're worried, though."

"Fine, but I'm coming for lunch, not breakfast."

"Agreed."

She stood there watching him walk away. Realizing that he was entirely correct—she was afraid of letting Justin in because she knew deep down that love was a losing game, at least where she was concerned.

Ten

It had been a long day, Justin thought as he drove through the quiet tree-lined neighborhood to Selena's house. The buildings around here were relatively new since this area had been hit hard by Hurricane Andrew back in '92 and completely rebuilt.

He felt good about all he'd accomplished today. Normally at this point in a negotiation he'd be chomping at the bit to close the deal, but this time he knew as soon as everyone was happy, Selena was out of here and that was the last thing he wanted.

Her suggestion that the Luna Azul Mercado committee go to the club tonight was genius. Nate and Cam were going to ensure they all had a good time; Nate had even invited his good friend, the rapper and movie star Hutch Damien, to join them. Nate's fiancée Jen Miller was going to teach them all a few salsa steps and use them for the opening conga line.

He pulled to a stop in the driveway of the address that Selena had given him. She was going to cook him a traditional Cuban meal.

He rubbed the back of his neck and sighed. As far as business decisions went, his being here wasn't his best. That was it. He could tell himself that he was doing this to blow off steam or to learn his enemy a little better but at the end of the day he knew he was here for one reason and one reason only.

He wanted to be.

Selena was changing him. And he knew that she didn't want to and was probably not even aware she was doing it. She had her own agenda and her own secrets. Secrets he was determined to find out tonight.

The front door opened and she stepped out onto the small porch. She was barefoot and wore a pair of khaki Bermuda shorts and a patterned wraparound shirt.

"Are you going to come in or just sit out here all night?" she asked.

"Oh, I'm coming in," he said, pushing the button to put the top up on his car and gathering the flowers and wine he'd brought for her.

Though his parents' relationship wasn't the best, his father had always said that you don't go to visit a woman empty-handed.

He came up her walkway noticing that the lawn was well kept but rather plain. There were no flowers in the beds at the front of the house and compared to her neighbors, this house seemed a little…lonely.

As did Selena as she stood there on her porch with one arm wrapped around her waist. She stepped inside as he came toward her and he followed her into the tiled foyer, which was done in deep, rich earth tones in a Spanish design.

As they headed farther into the sparsely furnished house, the walls were painted a muted yellow. There was a family portrait hanging in a position of prominence in her formal living room and the dining room was to the right.

"Whose house is this?" he asked.

"Mine," she said.

"Where you grew up?" he asked.

"No. I...I inherited it from my great-aunt. I usually rent it out and give my grandparents the income from it. But since I was back in town, my *abuelita* didn't book anyone for this summer."

"So why are you staying at the Ritz instead of here?" he asked. This home was warm and welcoming, though he could tell that she didn't live in it. There was a formal feeling that didn't fit with the Selena he'd come to know.

"I just...there are ghosts of the past here and I really want to focus on doing my job and going back to New York. Besides I can't pretend to be on vacation if I'm staying here."

"Fair enough," he said. "I brought these for you."

He handed her the flowers, which she raised to her nose to sniff. The bouquet held roses and white daisies.

"Lovely," she said without looking up from the flowers. "I'm going to put them in water. Want to come in the kitchen with me? Or you can wait outside back by the pool."

"I'll stay with you," he said, following her through the living room into the eat-in kitchen, which was made for entertaining. There was a breakfast bar with two stools and place settings. She walked around and opened a cabinet to find a vase and put the flowers in water. Then she leaned on the counter and looked at him.

"Thank you. I think my dad was the last man to give me flowers."

He knew her parents were dead so that meant it had been too long since a man had treated Selena right.

"You are very welcome," he said, putting the bottle of red wine on the counter.

"Dinner's almost ready. I thought we could have a drink and sit outside by the pool," she said.

"Sounds perfect to me," he said. She mixed them both mojitos and then led the way out to the pool deck. There was a fountain in the center of the traditional rectangular pool. She sat down on one of the large padded loungers and he took a seat next to her.

"So…how did things go today with my brother?" he asked. "Why didn't you mention your meeting was with him?"

"Probably the same reason you didn't tell me you were golfing with Maxwell this morning."

He laughed at that. "I guess we both are doing what we have to in order to win."

"Indeed. One thing I observed at the club today was a true love and appreciation of Cuban American society and history."

"We are definitely indebted to the community, which is why we want to make the marketplace the best it can be."

"I can see that. Your brother told me about your nanny."

"Maria? She was a great storyteller. She had a gift for making everything she said seem real."

"My papa was like that. He'd tell me grand stories before bed every night about a tiny girl who would fly to the moon and the adventures she'd have there." Selena smiled to herself. "He made me feel invincible."

Justin sat on the edge of his chair facing her. "What or who made you realize you weren't?"

Selena didn't want to talk about her past but with Justin she knew she would. Normally, she didn't date. That was pretty much how she'd avoided talking about her family and Raul for the last ten years. She'd had some casual boyfriends but those relationships had been brief, defined by their jobs and busy schedules.

Being back in Miami had awakened something long dead inside of her and she knew that she wasn't going to be able to just shrug this off.

"It's a long story and not very flattering," she said.

"I'm listening," he said. "Not judging."

She was glad to hear that but it didn't make finding the right words any easier. In her head were all the details, she knew the facts about what happened but she realized that she'd never had to really talk about them out loud.

"You are the first person I've attempted to tell this to," she said.

"I'm flattered."

She shrugged. "I'm not really sure I can talk about it now."

"This is the reason that your grandparents sold the marketplace?" he asked. He'd respected her privacy and stayed away from digging into her past on his own. He trusted her to tell him. Selena was nothing if not a woman of her word and he'd come to really respect her during the time they'd spent together.

"Yes, it is. I guess I'm making this into something more than it really is...I fell in love with a con man and it took a lot of money to make him go away. My *abuelito* went to the cops and they set up a sting to capture Raul—that's the man I was conned by—and he eventually was arrested and convicted. I made sure my grandparents got their money back but it took too long for them to buy back the marketplace."

He took a deep breath as anger exploded inside at the way she'd been treated. He was glad that Tomas had had the foresight to make sure that the man who'd hurt her had been caught and prosecuted.

He didn't want to say the wrong thing but he was so angry that a man had betrayed her love that way. He could scarcely sit still. He stood up and paced around, wanting to do something to make it right.

"I don't know what to say. This isn't what I expected to hear from you about your past."

"I'm not the girl I used to be. I don't…I don't get involved with men on such a deep level anymore. It happened right after my parents died."

"That bastard took advantage of you when you were vulnerable," he said.

He got out of his lounger and scooped her up into his arms before sitting back down on her chair and cradling her. "You are a very strong woman, Selena. I think you should take great pride in the fact that an event that could have made you bitter and resentful instead made you stronger."

She tipped her head up to look him in the eyes and he realized it would be so easy to get lost in her big brown orbs. "Do you mean that?"

"You know I don't say things I don't mean."

"That is true," she said. "You shoot straight from the hip, don't you?" She smiled and gently stroked his cheek.

He smiled at her because he knew she wanted to lighten this moment but it didn't change the fact that he was still angry on her behalf and he wanted answers. He wanted to make sure the person who hurt her never came near her again. Make sure that she was never hurt again. Make sure that she was protected.

The intensity of his feelings surprised him. But a few minutes later when she told him she had to go check on dinner, he finally let her go. He sat there by her pool realizing that no matter how much he'd been trying to tell himself that she wasn't going to matter to him, she did. Selena wasn't just his vacation fling; she meant more.

He should have acknowledged that from the beginning. He didn't flirt in waiting rooms or go out of his way to date women he had business dealings with. She was different.

She called him to dinner a few minutes later and they ate at her patio table with soft music coming from the intercom. He tried to keep the conversation light but it was harder than he'd thought it would be.

"I guess you are looking at me differently now," she said as they finished their meal.

He nodded. "Yes, I am. I'm sorry but I wish that I had five minutes alone with that bastard Raul."

"I shouldn't have told you," she said.

"You needed to," he said. "If you have never talked about it until now, then it was past time. Have you been back to Miami since everything happened?"

"For Enrique's high school graduation. But I flew in on a Friday night and out on Sunday morning. I didn't really have time to do anything but marvel over the fact that my baby brother had grown up."

"So how does it feel being in Miami this time

around?" Justin asked. "I guess that you're ready to deal with it."

She shrugged delicately and looked away from him. "I thought so...actually that's a lie. I figured what happened ten years ago wouldn't bother me anymore. But being here...dealing with you and knowing that if I hadn't fallen for Raul's sweet lies my grandparents wouldn't have to be negotiating with your company for their livelihood, well that forced me to face the fact that this is all my doing."

"I don't think it's that bad. Your grandparents don't blame you for anything and I know you are smart enough to realize now that Luna Azul isn't the devil."

She tipped her head to the side studying him. "I'm not sure. I fell for a smooth-talking man once and I don't want to make the same mistake again. Especially since it will be my grandparents who pay the price once again."

He didn't like the fact that she'd put him in the same category as a con man. "I've never lied to you and I'm not trying to cheat you or your grandparents out of anything. I resent the fact that you said that."

Selena rubbed the back of her neck. The last thing she'd intended to do was to offend him, but he had to understand that she was trying to protect herself.

"I didn't mean to say that you were swindling me or my grandparents," she said.

"Yes, you did. You wanted to make sure that I understood that you don't trust me."

"You? It has nothing to do with you," she said. She wasn't thinking, just reacting, and she realized she was being truer with Justin than she'd been with any man before. "I don't trust men. That's it, period, end of story.

I want to believe you when you say you are dealing honestly with me, but then I find out you are meeting with the zoning commissioner behind my back."

"Maxwell and I are friends. And you did the same thing to me. Going to meet my brother. What did you think that Cam would do, offer you better terms?" he asked.

An argument was brewing and she knew she was responsible for it. She'd simply wanted to tell him that trusting him wasn't easy for her and now she'd somehow gotten them into a mess that she had no idea how to get out of.

"I thought he'd give me some insight into whether he was the same kind of man you are. The kind of man I can trust. Because you aren't the only Stern brother that my grandparents and the other business owners are going to have to deal with."

He leaned back in his chair. "Damn, I'm sorry I got a little hot under the collar."

"A little? That's an understatement."

He shook his head. "You make me passionate, so of course I'm upset that you'd lump me in the same category as a guy who'd bilk your grandparents out of their fortune."

"I'm sorry about that. I didn't mean it that way," she said, then paused. "Do I really make you passionate?" she asked.

"Hell, yes. I know we just broke our number one rule about not talking about business when we are alone—"

"That was a stupid idea. I can't keep up two lives. I mean it would be nice to think that I could do it but to be honest I feel too much when I'm here. And it's clear to me you do, too."

"Yes, I do. In the spirit of open communication, I knew I wouldn't be able to think clearly unless I got the passion I felt for you out of my system."

"Oh, really?" she asked, getting up and coming around to his side of the table. He scooted his chair out and pulled her down on his lap.

"Yes, really."

She toyed with his collar, caressing the exposed skin of his neck. "Is it working?"

"Not yet. The more I get to know about you, Selena, the more I need to know. I feel like I will never be able to know enough about you and that's not acceptable. I never let anyone have that much control over me."

"So I can control you?" she asked, trying to keep things flirty and light because otherwise she was going to have to face the fact that Justin was more of a man than any other guy she'd ever let into her life.

For one thing, he was willing to admit that this was confusing him as much as it was confusing her. That shouldn't turn her on, but it did. It made her want to wrap her entire body around his and make love to him here on her patio. But she wasn't going to do that. She couldn't.

Already he was starting to become more important to her than she'd expected him to be. She had to remember that she was leaving in a few weeks.

"About as much as I can control you," he said. His hands settled on her waist and she looked down into his eyes.

There was something so pure about the color of his eyes and she felt like she could get lost in them. Get lost in the life that she once had and the life that she'd always dreamed of having. Dreams that had been swept away by Raul's actions.

"I'm afraid," she admitted in a soft whisper and put her head down on his shoulder.

"Afraid of what?" he asked, his hands moving smoothly over her back.

She didn't know if she could put it into words but then the simple truth was there. "You…me. I guess I'm scared of the way you make me feel. I've been so focused on my career and I've found a way to live with the past and with my mistakes. But now you are making me want again."

"Wanting is good," he said.

She turned her head on his shoulder and kissed his neck. "Wanting is very good. But I'm afraid that it is changing me. I thought I knew who I was. I thought that the woman I'd once been was completely gone but being back here has made me realize I'm not sure who I am."

He tipped her head back so that he could look down in her eyes. "You know who you are, you just didn't want to admit that there was still a part of you that could be passionate about a man and about this place."

She leaned up and kissed him hard on the lips. "Why do you think that?"

"Because it's in your eyes. I don't see a woman who doubts herself at all."

"I'm not talking about confidence," she said.

"What are you talking about then?"

"I'm talking about dreams," she said. "I thought that I was the kind of woman who would be happy with a career and a life in the big city…not the city of my childhood but a new place. A place where I'd carved out my own life. But I think I just realized that I haven't been living."

"You haven't?" he asked.

She shook her head, letting her hair brush over his hands as she leaned forward and kissed him gently. No matter what else came from her time with Justin she'd always be grateful to him for making her realize what had been missing in her life.

"No, I've been hiding and I'm just now realizing that I let Raul steal something from me. And you, Justin Stern, my *abuelito*'s silver-tongued devil, are slowly giving it back to me."

Eleven

Justin carried Selena back over to the lounger where he'd held her earlier. He'd had enough of talking. What he needed was something that made sense to him. Something he didn't have to dissect and analyze. He needed to have her body, naked and writhing, under him.

He needed them both to get out of their heads and he needed that right now. He lowered her onto the lounger and sat next to her hip.

"What are you doing?"

"If you can't figure it out then I'm not doing it correctly."

She shook her head. "It feels like lovemaking."

"Then that's what it is," he said. "I was hoping you'd say it felt like an erotic dream come true."

"It's more than that. Last night was so much more than I thought I'd find with a man…"

"That's what I wanted to hear," he said.

"I'm glad. I didn't expect to like you."

"Same here. But I knew from the moment I sat down next to you in the zoning office that you were different."

She smiled up at him. "Really. I thought you were just this crazy guy who thought with his libido instead of his head."

She made him feel good and happy, he thought. It didn't matter what the future held at this moment—he was more relaxed and turned on than he'd ever been.

He reached for the tie that seemed to hold her blouse together and undid it. He pulled the fabric open and found there was a little button on the inside that still had to be unfastened. But he was distracted from getting her completely naked by the one breast he had already uncovered.

She wore a nude colored mesh bra that was almost like a second skin. He growled low in his throat and caressed the full globe of that revealed breast, moving his fingers up to her nipple. "I love this bra."

"I'm glad. I wore it for you."

"What else did you wear for me?"

"Why don't you make yourself comfortable and I'll show you?" She stood up and he moved so he was lying back on the lounger. Selena was innately sensual and despite what she'd said about not knowing who she was, he knew she was one of the most confident women he'd ever met. There was something very sure about her, as she slowly removed her blouse and dropped it on the other chair.

"So you like this?" she asked cupping her breasts and leaning forward.

"Very much." Not touching her was torture but he

was determined to let her have this moment. And to let her seduce him.

She put her hands to her waistband and slowly lowered the zipper. Through the opening in her shorts he saw her smooth stomach and belly button before she slowly parted the cloth.

"I'm not sure you really want to see this," she said.

"Trust me, I do."

"Then take off your shirt."

"Show me a little something and I'll consider it."

She turned around and swiveled her hips at him. She lowered the fabric of her shorts the tiniest bit so that he saw the indentation at the small of her back and the thin nude colored elastic at the waist of her panties.

"Whatcha got for me, Justin?"

He stood up; being passive wasn't in his nature. He toed off his loafers and started unbuttoning his shirt. He let it hang open as he came up behind her. He wrapped his arms around her waist and bent to taste the side of her neck.

"This is what I have for you," he said. Taking her hips in his hands and drawing her back until her buttocks was nestled against his erection. He rubbed up and down against her.

She shivered delicately and tossed her hair as she turned her head to look back at him. "That's exactly what I need."

"I'm glad," he said, nibbling against her skin as he talked. He moved his hands over her stomach, feeling the bare skin. He dipped his finger in her belly button and her hips swiveled against his.

He pushed hands lower into the opening of her shorts and cupped her feminine mound in his hand. She was humid and hot and she shifted herself against his palm.

He pressed against her and she swiveled her hips again, this time caressing him.

He loved the feel of her against his erection. He pushed her pants down her legs and then reached between them to open his own pants and free himself.

He groaned when he felt the naked globes of her ass against his erection. She had on a thong.

"God, woman, you are killing me," he rasped in her ear.

"Good. I have thought of nothing else but you and me like this since you dropped me off this morning."

"Me, too," he admitted. He kept caressing her between her legs and used his other hand to push the thin piece of fabric that guarded her secrets out of the way.

She moaned his name and parted her legs, shifting forward so that he could enter her more smoothly. He held her hips with both of his hands as he pushed up inside her. He started moving, listening to the sounds she made.

He loved her sex noises and had a feeling he'd never tire of hearing them. Her velvety smooth walls contracted around him with each thrust he made. He felt his orgasm getting closer with each thrust into her body.

Everything started tingling, and then he erupted with a deep pulse. He heard her cry out as he emptied himself into her. She slumped forward in his arms and it took all of his strength to keep them on their feet. As soon as he was able to, he pulled out and lifted her in his arms, carrying her into the house.

"Where's your bathroom?" he asked. She liked the way that sex roughened his voice and made it low and raspy. At this moment she felt like the other things she spent all day worrying about didn't really matter.

"Down the hall, first door on the left."

He carried her down the hall, but she hardly paid attention to any of it. Just kept her head on his shoulder and thought about how nice it was to have a big strong man to carry her. It wasn't that she couldn't take care of herself because she could; it was that she didn't have to do anything right now.

She felt safe and…cherished. That was it. She'd never experienced it before. He made her feel like she was the most important person in his world at this moment. And she wasn't going to allow herself to analyze it and dissect it and figure out why she shouldn't just enjoy it.

He set her on the counter. Her bathroom had a large garden tub with spa jets. He turned the tap and adjusted the temperature.

He was a very fine-looking man. She'd be happy to watch him move around naked all day long.

"Bubble bath?" he asked.

"Under the sink. I can get it," she started to hop down.

"No, stay where you are. I want to do this for you," he said, standing up and coming over to her. Wrapped his arms around her waist and tugged her close to him for a hug.

She rested her head against his chest and had the fleeting sensation that this wasn't going to last. Like she should hold on to him as tight as she could right now. She squeezed him to her and he pulled back.

"You okay?"

"Yeah. Ready for this bath."

"Me, too."

He found the bubble bath and poured it into the running water. Soon there was a sea of bubbles as he turned the faucet off. He lifted her up and then stepped into the tub.

He sat down in the water, which was the perfect temperature, and cradled her on his lap.

"Are you okay?"

"Yes, why wouldn't I be?" she asked.

"I was like an animal out there. You turned me on and I couldn't think of anything except having you. Damn, just thinking about it is getting me hard again," he said.

"I thought men of a certain age took a little longer to recover," she said.

"Not with you around," he admitted. He pulled her back against her, moving his hands over her body.

"Why aren't you staying here?" he asked after a moment. "The real reason."

"I told you…it doesn't feel like home," she said. "And to be honest every time I'm here I remember all the bad things that happened. It makes me feel guilty and sad."

He hugged her close, and he was so sweet in that moment that she felt her heart start to melt. She knew she couldn't give in to that and let herself start to care for him—hell, who was she kidding, she already cared for him or she wouldn't have cooked for him. She was starting to fall for him and that was more dangerous than anything else she could do.

"I hope you will be thinking of me in this place now," he said.

"I definitely will be," she said. And that was a big part of her problem. He was slowly making himself a part of her time here. Making her want to stay in the one place she vowed she'd never make her home again.

They finished their bath with lots of caressing and

touching and Selena felt very mellow after they dried off. She found the dressing gowns that her grandmother kept in the closet for guests who rented the house and they put them on. He led her back outside to the pool and she wasn't surprised when he offered to clean up the dinner dishes for her.

"You don't have to do that. Why don't you mix us some drinks while I take care of those," she said.

He went to the bar, stopping along the way to pick up his cell phone. She suspected he was checking his email and she didn't like it. It was like he was going back to the businessman he essentially was.

She wondered if the sweet guy stuff was an act. Was that part of how he was playing her to make sure that she went along with all of his suggestions?

She piled their dinner dishes on a tray and took them inside to the kitchen putting them away before rejoining Justin.

When she got out on the patio, Justin had put his pants back on and was buttoning his shirt.

"I'm sorry but something has come up and I have to go."

She nodded. "No problem."

He stared at her for a minute. "Okay, good. So I will see you in a couple of days to start our meetings with the tenants of the marketplace."

"Sure."

It felt to her like he was running away and she didn't want to let it upset her but it did. It bothered her that she'd spent the evening with him, seduced him and shared the secrets of her past with him and now he was running out the door as fast as he could.

"I wish I could stay," he said.

"It's not a big deal," she replied. If he truly wanted to stay he'd stay.

"It is. Listen, I can't ignore this page," he said. "Are you spending the night here or at the hotel?"

"The hotel, why?"

"Let's meet for a nightcap. Say, eleven?"

"Why?" she asked again.

"I don't want you to think I'm the kind of man who runs away."

She wrapped her arm around her waist and then realized what it was she was doing and dropped it. "I don't know what kind of man you are."

"Yes, you do," he said. "I will remind you when I see you later tonight."

He kissed her hard on the lips and walked through her house and out the front door.

Justin didn't have an emergency waiting for him—he was a businessman not a surgeon—but he'd had to get out of there. Had to breathe and remind himself that as far as Selena was concerned they were having a vacation affair.

And he needed to remember that. He wasn't looking for the future Mrs. Justin Stern. He wasn't getting married ever and if he did change his mind…well, that wasn't going to happen, at least not now.

He drove aimlessly, finding himself in the parking lot of Luna Azul. Sitting in his car he wondered why he was still here. Cam didn't need him in Miami to continue helping to run the company. Not like he had in the beginning when they'd all three bonded together and did every job they could themselves to cut costs.

He could be anywhere else he wanted to, even New

York. But he knew he wouldn't leave. He couldn't leave. This place was in his blood. This was home.

Someone knocked on his window and he glanced up to see Nate standing there. He turned off the car engine and got out.

"What are you doing?"

"Thinking."

"I guess I can see why you were alone. Takes all your concentration, right?"

"Ha."

"Ha? Damn, man, you don't sound like yourself. What's up?"

He shook his head. No way was he going to tell his little brother that he was confused and a woman was responsible. Nate would laugh himself into a stupor if Justin admitted such a thing.

"Do you ever miss baseball?"

Nate shrugged his muscled shoulders. "Some days, but I don't dwell on it. It's not like I'm going to ever be able to go back."

"What about that high school coach from Texas who made the majors in his forties?"

"He was a pitcher, Jus. I'm not. Plus I like this life. I don't know that I'd be committed enough to work out every day and do all the traveling," Nate said then tipped his head to the side. "Besides, you'd miss me."

Justin smiled at his little brother. "I would. I never thought we'd all end up working together."

"I didn't either, but I bet Cam knew," Nate said.

"What are you doing out here?"

"I …I have a date."

"With Jen? I thought you were engaged, so dating was a thing of the past."

"She likes it when we meet up after she gets done with work and then we have a little alone time."

"Alone time? Seriously. You crack me up," Justin said but to be honest he was envious of his brother and his fiancée. Until this moment he hadn't realized that he wanted what Nate had found. And he knew it was because of Selena.

"I still have to head out after our 'date' to schmooze more celebs but this gives us a little time together."

"Sounds nice," Justin admitted.

"Thanks, bro. So are you going inside?"

"No. I have to head back to my office. I want to review some notes I made earlier."

"At this time of the night? I know Cam is a bit of a pain about this marketplace project but I think he'd let you have a night off."

"You know he doesn't want me to take any time until this is all wrapped up."

Nate arched one eyebrow at him. "You're not big on vacations."

"No, I'm not. I'm a workaholic so I guess it shouldn't surprise you that I'm heading to the office."

"Normally no, but I've never caught you sitting in the parking lot before."

Justin realized that his brother was now concerned. "I'm just looking at all we've accomplished."

"It always makes me proud, too," Nate said, glancing at his watch. "I've got to get inside. I'm hosting that group from the marketplace for drinks after the last show and I don't want to be late to meet with Jen."

"Don't let me keep you. I'm heading to my office."

Justin hugged his brother and then got back in his car and drove away. He needed to pay attention to the deal with the Luna Azul Mercado and get that finalized. Then he'd figure out what to do with Selena.

He wasn't going to allow her to continue to control him the way she had tonight. The only thing that made her power over him acceptable was the fact that she seemed unaware of it.

He pulled into the parking lot of their office building and didn't want to get out. For the first time in his adult life he wasn't interested in working. In fact, only one thing was on his mind and it was Selena.

He'd been an idiot to leave when he had. What had he proved?

He realized he'd proved to himself that he could be the one to leave.

And that was important. His father had never been able to leave their mother and that had been his greatest flaw. It had made the old man weak and Justin had decided at a very young age that he wasn't going to be like his old man. At least not when it came to love.

He wasn't going to fall for the wrong kind of woman. To be honest he'd vowed to never let any woman mean more to him than business.

He forced himself to get out of the car and go up to his office. He spent two hours going over numbers and sending detailed notes to his assistant for the meetings they'd be having over the next few days. By the time he'd left the office, he knew he was a much stronger man than his father had ever been and that Selena Gonzalez wasn't going to find the same flaw in him that his mother had found in his father.

Twelve

Selena changed her outfit about six times but finally went down to the lobby bar a little after eleven. If Justin weren't there, she'd know he was a bit of a con man just like Raul had been. But instead of going after her grandparents' money, Justin was going after—what?

That was the question she didn't know how to answer. She was pretty sure he wasn't after her heart, which she'd like to know more about. She knew most men were commitment-phobes but he took it to extremes, from what she'd observed.

Why then was she standing at the entrance to the mood-lit bar so tentatively? Hoping for…

Justin.

He'd come. To be honest, until she saw him she'd been afraid to hope that he would be here. She just had figured he wouldn't show up.

He waved her over to the intimate banquette where

he was sitting. She sat down and slid around the bench until she was next to him.

He leaned over and kissed her cheek. He'd had time to go and change and he'd put on aftershave but he hadn't shaved because a five o'clock shadow darkened his jaw.

She didn't to talk about the way he'd left. She'd spent most of the night reliving those moments and trying to ascertain if it had been something she'd done.

"Business emergency handled?"

He flushed and nodded. "It wasn't a big deal—just some paperwork that needed signing."

That didn't sound like a reason for him to rush out of her house but she wasn't going to call him on it. She'd see how the rest of the evening went and then make up her mind if he was playing her for a fool or just in over his head like she was.

But Justin didn't seem like the type of man to be overwhelmed by anything.

"What do you want to drink? They make a nice Irish coffee here, but I've always been partial to cognac."

"Me, too," she said. "My *abuelito* used to pour me a small snifter after I turned sixteen to share with him on Sundays when we'd go over to his house for dinner. I always felt very grown-up drinking it."

"My dad always had cigars with cognac, but I don't think we can smoke in here."

"Not at all. Do you smoke?" she asked, realizing that she really didn't know him all too well.

"No. I mean, the occasional cigar. When we first opened Luna Azul it was right at the height of the cigar club phase and we toyed with making it one, but in the end we wanted something that would stay in fashion."

"Good call."

"It was Nate who pointed out it was a fad. That guy has his finger on the pulse of what's hot and what's not."

"I would imagine so—I see him on the society page of the newspaper almost every day."

Justin signaled the waiter and ordered their drinks. "Nate does a lot of that socializing for the club. We get a lot of tourists and locals in the club because they want to catch a glimpse of Nate and his A-list friends."

"I noticed that you and your brothers are close, what about your parents?" she asked. She wanted to know everything about him, the personal stuff that she hadn't thought was important before. She knew from Cam that his parents were gone but she wanted to know more about the brothers' relationship with them.

"My parents are both dead."

"I know—Cam told me. I'm sorry. I know how it is to lose your parents."

"It wasn't that bad. I had a little bit of high school left and Cam stepped in to fill the void."

"I guess you weren't that close to them, then," she said.

"No, I wasn't. Well, my dad. He always took my brothers and I out all the time."

"Where did he take you? Were you rough-and-tumble boys?" she asked.

"He mainly took us to the golf course or out on his boat. Just out of the house. My mother was often socializing and didn't want noisy boys in the way."

It didn't really sound bitter when he said it but she was surprised and a little hurt for him. "My mother loved having us in the house and under her feet. My brother is ten years younger than I was so to keep me from being lonely my mom would always have my cousins over for me to play with," Selena said, remembering the crazy games she used to play with her cousins and how much fun it had been.

"My brothers and I are all two years apart, I guess it was too much for my mother. My dad enjoyed having us with him. I think we learned about living from him."

Their drinks arrived.

"Salud!" she said raising her glass toward him.

"Cheers," he replied.

They both took a sip of their drinks. She set her glass on the table in front of her.

"What did you think of your dad being a pro golfer?"

"Why are you asking me so many questions?"

She didn't know how to answer that. The truth was it had hurt when he left and she wanted to figure out what made him tick so he'd never hurt her again. Frankly, there was no way she was going to tell him that. "You know my family but I really don't know much about yours."

"Fair enough."

"What was your dad's name?"

"Kurt Stern."

"I've never heard of him."

"Most people who aren't very familiar with golf haven't. But he made a very good living playing for all of his life. He and my mother were killed when their private plane crashed on the way to a golf tournament."

Suddenly she did know who his father was. She remembered reading the story about the tragedy. "Of course. I remember seeing that in the news."

"I should have led with that part. He was more famous in death than he was in life."

"I'm sorry I didn't realize who he was."

He took her hand in his. "It's okay. Most people don't."

Justin felt like today had gone on too long. He was ready for it to end but not ready to leave Selena. Yet he knew he'd have to. Spending the night with her when they were on his yacht was one thing, spending the night with her here at the hotel something else. He just wasn't ready for it tonight. He didn't trust himself.

"Thanks for meeting for this drink," he said.

"I guess you are done talking about your family?"

"Way done. I don't like to talk about the past. I prefer to look to the future, which we are doing with our partnership."

"Which one?"

That was the question. "The Mercado is what brought us together."

"That is so true. If my *abuelito* hadn't thought you were a silver-tongued devil our paths never would have crossed."

He frowned as he realized how right she was. It had been chance that had put their paths on a collision course. "I guess it was fate."

She smirked. "Only if you count me falling for Raul as part of fate's ultimate plan. And I'm not sure that our destinies are that spelled out."

He wasn't either. "I've made everything in my life happen by hard work and determination, so I'd have to agree with you."

"Still…for me it would be reassuring if I thought all the heartache and trouble with Raul was so that my grandparents could have an even better place now. I mean that would be worth it."

He wondered if she thought he'd be worth it. What was the man of her dreams? Or had those died when she'd been twenty and betrayed by love? Tonight wasn't the night for asking that type of question.

"It would be worth it. I hope you know it was never my intent to swindle anyone out of anything."

"I think I do know that now. At first I wasn't too sure what to think of you."

"Why?"

She took a deep breath and then leaned forward, crossing her arms on the table. Her arms framed her breasts—he tried to keep his gaze on her face but he was distracted. He liked this woman. He loved her body and he wanted nothing more than to spend every night wrapped in her arms.

"I guess it was the way you came on to me. I thought 'this guy has got to be after something.'"

"Selena," he said, taking her hands in his and looking into those deep chocolate-colored eyes of hers. "I was after you. I didn't know who you were when we were sitting next to each other. I only knew that I wanted you."

"Lust," she said. "The mighty Justin Stern was floored by lust."

He squeezed her hand and lifted it to his lips to kiss the back of it. "I wasn't floored."

"Oh, what were you then?"

"Enamored. I had never seen a woman as beautiful as you," he said, meaning those words more than any he'd ever spoken before. There was something about Selena that struck him deep in his soul. He wasn't the kind of man who made soul connections or thought he'd find his other half but a part of him—the part that had run away from her house earlier—knew that he had. That there was something between the two of them that just couldn't be stopped.

"It was a force of nature," he said.

"You do have a silver tongue."

He didn't like that she thought so. "I don't. I'm known for being blunt and to the point. There is something about you that has captivated me."

"I wish I could believe you," she said, her eyes big and almost sad.

"Why can't you?"

"Men—"

He knew she was going to make a blanket statement that wouldn't be flattering. He knew he should let it go, it was late, they both had a full day of meetings tomorrow and to be fair she'd let him escape her house earlier without asking too many questions. But he wanted to know what she thought of men. Wanted to know the exact company he was keeping.

"Men what?"

"Some men lie. And they do it so well that a person never knows that they aren't telling the truth," she said. She shook her head. "I'm sorry, Justin. I wish I was a different woman who didn't have baggage."

"I don't," he said. He knew she'd been badly used and that the effect was one she still hadn't shaken. Raul's betrayal wasn't just of Selena and her heart but also of her family and he suspected that hurt her even more.

"Why not?"

"You wouldn't be the woman you are today without the past."

She leaned over and hugged him. "Thanks for saying just the right thing."

"Ha, I knew if I blundered around long enough I'd come off as suave."

"I didn't say you were suave."

"You implied it," he said. "I think we should call it a night before you change your mind."

She nibbled on her lower lip and he wondered if she was hesitating over tonight the way he was. When she didn't offer for him to come up to her room, he realized she was just as shy about where this was heading.

"I've got an early meeting so maybe we could have lunch?"

She shook her head. "I can't. I'm due to be grilled by my grandparents for lunch."

"Grilled about what?"

"You. Everyone on the committee guessed I had a date since I didn't come with them to the club and now I'm being called back home to answer for myself."

"Are you going to tell them your date was with me?" he asked.

"Definitely, I'm not lying to them."

"Would you like me to come with you?" he asked.

"That's sweet but I think I better handle this one alone."

"Very well, but let's meet for breakfast."

She nodded and they went their separate ways at the elevator. He down to his suite and she down to hers. He felt like he'd created a barrier between them tonight by running away. And as he fell asleep he realized that he wanted her in his arms. He needed her in his arms and he was going to make sure she was back there as soon as possible.

Selena woke up with the sun streaming through the windows and her thoughts on Justin. He knocked on her door at seven-thirty and she was surprised to see he wore his robe and was pushing a room service cart.

"This is as close as I could get to breakfast in bed, considering that you didn't invite me to spend the night," he said.

"You didn't seem like you were interested," she said.

"My mistake," he said, pulling her into his arms. He walked her back toward the bed.

He didn't say anything but pulled her under him. His robe fell open and he shrugged it off his shoulders revealing his nakedness. He pushed her nightgown up to her waist and slid into her body. He rocked them slowly together.

The sensation of having him inside of her again was exquisite.

She'd grown accustomed to his touch and it felt right to have him here between her legs. In her again. She no longer felt like she was alone.

She knew she was drawn to the feel of him. His body under her fingers, his chest rubbing against her breasts and the feel of his mouth on her neck with that early morning stubble abrading her. She shivered as he whispered darkly sexual words against her skin and rocked his hips leisurely against hers.

The first time they'd made love had been intense and explosive, the second time sweet and sensual, but this morning it felt like coming home. She was awash in feelings of Justin as they slowly moved together.

She scraped her nails down his back until she could cup his butt and pull him closer to her. He paused buried hilt-deep inside of her.

He lifted his head and looked down at her. "Good morning."

"Yes, it is," she said, feeling more relaxed than she

had in a long time. There was something nice about making love first thing in the morning.

"I like the feel of your hands on me."

"Me, too," she admitted. "From the moment I saw you in the lobby of the zoning office I wanted to touch your butt."

He gave her a wicked smile. "I wanted to touch your breasts."

He lowered his head and took the tip of one of her nipples between his lips, suckling her softly in the early morning light.

His hands moved over the sides of her torso and he cupped her other breast in his hand then rotated his palm over it. Stimulating it until the nipple hardened.

She shifted her shoulders as he started to suckle more strongly. She put her heels on the bed trying to get him to move in her but he wouldn't be budged. This morning he was determined to take his time and drive her slowly out of her mind.

"Please…"

"Please what? Doesn't this feel good?"

"Yes, it feels too good," she said.

"How can something feel too good?" he asked, tracing the edge of her areola with his tongue.

She couldn't think. The humid warmth of his tongue contrasted with the slight abrasion of his stubble and it was driving her mad.

"Just please…"

"Please what?" he asked.

"Make love to me," she said at last, looking into those clear blue eyes of his.

"My pleasure," he said. He started moving his hips again and the movement this time was more purposeful. He wasn't teasing the both of them now. The beast within him had been woken and he held her hips with the strong grasp of his hand as he drew in and out of her body.

He did it slowly, letting her feel each inch as he pulled it out, then plunged back in until he was buried inside of her.

"Is that what you wanted?" he asked, his raspy voice sending chills down her spine.

"Yes, but more. Yesss…"

"Selena, you feel so good to me," he said, then lowered his head and kissed her deeply, his tongue thrusting into her mouth with the same rhythm of his hips. She held on to his shoulders to lift herself more fully into his embrace.

Every particle of her being was crying out for release but he was keeping her right on the edge. So that little climaxes feathered through her, making him thrust faster and harder. Plunging into her and driving her over the edge. She tore her mouth from his and screamed his name as her orgasm rushed through her.

Justin held her hips and drove into her three more times before shuddering in her arms and emptying himself in her body. She lifted herself against him once more to draw out the exquisite feeling of pleasure.

He leaned off her body to the side but still held her close and she liked it.

She turned her head to look up at him. "I…"

"Don't," he said. "Don't say anything."

"Is this a mistake?"

He rolled over and pulled her into his arms so she rested on his chest, right over his heart. It beat loudly under her ear. "You don't feel like a mistake to me. But I think objectivity is gone."

She knew he was right. "We can't pretend we are just vacation lovers."

"No, we can't. I've never been good at lying, even to myself and you feel like more than a temporary affair."

It felt the same to her. She wanted more.

Thirteen

A week later, Selena still hadn't made sense of anything with Justin. He was keeping his distance and on some levels, that worked for her. Her grandparents and the other vendors had all had their meetings with him at Luna Azul. Selena had participated in some of them but for the most part had stayed back.

She needed to read every contract that was offered and go over the details very carefully. She'd also spent a fair amount of time at the zoning office and realized that Justin already knew that as long as he hired a local contractor he was within his rights to start construction.

Selena advised everyone of this fact so that they realized at some point they needed to concede some of their dream-list demands.

Her cell phone rang just as she was driving away from her grandparents' store. She glanced at the caller ID and saw that it was Justin.

"Hello." She put him on her Bluetooth speaker-phone.

"Put on your dancing shoes tonight, I'm taking you out."

"Really? Don't you think you should ask me first?"

"Nah, you'd just debate about it and then agree. I'm saving us a little time."

"Okay, then I guess I'll agree to go out with you. Where are we going?"

"Luna Azul. It's celebration time and you and I have never been to the club."

"Celebration?" she asked.

"Yes, ma'am. I finished the last of the appointments ten minutes ago and everyone is on board. Thank you for your hard work in making this happen."

"Not a problem. It is as important to you as it is to me."

"I know," he said. "That's why we need to celebrate. I will pick you up at seven and we can have dinner at my favorite restaurant first."

"Wait a minute. I can't do this," she said abruptly.

"Why not?"

She realized she was shaking and pulled the car over. "We were just a vacation fling, remember? We can't mix business and pleasure. We just can't."

"Why not?"

"Because if we do, I'm going to lose myself. I'm going to fall right back into the girl I used to be. I can't do that."

"You aren't going to turn into the girl you used to be. You're a woman now, Selena, successful and sure of yourself. There is no way you'd ever fall for a con again. And I'm not conning you. I've been nothing but honest with you."

That was true. "You have. But I haven't been honest with myself. I can't pretend that you mean nothing to me and I know we have no future. I can't stay here."

"Why not?"

"Because I have a life that I enjoy."

"Fair enough. Let's talk about this over dinner. I want to celebrate what we both worked so hard for. At least give me that," he said.

She realized that if she saw him again she was never going to be able to leave. He wouldn't let her and she was weak where he was concerned.

"Sounds good," she said, knowing that it was a lie. She wasn't going to meet Justin. In fact, if she played her cards right she'd never see him again. A clean break and she'd be back in New York in the heart of her safe life. Staying here…that wasn't an option no matter how tempting it might be.

She disconnected the call. She already knew about her grandparents' agreement with Luna Azul. There were only a few things left for her to do and then she could head home.

It was beyond time for her to leave. She was beginning to forget she had a life somewhere else. She'd fallen back into her old Miami routines but it wasn't the way she'd been before. She was eating breakfast with her grandparents, spending the afternoons with her brother and enjoying an idyllic life. But that wasn't realistic. If she moved back here, she'd be working all the time like she did back north. And why would she move here…for her family or for Justin?

She shook her head as she drove up to her hotel. It

had helped her keep her perspective that she was here temporarily, or had it? It was hard to stay because Justin had changed the way she looked at life here.

Granted, she was no longer the twenty-year-old woman who had left home with her tail between her legs. Helping her grandparents reclaim their grocery store and have a say in the new Mercado had helped resolve her leftover feelings of guilt.

She pulled the car over as the emotions she'd been burying for so long came to the surface. She started to cry.

She put her head down on the steering wheel. The flood of tears was gone and she felt vulnerable now. Justin had done this to her. He'd helped her make things right for her grandparents and for herself. She knew no one had blamed her for what Raul had done. But his actions had been a black specter over her for too many years and finally she was free.

She wiped her tears as she lifted her head. She had to get back to the hotel and get changed if she was going to actually go through with it and be on time to meet with Justin.

Justin.

He made her feel things she'd never experienced before. Not just sexually, she realized. Sex she could handle because that was lust and hormones—she could explain her attachment sexually to him. But the other bonds. The way she'd missed sleeping in his arms after only doing it one night—that wasn't right.

She was falling in love with him.

Love.

Oh, God, no. She wasn't ready to be in love with Justin Stern. She wasn't ready to face the future with him by her side…if he even wanted that. And what if he didn't?

She needed to get away. She drove to her hotel and handed her keys to the valet. Telling him to keep the car up front because she was checking out.

She went up to her room, packed her bags and called for a bellman. She wanted—no, needed—to get back to New York. Once she was away from Miami, the tropical fever that had been affecting her would go away. She'd be back to normal and whatever emotions she thought she was experiencing would go away.

It was just the vacation mind-set that was making her feel this way. She jotted a short note to Justin on the hotel stationery telling him she was needed at her job and left it at the front desk for him after she checked out.

Ten minutes later she was back in her car and headed to the airport. She knew that Justin would be upset that she left him that way but hey, he'd done it to her the other night, so…

She knew that leaving town wasn't the same as leaving her after a dinner. But at this moment it felt pretty darn close and though she knew her grandparents would be upset that she'd left again, she knew it was time to get out of here. And they at least would always love her.

Justin hung up the phone and leaned back in his leather executive chair. He glanced up at the portrait on the wall of him and his brothers with their father. It was the one thing he'd used as a talisman to keep himself focused on business.

But no matter how long he stared at it now, he knew that he'd been changed by this Mercado deal. He also realized that now that most of their business was concluded there was no real reason for Selena to stay in Miami, but he decided that he was going to ask her to stay. He had tried to keep things light but to be honest it wasn't his nature to be so casual. That was the main reason why he'd always limited himself to short-term affairs. But Selena wasn't that type of woman and with her at least he wasn't that kind of man.

He knew he wasn't ready for marriage…because he'd promised himself to never take that step. But he already knew that Selena meant more to him than any woman ever had.

She made him feel the same loyalty and devotion that he felt for his brothers but there was more than that where she was concerned. He didn't want to admit it to himself but he had fallen for her. He refused to say that it was love because he wouldn't be that weak. But it was pretty damned close.

Maybe knowing that was the key to not being like his father. The last thing he wanted was for Selena to realize how much she meant to him and how much control that gave her.

He got to his feet and walked to his office window. Miami was his hometown but he had seen a different side of it while he'd been with Selena. A side that made him realize that he'd been missing out on a few things.

Important things. He'd isolated himself here in the office. Tonight he was going to take the first step to break down the walls he'd used to shield himself all these years.

It was silly really but being a workaholic had meant that no one expected anything from him when it came to family. His brothers knew they'd have to call him at the office; his "friends" had all been colleagues. Until Selena. Now he was getting to know Enrique and Tomas and Paulo as friends.

He owed that all to Selena. Even though she thought she was no longer entrenched in her family, he'd seen that she was and she'd brought him into that group as well.

There was a knock on his door.

"Come in," he said.

Cam stood there looking tired but holding a bottle of Cristal in one hand and two champagne glasses in the other. "I figured it was time to celebrate."

"Definitely. I sent the last contract to legal and have a verbal confirmation from all of the vendors. To be honest, things worked out even better than I anticipated."

"I knew they would," Cam said. He put the glasses on the desk and opened the bottle of champagne.

"Is Nate coming?"

"No. He… I'm not sure what's going on with him. I think that he is doing something with Jen."

"Doesn't he always these days? He's taken to being a committed man like a fish to water."

"Yes, I hope he doesn't run into the Curse of the Stern men. We just aren't good with women and relationships," Cam said.

Justin took the champagne flute that Cam gave him. "To our success."

They both took a sip of the drink. Justin wished he could say that his mind was still on business but he knew that he was thinking of Selena and the Stern curse.

What if he was destined to screw up the relationship with her?

"Now about the tenth anniversary celebration…"

"Yes, we can get to work planning the details of the ground-breaking. Nate tells me most of the pieces are falling into place for the outdoor festival and concert."

"Excellent," Cam said. "That's exactly what I was hoping you'd say."

"I know. You are an even worse workaholic perfectionist than I am," Justin said.

"I'm not a workaholic," Cam said. "I just put the club and our company first."

Justin reached over and squeezed his brother's shoulder. "I know you do, but you're not on your own supporting us anymore. We are wealthy men, we're here to help. You could relax."

Cam nodded. "I don't know how to relax…or so I've been told."

"That's BS. I've heard the same thing said about myself. The problem with people who make those comments is that they don't understand what it's like to work hard to make their own business successful."

"I see your point, but I am almost always at work or at the club. I was thinking I might take a few days off."

Justin looked at his brother shrewdly. "Is there a woman involved?" Not because Justin was psychic or anything but Selena had made *him* behave that way.

"Maybe. Not sure. Why?"

"Don't you remember me moving into the Ritz?"

"Hell, yes. A woman?"

Justin nodded. "Selena Gonzalez."

"I like her," Cam said. "She's smart and funny. Is she staying in Miami?"

"I hope so. Now that our business is over I can concentrate on her…but I'm not sure that is the wisest thing to do."

"Why not?"

"The Stern curse. Look at Dad."

Cam shook his head. "You're not like Dad. Dad married our mother for business reasons. Even though they didn't get along, I think he liked not having a woman who'd take up his time."

"Why did he stay with her?"

Cam looked over at Justin. This was a subject they'd never spoken of before. "I think he stayed for us. I think having sons was something he hadn't expected."

"How do you know?"

"Just an educated guess. And I know you aren't like Dad when it comes to women," Cam said.

"I don't even know that."

"Jus, look at the life you have led," Cam said. "Then look at the fact that you went through a tough negotiation with Selena and kept your personal life separate. You got the job done. That takes a strong man. And I've always known you were that."

"Thanks, Cam. I…I'm scared to admit how much I need her."

"If she's half the woman I think she is, that won't be a problem. It wasn't Dad's devotion that was the issue with our parents but rather Mother's coldness. Selena isn't like that, is she?"

Justin thought about that after his brother left. If there was one thing he knew for sure it was that Selena wasn't cold. And he wasn't a man who gave up when he wanted something as badly as he wanted her.

* * *

As much as Selena wanted to just escape to the airport and head back to New York, she knew she had to at least read over the contracts with all the vendors for the Mercado one last time. So she was sitting in the back room of her grandfather's grocery store, poring over the documents.

She'd gotten lucky that her grandfather was busy with customers and hadn't had a chance to notice her suitcases in the rental car. She knew she'd have to tell him that she was leaving, but right now she just needed to focus on business. So she read the contracts and existed in a world where emotions weren't a part of the equation. The Stern brothers had been more than fair in the agreements, but she refused to let herself dwell on that or on Justin.

She had had to pay an insane amount of money for the ticket and even then her flight didn't leave for another six hours. Once she was on the plane and back in her Upper West Side apartment, she'd relax. Until then she was swamped with an overwhelming sense of panic. She was afraid. Not of her family or Justin or even how they'd react when they realized she'd left, but of herself.

She didn't want to go. Last time she'd left she wanted to leave. Couldn't have gotten out of Miami fast enough. But this time she wanted to stay and that was even more dangerous.

She knew that the life she'd been living here wasn't real and that getting back to her routine was the only thing that would wake her up. Smiling and laughing and doing things that made no sense like sleeping with Justin Stern…that wasn't her and she needed to get back to New York where she could remember who she was.

"Selena?"

She started as she heard her name and turned to see Paulo standing there. She got up and gave her cousin a hug.

"I think I already reviewed your contract," she said.

"You did," he said. "I noticed your suitcase in the car. Are you leaving?"

"Yes, I am. I was just here to make sure that Luna Azul didn't take advantage of you all in the fine print. I'm almost done."

"I must have missed *abuelita*'s call. I thought she was going to have everyone over before you went back home."

Selena flushed as a weird sensation made her stomach feel like it was full of lead. "Uh, I kind of haven't told her I'm leaving yet."

"What? What's going on? Are you okay?" he asked.

"Nothing is going on. I just got word that all of the vendors at the Mercado were ready to sign their contracts and there is no reason for me to stay anymore."

"No reason…what about family?" Paulo asked.

"I am not leaving the family, Paulo. I'm—"

"Is this about that guy you were dating?" he asked.

"No. The guy—Justin—he's not responsible for this," she said. She needed to make sure her family understood that what was going on had nothing to do with Justin and everything to do with her. "I have to get back to my job, that's all."

"Your job?" Paulo asked. "Maybe if I hadn't known you since we were in diapers I'd believe that. But to leave without saying anything to our grandparents… *Tata,* that is not like you. Even after Raul you said goodbye to them."

She shook her head. "If I don't leave now, Paulo, I think I'm going to make an even bigger mistake than I did before."

He hugged her close to him. "What kind of mistake? I can help you."

She pulled back and realized how much she really loved her family. "You can't. I wish you could."

"There is nothing that is so big that you have to run away."

"I know it seems like I'm running away, but truly I'm not, Paulo, I'm simply going home."

"Is New York really your home?" he asked.

"Yes," she said with all the confidence she could muster. She wanted Paulo to believe it because maybe if he did, she would.

"That's a lie, *tata,*" he said. "When you came down here you were buttoned up, wearing all black and looking like anyone else from up there. But after a few days your hair was down and you blossomed back into the woman you really are."

"I haven't changed," she said.

"Then you aren't being honest with yourself. I hope you wake up to the fact that you can't ever really be comfortable in your own skin unless you acknowledge that your family is a huge part of who you are," he said.

Paulo was being hard on her. Almost as hard as she was sure her grandparents would be. "I'm not going to change my mind."

"I hope someday you do. When are you calling *abuelita?*"

"I will do it in a few minutes when I've finished reviewing this last contract."

"Make sure you do. I don't want to keep secrets for you."

Paulo walked away and she shivered. If she wasn't so afraid she'd try to find a way to stay, but there were no doubts in her mind that she needed to go back home and get some perspective. But Paulo had a point and for the first time she'd seen how badly it had hurt her family the way she'd left before, but they had understood. If Paulo was that mad, how would Enrique and her grandparents react?

How would Justin?

What was she running from? Was she making a huge mistake?

She rubbed the back of her neck. She shouldn't leave without at least saying goodbye to her grandparents. She couldn't. "Paulo!"

"Si, tata?"

"Will you come with me to *abuelita's*?"

"Definitely. I think this is the right thing to do."

"Paulo, I'm so confused. No one has ever made me feel this way."

"You mean Justin?"

"Yes. And he's not…he's not like anyone else I've ever known. I'm afraid to trust myself."

"You shouldn't be. You are a very smart woman, *tata*," Paulo said. A few minutes later they were in his car driving toward her grandparents' house.

Selena wanted to pretend that she was still getting on that airplane and leaving Miami but a part of her no longer wanted to go.

* * *

Justin arrived at the Ritz twenty minutes before he was supposed to pick Selena up. He went to his room and packed up his luggage and had it taken to his car before he went to check out. Selena was going to look right at home in his waterfront house on Fisher Island. It would be nice to see her there.

"How can I help you, sir?"

"I'm checking out," he said. "Justin Stern."

The front desk hostess nodded and started working on her computer and a minute later glanced up and smiled at him. "It says we have a letter for you. Let me grab that while you look over the folio."

She handed him his resort bill and he glanced down at it before signing his name. Then she passed him an envelope and told him to have a nice day.

The handwriting on the front was Selena's and he knew what it said before he even opened it.

But he tore it open anyway. He glanced down at the note on the hotel stationery.

Justin,
I have an emergency back in New York and had to catch a flight out today. Thank you for all of your hard work on making the Luna Azul Mercado a true part of the Cuban American community. I wish you much success with this endeavor.
    On a personal note, I'm sorry to leave without seeing you again but I think this might be easier. I have come to care for you and am questioning my own judgment where you are concerned. Forgive me. I know deep down you'll understand.

Please accept my apology for not calling you
but I was afraid to hear your voice again before I
left.

Take care,
Selena

Justin refolded the letter and put it in his pocket as
he walked out of the club. He got in his Porsche 911 and
drove like a madman away from the Ritz. He had no
real destination in mind until he found himself parked
in front of Selena's house.

He remembered the night they'd made love by her
pool. The night that had changed everything between
them and though he'd thought he had the luxury of time
to make up his mind about her and what he wanted
from their relationship, he just realized that Selena was
battling the same things he had been. And she'd decided
that a quick, clean break was the simplest solution.

But he knew it wasn't. She thought that now that she'd
gotten everything she wanted that she could walk away
from him, and he felt used.

He'd been the one who'd started this and he'd be the
one to end it. Justin Stern wasn't her lapdog…he wasn't
about to let Selena get what she wanted and then walk
away.

He fired up the engine of his car and drove back to
his office building. If that was the way she wanted to
play things then he would show her that he was more
than willing to play her game. And he would beat her
at it.

He pulled out the contracts and then had his assistant
bring him the list of other local business owners who
weren't in the Mercado. The zoning ordinance simply

said that it had to be a local vendor, not that it had to be the same ones.

He drew up a list of comparable businesses and then called Cam to tell him to hold off on celebrating.

"Why?" Cam asked.

"Because we're not going to be lying down for the committee. If they want to be a part of the Mercado they will have to meet our terms," Justin said.

"What has changed in the last two hours? And how much is it going to cost us to break the contracts with our current vendors?"

Justin knew he had to tell his brother something but he didn't have the words right now. "I will tell you later. Let's just say that I think an expert played us. And that makes me mad."

"What does Selena say?"

"I have no idea, she's gone back to New York."

There was silence on the line and Justin knew he'd said too much.

"You can't go back on the deals we have in place. I know you are angry. Hell, I'm pissed for you, but there is no way we are going to let a woman ruin the good thing we have going."

"I know. I really know that it's not the best idea, but I want to hurt her, Cam."

"I understand that," Cam said. "I'm coming back to the office. Don't do anything rash."

When Cam ended the call, Justin stood up, trying to get rid of the restless energy that was making him feel like he was going to punch something. He wasn't in the right frame of mind to work right now, he knew that, but he had no idea where he would go.

The gym. He needed physical exercise and a lot of

it. He would love it if he could go to a boxing ring but the closet one was thirty minutes away and he wasn't in any shape to drive right now.

He kept a bag of workout clothes at the office and grabbed them and his iPod and left. The gym was only a block away and he walked there, got changed and was on the treadmill in less than twenty minutes.

He put his headphones on and ran. It took about two miles for his mind to settle down and he realized that revenge was not the smartest reaction to have to her leaving.

He cared too much for Selena. He knew that he wanted to hurt her the way she'd hurt him by leaving with only a note to explain her actions. But he also liked Tomas and Paulo and all of the other business owners. Hurting them might succeed in getting Selena's attention but he wasn't interested in ruining Luna Azul and his new friends in the process.

"Want some company?" Cam asked as he walked up. He got on the treadmill next to Justin and started running.

"No, but I don't think you are going to listen to me."

"I'm not," Cam said.

"How did you find me here?"

"You're pretty predictable, bro." Cam took a long look at Justin before he started up the machine. "Are you still thinking like a knucklehead?"

"No. I know I can't throw away everything we've worked for because of a woman."

"Good. What else have you figured out?"

"I still want her, Cam. Maybe this is what Dad felt

about Mother. Maybe he realized that he couldn't live without her."

"Maybe, little brother, I never understood the two of them. But this is about you."

How true. He didn't care about his parents' relationship; it was time to break the cycle. He realized he wasn't interested in doing anything that was going to harm Selena. He wanted her back. When he had her in his arms again, he'd make damned sure she never left.

Selena was his. She'd made that choice when she'd given herself to him on his yacht. He hadn't realized it at the time but a bond had been formed.

It took him two more miles of running on the treadmill until he had the seeds of a plan. Normally he'd play his cards close to his chest and keep this wound private but he knew to win Selena he was going to have to pull out all of the stops and involve not only his family but hers as well.

As Justin stepped off the treadmill, he turned to Cam with a smile on his face.

Fourteen

Selena was cold. It was almost April and though spring had definitely been present in Miami, it wasn't very warm here in Manhattan. She'd been back for one weekend. That was it, even though it felt like a life-time.

She pulled her coat a little closer as she exited the subway station nearest her office and started walking. There were a lot of people on the street but she kept her head down and just walked.

Selena's talk with her grandparents and brother the day she left had been…somber, but she'd done what needed doing. Her boss had been very happy to see her back from her leave of absence so soon and had immediately put her on a project.

The kind of project she loved, one where she just worked 24/7 and was consumed with all the research she had to do. Being a corporate lawyer meant lots of time reading case studies and finding precedence.

She wanted to believe she'd made the right choice but she felt alone and missed Justin. He hadn't called her and to be honest she hadn't expected him to. She hadn't really given him an opening to.

She entered her office and walked past the security guard flashing her badge. He smiled at her as he did every day and called good morning to her. But she didn't smile back. She just didn't have it in her to pretend to be happy when she wasn't.

She took the elevator to the seventh floor where her office was and when she was seated behind her desk she looked around.

She shook her head as she waited for her computer to boot up.

What was she doing here?

Waiting.

She'd spent her entire life waiting.

Her phone rang and she glanced at the caller ID. It was her brother.

She picked up and said, "Hi, Enrique."

"I'm sorry to bother you at work but we need you back in Florida."

"Why? What is going on?"

"The Stern brothers have offered me a gig. I want you to be here. It's my first legit gig," Enrique said.

"When is it?"

"This weekend. I know you said you needed to be back in New York, but I really want you here for this."

"Let me see what I can do," she said. She couldn't avoid the important events in her brother's life. "I will let you know if I'm coming."

"*Tata,* I need my sister there. We are all each other has."

"Enrique, you have *abuelito* and *abuelita* there."

"It's not the same. I want my big sister to be here."

"Okay, I'll do it."

"Good."

They hung up and she stared at the phone. It was odd that her grandfather hadn't told her about the gig when they spoke on the phone last night. But he was still mad she'd left and had refused to tell her anything about the Mercado, so that might explain it.

She went online to research airfares and almost booked her flight, but she realized if she was going back she wanted to see Justin. She needed to see him. She picked up the phone and dialed Justin's number. Something she'd done numerous times in the past. But this time she hung up before he answered. The same thing stopped her now, as had each time over the last several days.

What was she going to say to him? She honestly had no idea what he was going to be like when she phoned. If she knew she'd get his voice mail she'd stay on the line even if just to listen to his voice. And if he answered she could make up some excuse about wanting to read Enrique's contract for him or find out how the Mercado was progressing but that wasn't the truth.

She missed him.

There, she'd said it.

Since she'd been back, she'd been existing.

Existing…hadn't she always wanted more from her life?

Her boss walked by and paused in the doorway.

"You look like you are pondering something big."

"I am. I think I am going to resign."

"Why?"

"I don't belong here, Rudy, I need to be back in Miami."

He shook his head. "I knew I shouldn't have let my best lawyer go to Miami in March."

"It's not the weather," she said.

"What is it then?"

No way was she going to tell her boss that it was a man. A man who might not even want her after the way she'd left. She'd made a mistake but if Justin had cared for her even a tenth as much as she loved him, then he would at least listen to her and that was all she needed.

Her time in Miami had reawakened her fighting spirit.

"It's my heart. I left it down there and I don't think I'm surviving very well without it."

He nodded. "That I understand. Can you at least finish the case you are working on?"

If she worked around the clock she could get her research finished and her notes in order so that she could pass it on to another attorney. She nodded and got to work.

Suddenly she didn't feel so lethargic. She looked out the window, realizing soon she'd be back home in Miami and that was really all she needed.

She decided she'd go to Miami for Enrique's gig this coming weekend. It would give her a chance to find Justin and try to make amends before she moved back there permanently. And if she hustled, she could finish her move by the time Luna Azul's tenth anniversary party rolled around.

She didn't want to waste any more time now that she'd decided what she wanted. She felt silly that it had taken her so long to realize that Justin owned her heart. She suspected she'd known it when she'd gotten on that plane in Miami to fly back here.

When Justin got off the private plane Hutch Damien had loaned him and walked across the tarmac to the heliport, he thanked his lucky stars. Nate's celebrity friends sure came in handy.

Flying to New York City had been his last resort. At first he'd harbored a few fantasies of Selena coming crawling back to him but those had died quickly.

Given her past with men, he knew he was going to have to compromise and be the one to make the first move. He was still mad at the way she'd run off. But he loved her. He'd known that almost the instant he'd read her letter and realized that she was leaving him.

It had taken him one lonely night before he was able to admit it out loud and then he knew that he had to get her back. On his own. He knew her family was more than willing to help him get her to come back, but this was strictly between him and her.

There was no way he could spend the rest of his life without her.

His cell phone rang before he got on the chopper for his ride to midtown Manhattan and Selena's office.

"Stern."

"It's Tomas. Enrique called Selena this morning and… told her about the gig. I think she is coming home."

"Dammit. I told Enrique I could do this without his help," Justin said.

"He loves his sister and he wants her to be happy."

Of that Justin had no doubt. "I thought I said I was handling this."

"You did but our family doesn't want to leave anything to chance."

Justin shook his head. "Thanks for letting me know. I will call as soon as I have some news."

"Just bring our *tata* home," Tomas said.

Justin had every intention of doing just that. Selena belonged by his side. Together they had made a good team but they had also completed each other. This wasn't some big show to convince her to overlook his flaws. She hadn't changed who he was at his core; she'd just shown him that the right woman was all he needed to be happy.

Years of short-term affairs had left him with the feeling that he was just like his father. But one month with the right woman had convinced him that he had been wrong.

He needed Selena the way he needed to breathe.

He got on the chopper and watched the views as he flew over Manhattan. Not bad. What he hadn't told her family but had told his brothers was that if Selena wouldn't come back to Miami, he was going to move here. He even had a possible apartment lined up just in case.

The chopper landed at the heliport and his driver met Justin. Soon they were on their way to Selena's office.

He knew her well enough to know that she would be at work even though it was almost six in the evening. She was the kind of person who poured herself into whatever task she took. But more than that, she'd run away not only from him but also from her family. It was going to take a lot of work to keep her mind busy so she wouldn't have to think of all she'd left behind.

Tonight she was going to have no choice but to think about it. He was back. And he was going to get the answers he needed from her about her actions and then he was going to find the key to both of their happiness.

He was sure it was in the both of them. That they belonged together. Now all he had to do was convince her of that.

His phone buzzed and he glanced down to see a text message from his brother.

Cam: Are you there?
Justin: Just.
Cam: Let me know how it goes.

Justin had to laugh. One would think a make-or-break business deal hung in the balance the way Tomas and Cam were anxiously awaiting news. But he knew that both men had his best personal interest at heart. This wasn't about business.

Justin: I will.

Cam had been worried, angry and then understanding when Justin had come to him and told him that he had to go to Manhattan and that there was a chance he was going to move there.

It had taken Cam less than twenty-four hours to figure out a plan to keep Justin in the business no matter where he ended up. He wanted to bring what he called "a taste of Miami Latin to the club scene in Manhattan" and Justin would be in charge of finding a new location and getting it up and running if he decided to stay in New York.

When the driver pulled to a stop in front of Selena's

building, Justin jumped out of the car. He entered the skyscraper and went right up to the security guard at the reception desk.

"Can I help you, sir?"

"I'd like to see Selena Gonzalez," he said, and gave the man the name of her law firm.

"Is she expecting you?" the guard asked.

"No, she isn't." Never in a million years. But then he figured she didn't know him as well as she should have. How much he needed her. If she had, she might not have ever left him in Miami.

"Have a seat over there, sir."

Justin walked a few feet from the desk but couldn't sit down. Not now. He was ready to see Selena and no matter what happened he wasn't leaving this building until he did.

The guard hung up the phone and motioned for him to come over. Justin did and was handed a pass and given instructions on how to get to Selena's office.

Selena hung up the phone and immediately pulled out her compact and checked her makeup. It was shallow, she knew, but she wanted to be looking her best when Justin got up here. She reapplied her lipstick but there was no disguising the dark circles under her eyes. She was tired and he was going to be able to tell without much effort.

She could hardly believe he was here. What if she'd imagined the call? All day she'd thought about the fact that if she moved back to Miami there was a very real chance for her to reconcile with him.

Reconcile? She would probably have to get down on her knees and beg him to give her another chance. And she was in a place in her life right now to do that. She wanted Justin. He was the reason she was quitting her job and moving back to Miami.

She heard the outer door of her office open and got to her feet, poking her head around the corner.

Justin.

He looked better than she'd remembered. His hair was casually tousled, his skin tanner than the last time she'd seen him and his eyes very intense.

She had to force herself to stay in the doorway and not run to him. But she wanted a hug. She needed one. She hadn't had a single good night's sleep since she left him and she craved the feeling of those big strong arms around her.

"Hello," she said.

"Thanks for agreeing to see me," he said.

She stepped back and retreated behind her desk as he walked toward her. But when he entered the room she realized she wasn't in a position of power, not anymore. She'd tried to protect herself by leaving Miami but she was completely vulnerable where Justin was concerned.

She'd give him whatever he wanted if he forgave her.

"I figured it was the least I could do."

He tipped his head to the side. "The very least…why did you run away?"

"I was scared. I guess I didn't want to take a chance on staying and letting you hurt me."

"Why would I have hurt you?"

"Because all the men in my life have. Maybe not my *abuelito*. But my papa died when I needed him the most and Raul took my heart and my money and then he left. I didn't want to give you the chance to do the same thing to me. So when I realized our business was done and that I had a small window of time to get out of Miami—I took it."

"Have I ever done anything to make you think I would leave you like that?" he asked.

"You suggested we have a vacation affair. That we pretend that our lives were separate. That isn't exactly a ringing endorsement for giving your heart to someone."

"You were afraid of me and what I made you feel. From the beginning it was me coming on strong and you backing up. I guess I should have expected you to run."

Selena looked at him and saw the man she loved. Saw the pain she'd caused him when she'd left. If she had to guess, she'd say it wasn't just the leaving but the way she'd done it. Sneaking out of Miami the way Raul had done to her.

"I'm sorry."

"Me, too."

"Why are you sorry?"

"That you felt you had to leave like that."

"I care for you—hell, I love you, Justin, but I'm not sure I can trust any man with my heart. I ran away from everyone because the desire to stay was so strong I couldn't trust it."

"You love me?" he asked her.

She nodded. There was no way she was going to deny it. She wanted Justin back in her life and he realized it would take a lot for him to trust her again but it was what she wanted more than anything else.

"Yes, I do."

"I'm still angry at you for running away," he said.

"I expected as much. I don't know if I'd be able to forgive myself."

"I can forgive you, I understood why you left even as you were running away. But the anger is still there."

She nodded. "I understand. By the way, why are you here? Enrique said you gave him a gig. I was going to call you and tell you I'm coming back to Miami."

"That is good to hear. Enrique is trying to be helpful. I guess I didn't move fast enough for your family. They want you back."

"Of course they do," she said, relieved that Justin was the kind of man she'd believed him to be. Not a man who would try to hurt her family because she hurt him. "But do you?"

"I wouldn't be here if I didn't."

She smiled over at him. "Thank God. I know it's going to take time before you and I can be back to the way we were…I've already talked to my boss about resigning and moving home. I think—"

"No. You don't have to resign and move back to Miami. I am here because I can't stand another day without you. Together we will figure out what works for both of us because I'm not letting you leave me again."

"Why?"

"Because I love you."

She jumped up and ran around her desk and threw herself into his arms, kissing him. He squeezed her tightly to him and she started crying. She'd thought she could control her emotions but she couldn't.

"I was afraid to dream this could happen. I really didn't know what to expect."

"I knew what was going to happen. I have fallen in love with one woman in my life and that's you. There was no way I was going to let you go. I need you, Selena. You are the one person who grounds me."

She cupped his face with her hands and kissed him again. "I need you, too, Justin. You make it possible for me to believe in my dreams again."

"Good. Now what do you say we get out of here so I can make love to you."

"Sounds like a very good idea," she said.

Justin took her hand in his but stopped. "I am not leaving here until you answer one more question."

She took a deep breath. "Yes."

"Will you marry me?"

Justin wasn't playing around. He wasn't about to get Selena back in his life only to let her walk away again. He needed her to not only be his but to show the world that she was.

"Are you sure?"

"I wouldn't have asked if I wasn't," he said. He reached into his pocket and pulled out the ring box. He opened it and took the ring out. "I know that proper form means I should be down on one knee, but I wanted to look into your eyes when you answer me." He'd had it specially made for her. A marquis-cut diamond that he knew would look perfect on her hand.

She nodded. "Yes, I will marry you."

He slipped the ring onto her finger and then pulled her close for a kiss. She moved against him.

And he leaned back against the door pulling her closer to him. He wanted this woman. She'd turned his world upside down and now that he had her back in his arms, he needed to reinforce those bonds by making her his.

"Are you really mine?" he asked.

She smiled up at him, grinning ear-to-ear. "I am."

She shifted against him and he hardened instantly. "Then let's get out of here and find a proper bed so I can make love to you."

She flushed and raised an eyebrow at him. "You drive a hard bargain. Give me a minute to get my bag and shut down my computer and we'll go to my place."

"Okay," he said. "Are you ready to go yet?"

"I am."

The ride across town to her apartment took too long and he held her on his lap and kissed her the entire time. He didn't want to stop touching her and luckily didn't have to.

She shifted around so that she was facing him instead of lying in his arms. "Thank you for coming after me. I mean, I was going to come to you, but thanks."

"You're welcome. I was angry at first and wanted revenge. But that just made me realize how much I love you—because I could never do anything to hurt you or your family."

She hugged him close. "I know you couldn't. Even though you are tough in business, you have a good heart."

"Selena, I thought I was the Tin Man until you came along and showed me that I had one."

The car came to a stop. "This is my place."

"About damned time," he said.

The doorman came and opened the door for them. Justin followed Selena into the lobby and onto the elevator. He couldn't resist caressing the curve of her hips and pulling her into his arms for another kiss. Then he lifted her in his arms as the elevator doors opened and carried her down the hallway, following her directions.

As soon as she unlocked her apartment door and then stepped inside he leaned back against it and kissed her with all the carnality he'd been bottling up since she'd agreed to be his wife.

She dropped her bag and kicked off her shoes as he walked into the apartment.

"Bedroom?"

"Down the hall. Take your jacket off," she said.

"I'd have to put you down and I'm not ready to do that yet."

He walked into her bedroom and set her in the center of her king-size bed. It was covered with pillows. When she turned on the bedside lamp he saw that her room was done in warm hues of green and gold.

He toed off his shoes and socks and then took off his jacket. She reached for the buttons at the front of her blouse but he brushed her fingers aside and undid them himself.

He took his time stripping her. Each new bit of skin that was revealed he took the time to caress first with his hands, then with his mouth.

He lingered over her breasts and when she got restless and tried to hurry him, he refused. This time he wanted it to last and knowing that he had the right to make love to her for the rest of his life gave him the willpower to take his time.

"Now you are mine," he said.

She unbuttoned his shirt and pushed it off his shoulders onto the floor. Her hands roamed over his chest and traced the path of hair down to his belly button. She ran the edge of her nail around the circumference of it again and again. Each circle she completed made him harden even more. She reached for his pants and quickly had them open.

"Now *you're* mine, Justin."

Luckily, they would have a lifetime to work through the fine points of this negotiation.

Epilogue

At the end of May, after Selena had tied up all the loose ends in New York, she and Justin flew down to Miami for the ground-breaking of the Mercado and Luna Azul's tenth anniversary party. The guest list consisted of a glittering array of celebrities. But Selena didn't really care about that. This afternoon, she was enjoying herself in the warm Miami sunshine. They were having a party at her grandparents' house to celebrate her engagement to Justin.

"How's my fiancée?" he asked, coming up behind her and wrapping his arm around her waist.

"Good. I never thought I'd feel this at home in Miami, but moving back here with you…it feels right."

"We can always go back to New York. I'm up to the challenge of opening a Luna Azul club there."

"No, Justin. I'm here to stay." Selena was quiet for

a moment. Then, looking deep into his eyes, she said, "Thank you."

"For what?"

"For giving me back what I thought I'd lost forever."

"What was that?"

"My family and my heritage," she said.

"I didn't give it back to you, you helped me find it and now we can share that. I think we both ended up winning."

"I think so, too," Selena said, going up on her tiptoes and kissing Justin.

"I told you he was a good man," her *abuelita* said as she came up behind her.

"That's not all you said," Selena said with a grin.

"What else did she say?" Tomas asked.

"That he had a nice butt, *abuelito!*"

Justin flushed and everyone standing around them started laughing.

"Well, he does," her grandmother said.

"I guess you are part of the family now," Cam said to Justin. "They definitely like you."

"I like them, too," Justin admitted. He pulled Selena close and whispered in her ear. "I love you."

"I love you, too, Justin Stern."

* * * * *

"You may stay, Phoebe."

Cain's deep baritone voice riddled Phoebe with sudden sharp memories. She ignored them. "How magnanimous of you," she snapped, wanting him to face her. "But no thanks. It's obvious no one is welcome here. I'll make other arrangements."

It was humiliating that she needed a place to hide. It wasn't in her nature to back down, but she was desperate to keep her life from spiraling out of control…again.

"Phoebe." His sharp tone demanded her attention.

She went still, her heart in her throat. "What?"

"Forgive my reluctance," he said softly. "I'd be… delighted if you'd stay at Nine Oaks."

That sounded about as welcoming as a case of the plague, Phoebe thought. "How about you look at me and say that? Then I might believe you."

Cain stiffened then turned his head. His gaze slammed into hers. Nine years tumbled away, and they were again naked, skin to skin. Wanting the contact to be more intimate.

Phoebe tried to push those memories away. She didn't need sensual distraction. She needed peace and privacy. And Nine Oaks was the only place she'd find them.

SECRET NIGHTS
AT NINE OAKS

BY
AMY J FETZER

Published in Great Britain 2012
by Mills & Boon, an imprint of Harlequin (UK) Limited,
Eton House, 18-24 Paradise Road, Richmond, Surrey TW9 1SR

ISBN: 978 0 263 89105 8

51-0112

Harlequin (UK) policy is to use papers that are natural, renewable and recyclable products and made from wood grown in sustainable forests. The logging and manufacturing processes conform to the legal environmental regulations of the country of origin.

Printed and bound in Spain
by Blackprint CPI, Barcelona

Amy J Fetzer was born in New England and raised all over the world. She uses her own experiences in creating the characters and settings for her novels. Married more than twenty years to a United States Marine, and the mother of two sons, Amy covets the moments when she can curl up with a cup of cappuccino and a good book.

For the Henkels
Ryan, Mia and Miles

Family made us related
Life made us friends

Love you
Amy

One

Nine Oaks Plantation, SC

Cain Blackmon coveted his home and his privacy. So much so that he paid a fortune to keep people away from his estate. *People* should have included his younger sister, Suzannah.

The woman could drive a saint to violence.

She'd asked a favor; for the impossible. Not for him to leave Nine Oaks, that he wouldn't do, even for her, but to invite someone inside. To live. For *weeks*.

And that someone was Phoebe DeLongpree.

She might as well have dared him to name his most erotic fantasy and lay it out for the world to see.

"No." From a seat at his desk, Cain picked up a file. "There are plenty of hotels and spas in the area."

Suzannah blinked. "Well, that's just plain rude."

Cain didn't have any compunction about turning her down. He did not want that particular woman here.

Suzannah stepped nearer, her hands on her trim hips as she gave him a glare he remembered from their childhood. It signaled she was about to clamp down on a bone and refuse to let go. "This is my house, too, you know."

"Fine. When shall I expect your share of the restoration mortgage?"

"You're avoiding the issue."

"And you are refusing to accept the inevitable. I made myself very clear, Suzannah. I don't want a houseguest." Glancing at the closed door, he could almost scent Phoebe on the other side.

"You don't want *anyone* here, and for no good reason." He shot her a hard look and his sister wilted a little. "Fine—for reasons you won't discuss with *me*."

Her wounded tone gave Cain no more than a pin-prick of regret, yet he looked to the painted ceiling with its intricately layered molding and prayed for patience. "All right, Suzannah. Tell me why I should invite a stranger—"

"She's not a stranger."

No, he thought, she was Phoebe. Shapely, sexy-without-trying Phoebe. A man's erotic vision in a five-foot-two package of sensuality and combustible energy. He knew her from firsthand experience when she'd rocketed through his life and this house once before, briefly, but long enough to stir his desire to dangerous heights. Enough that he'd caught her under the servants' staircase and kissed her.

It had been one of the most electric, sensual moments of his life. And a mistake. She'd been liquid fire in his arms, dragging him into her unstoppable passion. And scaring him with it. Yes, Cain admitted with a bit of youthful recollection. Scaring him. Because one touch told him he'd delved into something that would consume him whole.

The memory of it tightened his groin, and he shoved out of the chair, turned to the window and brushed back the curtain. He stared at the landscape that hadn't changed in over two hundred years, his gaze flowing over the familiar live oaks draped in Spanish moss, the manicured gardens sloping toward the boats floating lazily down the river. The serenity of it didn't stop the memory of a single warm, wet kiss that left him raw and stripped.

Cain pinched the bridge of his nose, thinking that

Lily had never made him feel even a degree of what he'd shared with Phoebe in those few moments.

And he'd married Lily.

His expression darkened, the memory of his late wife compounding the guilt he stacked in a corner of his mind. He didn't want to share his isolation for the simple reason that Phoebe would end up hating him, and he didn't want that burden.

"I'm listening," he prompted, impatient to say no, again.

"She'd dated this guy three times, called it quits, but he wouldn't go away. Then he got mean."

Cain twisted a look back over his shoulder, frowning. "Go on."

"It was Randall Kreeg, the fifth."

Cain's brows shot up as the realization set in. Randall Kreeg, the son of the CEO of Kreeg Enterprises. A computer-generated imaging company all filmmakers used today. He'd seen a news report, yet hadn't paid it much attention, nor had he associated Phoebe with P.A. DeLong. Like most, he assumed this person was a man. "He's been arrested as I recall."

"Yes. She'll testify against him in a few weeks. But that wasn't the half of it." When he frowned, she asked, "Don't you read the papers?"

"Yes, several, daily."

"Phoebe is P.A. DeLong. The film writer?"

Good God, he thought. Sweet little Phoebe wrote those terrifying scripts?

"I see you understand. Add to that, the L.A. press twisted the whole mess, accusing her of staging it for publicity and ignoring the fact that Kreeg terrorized her."

Cain tried to imagine someone entering his life just to torment him. He almost laughed. What was Phoebe but a walking torture for him? "He's in jail, then she's safe."

"For how long? He can post any bail, and with his high-priced lawyers, who do you think they'll smear? She had to leave L.A., but the press has dogged her since she landed here. Though she covers it well, she's this far—" Suzannah pinched the air between her thumb and forefinger "—from collapsing from exhaustion."

Exhaustion? Phoebe? The woman had more energy than ten people, which made him doubt his sister's viewpoint on the matter. He faced the window again, unwilling to concede to her demands. Then he heard the door open.

"Enough, 'Zannah! Stop!"

Cain recognized Phoebe's voice instantly.

"I won't have you begging him for this, for pity sake."

"You heard?" Suzannah said, clearly mortified.

"I didn't press my ear to the door since my mama taught me better, but his answer was *quite* clear."

Good, it saved him from repeating himself, Cain thought, his gaze on the view, hands clasped behind his back. He didn't turn to look at Phoebe. He didn't have to. The energy level in the room went up a couple notches the instant she stepped inside. To look at her now, well, that was like anticipating a mortal blow. He knew it was coming, and there was no doubt it would have more impact than he expected.

Yet Cain knew when he was licked. Suzannah would never forgive him if he denied her request. He had so few people in his life, and he adored his baby sister. He didn't want to lose her, too. So, he said the words that would leave him in complete agony for the next few weeks.

"You may stay, Phoebe."

His deep baritone voice riddled Phoebe with sudden sharp memories. She ignored them. "How magnanimous of you, my lord," she snapped. "But no thanks. It's obvious no one is welcome here. I'll make other arrangements." Though she didn't know where. The press had a sixth sense, and had already forced her across the country and out of Suzannah's place.

It was humiliating enough that she needed a place to hide. It wasn't in her nature to back down, but she was desperate to keep her life from spiraling out of control again. Cutting herself off from the world that had been very unfriendly to her lately was the only way. She'd lost so much and needed it back or she wouldn't be able to recognize herself in the mirror.

She was ready to leave, wanting to pinch Suzannah when she kept appealing to him.

"Phoebe." His sharp tone demanded her attention.

She went still, her heart in her throat. "What?"

"Forgive my reluctance," he said a little more softly. "I'd be...delighted if you'd stay at Nine Oaks."

That sounded about as welcoming as a case of the plague, Phoebe thought, moving a step closer. "How about you look at me and say that? Then I might believe you."

Cain stiffened, then turned his head. His gaze slammed into hers. Nine years tumbled away. They were trapped under the staircases, pawing at each other like teenagers, wanting contact to be tighter, more intimate. Naked, skin to skin. When she moved closer and met his gaze, he felt ashamed that he'd hurt her that next morning. But where Phoebe was concerned, going cold turkey was the only way to deal with something that powerful.

It was the hardest thing he'd ever done. Because he'd wanted her like breath itself.

Green eyes pleaded with him for understanding. The same way she'd looked at him that morning, yet never asked for an explanation. Her look drove into him like a punch. My God, she was beautiful. Nine years had aged her from a girl to a breathtaking woman. Dark red hair framed her face in uncontrolled layers, much like her personality. The wild cut suited her, framed her elfin face, her big innocent eyes. His gaze lowered unconsciously to her mouth, to the lushest lips he'd ever had the pleasure to kiss and for a second he remembered the exotic taste of her. His gaze drifted lower, over her body wrapped in a frilly rust-colored top and matching leather skirt that was short enough to be illegal. Sexy without trying, he thought, catching a hint of something lacy under the sheer blouse. Right now he wanted nothing more than to be consumed by his own desire for her again. See if it had been a fabrication of his youth or still as real as his memories. He shoved the thought down. He couldn't afford to think or feel any of that. Not ever. Not for her.

"If it's refuge you seek, then Nine Oaks is at your disposal."

Phoebe wasn't listening. She was staring. He was bigger than she remembered, taller, broader in the shoulders. The pale sunlight shimmering through the windows silhouetted him against the sheer curtains, making his rich brown hair shine, the angled cut of his jaw stand out against his pristine white dress shirt. He gave off an aura of isolation, yet when he faced her fully, Phoebe couldn't breathe as his dark eyes clashed with hers.

Intense, assessing, edged with anger.

His mysterious hooded look was nothing like the man of her past, and the way he scrutinized her from head to toe made her feel peeled open and vulnerable. She smoothed her leather skirt and didn't like that he made her nervous.

But then, she was getting an opportunity that hundreds of people would kill for. A look at the South's most infamous recluse. He didn't look it, though. She wasn't expecting long hair and pale skin or anything like that, yet he looked…well, as heart-stoppingly handsome as he had nine years ago, but now, there was a dark gloom surrounding him. While it was sexy and mystifying, it made her want to pull apart the reasons he hid from the world. Even hid from his sister.

"*Is* that what you want?" he said, startling her.

Phoebe tried gathering her thoughts when she could taste the strain in the air. She knew the truth. He *really* didn't want her staying here. Normally, she'd have taken the hint and split. She wasn't dense, but she *was* desperate. Her life was in shambles and there was no sign that the press would leave her alone until the trial weeks away. She needed peace and privacy. To feel safe again.

"Yes," she said. "Just for a little while." She needed time to get a handle on her insomnia and, hopefully, regain her creativity.

"Do you have your things with you now?" he asked.

"No. To be honest, I didn't anticipate a yes."

Cain's brows knitted. His gaze moved to his sister standing behind Phoebe, her arms folded, a warning in her eyes. *Don't hurt her,* Suzannah was saying. *You've done that already.* He must be reading that wrong, Cain thought. Surely Suzannah didn't know about that kiss. But then, Phoebe and her sister had been friends for over a dozen years. They probably told each other everything. All the more reason to keep away from Phoebe while she was here.

Then Suzannah said, "Since I'm leaving for England," on business for him, Cain knew, "she'll be here this afternoon."

"Would you like me to send a limousine for you?" Cain offered, reaching for the phone.

Phoebe blinked. "Good grief, no. I wouldn't know how to behave in one."

"Not alone, at least," Suzannah muttered, a secret smile passing between the women. Phoebe's cheeks pinkened delicately, and Cain was instantly jealous of the man who'd had the pleasure of misbehaving with Phoebe inside a dark luxurious car.

Oblivious to the images rushing through his brain, Phoebe pushed Suzannah out the door ahead of her, then paused to look back around the edge. She met his gaze across the large room. "I appreciate this, Cain. I'll see you this afternoon."

No, you won't, he thought, yet nodded just the same.

The electronic sensors on the front gates sounded softly from Cain's computers, the relay reminding him of his promise to his sister. He'd thought of little else since this morning. His offer to Phoebe was gallant, but a mistake.

Cain pinched the bridge of his nose, then looked at the screen. Video cameras were positioned around the property, each one representing a separate block on the monitor. In the upper left square, Phoebe sat behind the wheel of a topless yellow Jeep, waving frantically at the camera, then looking behind herself. Her panic was full-blown, and the sudden urge to protect her shot through him.

Quickly hitting another key, he opened the gates

and she shot through with little room to spare. The gates closed behind her and he aimed the camera down the street to show a TV news van skidding to a halt. Photographers leaped out, snapping pictures. His irritation made him hit the speaker. "You are on private property. Please leave."

The man and woman looked startled. "It's a public road, pal."

"I *own* the road. The gates are now armed."

To bring the matter home, the Dobermans raced to the gate, their fangs and bark sending the couple into the van.

Unaffected, Cain turned from the console. Suzannah hadn't given him details of what Kreeg had done to Phoebe, and he suspected his sister was protecting her friend any way she could. Even from him. After Phoebe and Suzannah had left, Cain had done a search for any information. As much as the press was hounding her, it had more on Phoebe than on the police capture and Kreeg. The thought of her being hunted and tormented made Cain's anger rise.

Trying to distract himself from the woman racing up his driveway, Cain grabbed a sheaf of papers, and began making notes he really didn't comprehend. Temptation won and he glanced at the screen. She looked…well, comfortable in her own skin, he thought, dark red hair flying, her plush body in a tight tank top and jean skirt that hugged her delicious curves as she shot up the drive at full speed.

It didn't surprise him. She'd always been a bit untamed. That was the reason he hadn't pursued her after that kiss under the stairs. All that energy was dangerous. A strand of unwanted regret laced through him like a rope about to tighten, choking him. With more force than necessary, Cain tapped the intercom console. "Benson?"

"I saw her, sir."

Benson was always one step ahead of everyone, including Cain. "See that Miss DeLongpree has everything she needs."

"Yes sir. Will you be meeting with her, sir?"

"No." She wouldn't be pleased about that, but subjecting Phoebe to his lifestyle was out of the question. She'd asked for sanctuary.

Nine Oaks was a fortress, his private haven from the public eye. From anyone. For five years.

If Phoebe DeLongpree wanted solitude, then he'd give it to her. Only that. He'd already ruined one woman's life. He wouldn't take the chance of destroying another one.

Phoebe sped past two-hundred-year-old oak trees lining the nearly mile-long private lane to the house, their branches arching over the road like protective arms, welcoming her into seclusion. Into the ancestral home of Augustus Cain Blackmon the fourth. A bona fide recluse.

No one, including his sister, understood why he did the Howard Hughes thing, but there was a lot of speculation about why he hadn't shown himself in public or private since the death of his wife five years ago.

Though Cain never discussed his reasons with anyone, Suzannah believed it was because he loved his wife so much that he was still mourning her. But Phoebe, being a scriptwriter, came up with a dozen, slightly twisted scenarios, none of them as touching as a man who couldn't face the world without his bride. A real waste of a good-looking man, in her opinion.

In nine years, Cain Blackmon had aged to perfection, yet looks aside, why he cut himself off from the world nudged at her curiosity. Why lock himself up when he didn't have to? She'd have gone nuts being so confined. Besides, the newspapers had stopped asking why a couple years ago. At the thought of the press, she glanced in the rearview mirror as the news van pulled away. She understood Cain's need for privacy.

Sometimes, being alone was a good thing.

She wasn't used to publicity, either. Using the pseudonym of P.A. DeLong and being anonymous had suited her just fine.

Randall Kreeg had changed all that.

Needles of fear pricked her spine and she glanced in the rearview mirror again, half expecting to see him sitting behind her, looking smug and arrogant. Then she realized that no one stepped on this property without Cain's permission. *He can't touch me here,* she reminded herself and gripping the steering wheel, she worked her shoulders, refusing to allow her fear to ruin this opportunity to retrieve her creativity.

Yes, being alone was a good thing for her now.

Just not five years of it. Granted, Cain's seclusion was overkill in her opinion, but then she wasn't Cain. She'd never loved anyone that much. And she didn't have Nine Oaks to escape to. Till now.

As the house came into view, she felt as if she were in a time warp. Rolling to a stop in front of the antebellum mansion, she locked the brake and stood on the seat of her Jeep, then braced her arms on the top of the windshield. She just stared.

It hadn't changed in about two hundred years, if she had to hazard a guess. Suzannah told her that Cain had had the entire plantation restored to its former glory, even the stables. Porches wrapped the upper and lower levels of the mansion, a widow's walk was on the third floor. Painted white and trimmed with Charleston green shutters so dark they looked black, the house rambled, its stone verandas leading to a dock, the river and a pool. From the river, acres of land spread out in three directions opening on to fruit orchards, rice, sugar, peanuts, cotton and timber. While pictures of Nine Oaks graced local shops, hotels and restaurants, nothing compared to seeing it up close again.

She loved this house. Its serene elegance drew her. Suzannah had always brushed off Phoebe's awe and envy over Nine Oaks, but then she'd grown up here with Cain. For a second, she wondered where he was. The library again, she decided, her gaze skimming the house.

The front doors opened, and while she didn't expect Cain, she was a little disappointed when a young man dressed in a white shirt and dark slacks trotted down the steps. Another man, older and wearing a suit, walked sedately behind the first.

The young man smiled brightly. "I'm Willis, Miss DeLongpree. I'll take your bags up for you and park your car."

She thanked him, smiling as she pitched him the keys, cautioning him the second gear stuck a little. Silver haired and slender, the older man waited on the wide Federal staircase and Phoebe recognized him as she mounted the first few steps.

"Hello, Benson," she said. "How's it going?"

Not a fraction of Benson's distinguished expression changed as he nodded and said, "Miss DeLongpree. Welcome back to Nine Oaks."

"Thanks." Just because she knew it would fluster him, she popped up and kissed his cheek. "You're looking mighty good there, darlin'."

He blinked and cleared his throat, his ears glowing pink. "And you, miss."

"You still riding roughshod over the gang here?"

His eyes twinkled. "I will die doing just that, ma'am."

Phoebe had the urge to tickle him just to see if he knew how to smile. She liked him. Once, Suzannah had snitched liquor from her daddy's private stock and together they'd indulged too much. Benson had found them, drunk and silly, and managed to get them both to Suzannah's room before anyone discovered their crime. Then he went beyond the call, soothing their hangovers with some old-fashioned remedy, and never telling a soul. *You had to love a man who knew how to be discreet.*

Following him, she stepped into the coolness of the house, looking around at the familiar decor. Heart-pine floors stretched for yards in three directions, complementing the pale yellow walls and the carved pecan wood moldings and doors. But the real eye catcher was the twin sweeping wood staircases that led to the second and third floors of the east and west wings. *Eat your heart out, Scarlett.*

She looked at Benson. "So where's Cain?"

"Mr. Blackmon is very busy. Follow me, please." He headed for the stairs.

"Too busy to greet his guest?"

"He's aware you've arrived, Miss Phoebe."

Of that she didn't doubt, yet Phoebe stopped where she was and Benson paused on the stairs, looking down at her, then arching a brow. "Not even a hello?"

Sympathy clouded his dark eyes. "Mr. Blackmon doesn't receive visitors."

"He really is the ogre locked in his castle, isn't he?" Somehow, she'd hoped his extremeness was mostly rumor.

Benson's gaze narrowed, and in a heartbeat he went from majordomo to watchdog. "He does as he pleases, miss."

"Yes, well, so do I."

Phoebe turned to her left and walked toward the library, suspecting he was in there. Cain didn't owe her a thing—if he was going to ignore her, fine, he could. It was his house. But nine years ago, the man had kissed her into a bone-melting puddle, and now they were connected.

He owed her at least a "Hello, how's your mama?"

"Miss DeLongpree. I wouldn't advise opening that door."

Lord, he sounded afraid for her. "Duly noted, Benson. I take full responsibility."

She pushed it open and stepped into the grand library. She hadn't really taken notice of it this morning, yet her gaze landed first on the back walls lined with dark wood shelves and stuffed tight with leather-bound books. Her mouth practically watered. There were groupings of chairs, and antiques dotted the room. Rich heart-pine floors were covered with vivid carpets in a mix of burgundy, blue and gold. Masculine, opulent, the room spoke of aged brandy and Cuban cigars, soft conversations about finance and world affairs. It said *Cain,* she thought, quiet, reserved. For a second, she absorbed the history lingering like smoke inside the walls before looking around the room again.

He wasn't there.

The chair was turned away from the desk, and a bank of computer screens filled one side of a large U-shaped work center. On the bottom of one of the computer screens, the stock market updates ticked by. Yet aside from the usual desk paraphernalia, lamp, phones, blotter, there was a china cup and saucer.

And whatever was in it, was still steaming.

He'd heard her coming and left somehow.

Phoebe felt a hard punch somewhere near her heart.

She didn't bother looking further. Quietly, she backed out and closed the door. Benson didn't say a word, didn't show any emotion, but Phoebe suddenly felt like the morning after Cain had kissed her so thoroughly, then later behaved as if it had never happened.

She felt ignored. Unworthy. Used.

Disappointed, she followed Benson upstairs.

Two

A half hour later, Benson slipped into the library, posting himself at the edge of Cain's desk.

"Is she settled?" Cain asked, writing.

"As well as Miss DeLongpree can settle, sir."

Cain looked up, amused. "Still a little hyper?"

"Yes, sir. She's in the east wing, the yellow suite," Benson said. He added, "She was very determined to see you."

Cain said nothing, closing a folder. He'd heard her coming and slipped out through a secret passageway his ancestors had built into this house over a century ago to escape from the Union Army. It was devious and a bit cowardly, but Cain told himself he was sparing Phoebe. He wasn't the man she knew before, and she'd be expecting that.

"Where is she now?"

Benson gestured to the security screen, to the center block, and Cain watched as Phoebe, in a bikini, hopped on the diving board.

"Oh good God." His muscles locked, heat skimming his bloodstream. Cain swallowed. There wasn't enough bikini to cover that body, he thought, and watched her bounce on the board, then jackknife and plunge head first into the twenty-foot-deep water. She barely made a splash.

"Impressive," Benson said, and Cain spared him a glance. If he didn't know better, he'd swear the man was smiling.

Seconds later, she popped to the surface in a smooth arch, then started swimming laps, looking like a slim, hot pink torpedo shooting through the water. Cain watched her for a second, then tapped the keys and viewed another section of the property. He wasn't a voyeur, but the image of her round plump breasts spilling out of her top left an imprint in his mind.

And in his blood.

It confirmed what he knew—getting anywhere near Phoebe was dangerous.

"She won't give up easily, sir."

Cain rubbed his temple. "She doesn't have a choice."

"Sir…if you would simply—"

"Spare me the sermon, Benson. Please."

Once in a while, Benson made a plea for him to leave Nine Oaks. Since Benson had practically raised him, he wasn't offended. Yet Benson had been here the day his wife had died. He'd heard the horrible argument they'd had, had warned him when Lily had taken a boat out onto the river.

Cain didn't choose to be alone because he was grieving, as most people assumed.

He was alone, because he was paying for his crime.

Lily wasn't skilled enough to sail alone.

And that night, he knew it.

There was a fine art to being lazy.

Phoebe hadn't a clue how to begin. As a kid, her mom had instilled in her that "a flagrant misuse of time" was nothing short of criminal. Once Phoebe was on her own, she'd gotten over that. Well, mostly.

She'd always been a little hyperactive, which translated into her mouth running faster than her brain and getting her and Suzannah into major trouble when they were in college. But she'd needed to do something, even if it was wrong. Right now, she wished for anything so she could sleep tonight. After weeks without a good night's rest, the reflection in the mirror was looking pretty sad. She dreaded bedtime.

Although she could have done another twenty laps, she was waterlogged already. Maybe later, she thought, trying to clear her ears as she stepped inside the house. Maybe after one of Jean Claude's famous meals.

Entering the house from the south side, she wrapped the flowered sarong more securely around her hips and headed toward the foyer. Her heeled sandals clicked on the pinewood floors, almost echoing in the big house. The sound made her feel as if she were in a museum, that any extra noise was going to earn a reprimand from the guard.

That would be Benson, she thought, smiling. She passed several unused rooms, and knew she and Cain were the only people here who didn't work for the estate. It was sad to have so much room and not use it. The house screamed for a big summer party.

Suddenly she found herself staring at the library door. She hadn't meant to come this way, especially not dressed as she was. But Cain was in there. She could hear the low murmur of his voice. She thought about how he'd slipped out of the room when he knew she was coming in, and the sting of it skipped through her again. This need to see him irritated her. She didn't really want to speak to someone who went out of his way not to be near her, but just the same, the need was there. Being so casually dismissed pushed her to reach for the door latch. Her hand stopped midway. Whoever Cain was talking with, he didn't sound pleased.

When it grew quiet again, she rapped on the door. She heard his unintelligible response and pushed it open, her gaze sliding around the room, then focusing on the desk. He stood behind it, his hands clasped behind his back as he looked out the window. He stared at the water a lot, she realized.

"Yes, Benson?"

"It's me, Cain."

He stiffened, yet kept his back to her.

"What is it that you want?" Cain said more tersely than he intended.

She considered the wisdom of confronting him when clearly he didn't want her near. "Am I truly welcome here?"

Her voice sounded fragile, and Cain sighed softly and faced her. His gaze latched onto her face, to her pretty green eyes that looked so hollow right now. Then his attention slipped lower. Good God, he thought and swallowed, his pulse skipping a couple of beats. The skimpy bikini barely covered her smooth tanned skin while the sarong was tied low on her hips and showed the enticing dip of her navel. He'd never seen anything so exotic.

"Am I, Cain?"

He dragged his gaze to her face. "Of course you are."

She sagged a little. He didn't want to make her feel uninvited. He just didn't want her within touching distance. His moods had a tendency to rub off on people, and knowing she was here, simply reminded him that he'd made a terrible mistake before and would never risk it again. But the temptation just to look at her won out over his better judgment and Cain moved from behind the desk.

Phoebe watched his approach as if she were looking down a long thin tunnel. Her world narrowed. Cain. The man who'd made her world tilt years ago and never tip right since then. Her knees softened a little. Her tastes in men didn't normally lean to the suit-and-tie type, but lordy-my, a girl could change her taste, couldn't she? His white dress shirt pulled at his broad shoulders, his hair a dark, chocolate-brown that shone so much she wanted to run her fingers through it.

He stopped, and she looked up at him. "Thank you, Cain."

He only nodded. Silence stretched between them

and for a woman who normally didn't know how to shut up, she was at a loss for words. She tried for the ordinary.

"So are you going to have dinner with me or anything, or just keep this distance you're so fond of lately?"

"Perhaps."

That wasn't an answer. "Well, just so you know, I'm available for cocktails at five."

A smile barely curved his mouth. "I'll remember that."

Her gaze traveled over his face. "You're just so snappy with the pleasant conversation, aren't you?" Now that she was near him, her nervousness fled. Amazing, she thought. It was like staring into the face of someone she'd known for…centuries.

When he didn't say anything, kept staring, she said, "Out of practice?"

"Hardly."

"We can start at the beginning." She held out her hand. "Hi, I'm Phoebe DeLongpree, your sister's best friend."

He looked down at her hand. He knew what would happen if he touched her, felt her warm skin against his in something as mundane as a handshake. He'd want more, and that he couldn't have. Ever.

"Very funny."

Phoebe frowned, lowering her hand. "More than a physical recluse, I see." Miffed, she moved to the door.

"Phoebe."

"Yes?"

"This is a male household. I suggest you cover yourself a bit more."

Phoebe didn't bother looking down at herself. She knew what she looked like. She'd run nearly a hundred miles in the last couple weeks, worked out till she was sore and tired, doing anything to fall into a peaceful sleep. She faced him. He was behind his desk again, shuffling files.

"It's a bikini, Cain."

"Is that what you call that?" There was more cloth in a handkerchief than in that top, for heaven's sake. And unfortunately, Cain's imagination was easily filling in what lay beneath every sparse inch of fabric.

"Yes, I do. And I look good in it or I wouldn't be wearing it. And anyone on your staff could have walked outside and seen me, so I think the problem lies with *you*."

He snapped a look at her. She unwrapped the sarong, slinging it over her shoulder, and on heeled sandals the same shade as her bikini, she turned and walked to the door.

His gaze lowered and Cain groaned, feeling mortally wounded. The damn thing was a thong, and her slim hips and tight, round behind rocked in sexy motion as she left his office. He closed his eyes, the image replaying in his mind enough to make his ears ring and every muscle in his body lock up. His groin was so tight he thought he'd snap in two if he tried to sit.

Cain let out a long-suffering breath, rubbing his face, then scraping his hands back over his skull.

As much as he wanted her gone, he wouldn't go back on his promise. When he lowered gingerly into the chair, he resigned himself to the sexiest creature on the planet torturing him with temptation.

It was going to be weeks of pure hell.

Standing at the top of the staircase, Phoebe eyed the long curving banister, imagining descending the steps in a gown to a handsome escort waiting at the bottom. Chewing her lip, she leaned out, looking down the halls to see if she was alone, then hitched her rear onto the polished banister and slid her way down. She hopped to the floor, her sneakers squeaking, and she did a little wiggle before turning toward the hall.

Someone cleared his throat.

She flinched, spinning around. Willis stood nearby, grinning, and holding a tray. Phoebe flushed a little, put her finger to her lips, then moved closer.

"This is for Cain, right?" she said, scoping out the coffee service.

"Yes, ma'am."

She snatched the pad and pencil from the breast pocket of his jacket, and scribbled a note, then stuffed it under the saucer. Willis, blond and young, gave the plate a skeptical look.

If that won't get a rise out of Cain, nothing will, she thought, then winked at Willis before heading toward the heavenly scent of freshly baked bread.

Benson appeared out of nowhere. "Miss Phoebe, dinner is served." He gestured toward the formal dining room.

"Oh, great." She was looking forward to tasting one of Jean Claude's creations. She followed Benson into the dining room, its vivid red walls and white trim giving a casual feel to the austere surroundings. The older man pulled out her chair and when she sat, he lifted silver domes off the plates. Her mouth watered as the glorious scents of lemon, chicken and delicate vegetables wafted up to greet her.

She tipped in her chair, looking around. "Cain isn't joining me?"

"No, miss."

"Well, that stinks," she muttered under her breath.

Benson poured her some wine and offered her napkin, then said, "Enjoy," before he left her alone.

Phoebe stared at the wide empty room. "Hello, hello, hello," she said like an echo. She hated eating alone. It was boring and she always ate too fast. She felt a bit insulted that Cain couldn't be bothered to join her. She'd practically invited him to, in his own house no less.

Gathering her plate and utensils in the napkin, she walked to the kitchen, stopping in the doorway, and taking in the small bit of chaos. The Nine Oaks' kitchen had been modernized and she didn't know what half the appliances were used for, but then, a microwave was her best friend lately.

Around the edge of the granite counter, a few of the staff sat, eating dinner and watching the TV. She recognized Jean Claude, Willis and Mr. Dobbs, who handled the dogs and cared for the stables. The two others she hadn't met yet, but from the looks of their clothing, they worked on the grounds.

"Oh, I could just live at your feet, Jean Claude," she said, inhaling deeply. "You could just throw me some scraps and I'd be grateful."

Jean Claude glanced her way as he pulled a flat wooden paddle filled with steaming loaves of bread out of the stone oven. "Well, where y'at, Miss Phoebe?" His smile was big and bright.

"I'm just fine, Jean Claude. Do y'all mind if I join

you?" She nodded toward the counter. "It's dull eating with a flower arrangement for company."

"Yes, of course," the group said, and Willis hopped up to get her plate and make a spot for her.

She slid onto a stool at the granite counter.

"I was glad to hear you were coming for a visit, Miss Phoebe," Jean Claude said.

"Shocked you, I'll bet," she said, cutting her chicken. It was stuffed with crabmeat and shrimp and she was practically drooling over it before the first bite made it to her mouth.

His lips curved. "Yes'm, it did."

Jean Claude was raised in New Orleans, Cajun to the bone, tall, slim and handsome at nearly sixty. There was something terribly sexy about a man who could cook, and Jean Claude was the best chef in five counties.

"Suzannah invited me. I think she blackmailed Cain, though."

"Miss 'Zannah is a strong woman, that I'll say."

"I'd say pushy."

"More than you?"

She smiled. "She runs a close second." She gave him her best begging-to-try-it look. "You going to share some of that?" She eyed the fresh bread.

"What? You don't like my dinner?" He nodded toward the plate.

"It's great, but your bread, well…it's a spiritual thing."

Grinning, Jean Claude cut her a slice, slathering it with butter.

"Bless you, I was *so* prepared to grovel," she said, then sank her teeth into the warm bread and swore she'd just tripped into food heaven. The flavors of herbs and butter exploded in her mouth. "Divine, Jean Claude."

He flashed her a smooth smile, slicing and packaging up the remaining loaves as he introduced her to the others having dinner. The TV droned softly.

After a few minutes, the conversation grew lively as Jean Claude told stories of some of Phoebe and Suzannah's college antics. "I come down here, and they had the freezer wide open, and the two of them were sitting on the floor, eating ice cream. Just a spoonful here and there, mind you, but from every bucket I had." Jean Claude tsked and winked at her.

"We were bonding over both getting Ds on history term papers. But I paid for that ice cream with a stomachache for two days. But poor 'Zannah, she felt the need to go jogging." The group groaned, imagining the damage. "It wasn't pretty," Phoebe said.

"You would have been better served to study harder," Jean Claude said.

"Oh yeah, sure, but then, that would have been sensible."

"Did you pass the course?" a voice said from the doorway, and they all looked up.

Cain was leaning against the door frame and the room grew noticeably quiet. When Willis made to leave, Phoebe subtly put her hand on his arm, keeping him still. How long had he been standing there?

She tipped her chin up. "Yes I did. I didn't have much else to do but study for the exam with a stomachache. Your sister, however, didn't make higher than a C on the final."

"Tattletale," Cain said, amused.

"What are friends for?" She grinned hugely, then said, "You going to stand there or come join us?"

Cain recognized the challenge in her eyes. Everyone stared and waited. Never taking his gaze off her, he pushed off the door frame and came into the kitchen. Her triumphant smile was damned annoying.

"Sir, would you like your dinner now?" Jean Claude said.

"Sure he would," Phoebe said, nudging out a stool, and Cain hesitated before he sat beside her.

Jean Claude looked at him, waiting, and Cain nodded, too interested in feeling the heat of Phoebe's body, in smelling her perfume. It was intoxicating.

She was intoxicating. Dressed in a short denim skirt and a red top that scooped low enough to show come great cleavage, she looked fresh and incredibly desirable. But then, all Phoebe had to do was walk into a room and he was pretty much sunk.

Her note under the coffee service tray hadn't pulled him from his office, though her scribbled words *"Come out and play with me"* were evocative enough to give him daydreams for the rest of his life.

But he'd been drawn by the noise, the laughter that echoed down the hall. It had been a very long time since he'd heard that. He'd stood at the door for a couple of minutes, watching as Phoebe pulled everyone into the conversation, turning the focus off her and onto the men. She talked easily, smiled often, and looked right at home. But then she was the highlight of the house. Aside from his sister, there hadn't been a woman at Nine Oaks in five years. Cain's thoughts shifted to Lily and he instantly derailed them, unwilling to ruin his dinner.

Jean Claude served up a plate of dinner and Cain ate, listening as Phoebe told a joke. Laughing with them, one of the men said goodbye, and left.

"I saw you diving, Miss Phoebe," Willis said and Cain shot Phoebe a covert look. "You're very good. That jackknife was something else."

"Thank you, Willis."

For one pointed moment, she looked directly at Cain as if to say, "see, I told you so." But all Cain had on his mind was the sexy image of her prancing out of his office with her bare behind jiggling. He'd tried all day to banish that picture and failed. He sure as hell didn't need another reminder. His body wanted this woman. It damn near screamed when he was near her. And sitting beside her, feeling her arm brush his, was enough to shoot another wave of heat through his bloodstream. He was glad there were people around; he couldn't trust himself alone with her.

"I was on a team in college," Phoebe said. "Heck, I was on three. Track, 500-meter relay swimming, diving." She looked at the young man. "I've always been wound a little too tight."

"Well, there's a news flash," Cain said dryly, eating.

"No. Really?" Jean Claude put in and she laughed. "I'm surprised that you can sit still long enough to write."

She looked up, chewed, then swallowed. "You know?"

"We read the papers, *bébé*," Jean Claude said.

Cain felt a surge go through her, saw her shoulders go taut. He'd never seen her tense up so fast. And though he didn't know the details of the incident with Randall Kreeg, he decided it was time he found out more.

Phoebe glanced around at the group, flushing with embarrassment. "Yes, well, I guess the cat's out of the bag about that."

The sudden silence was interrupted by the TV and a news flash. Cain heard her name and looked up.

The broadcast recapped the arrest and incarceration of Kreeg and mentioned speculation that Phoebe or the last producer who'd bought her script had staged the incident. He looked at Phoebe. She was frozen, her attention riveted to the TV. He called to her, but she didn't respond.

All Phoebe saw was Kreeg, looking rich, handsome and so damn supreme as the police escorted him into the station. A wave of memories hit her, blanketing her thoughts, bringing back the terror of realizing that Kreeg had touched her things, had been in her car. Then in her house.

Her breathing quickened.

Beside her, Cain frowned, noticing her hands shake.

"Phoebe?" Cain called again.

She lifted her gaze to his and the scared look in her eyes fractured his heart.

And made it bleed.

Three

Cain laid his hand on her arm and she flinched, trembling, her gaze shooting around the room, panicked as if searching for an escape.

His features tightened, then he leaned closer, sliding his hand farther up her arm and whispering, "It's okay, darlin', you're safe here. I swear it."

Phoebe blinked, then let out a long, shaky breath, and looked at him. Her eyes were owlish wide, as if replaying the last seconds in her mind, and she looked so frail and small that Cain fought the urge to take her in his arms. Then just as quickly as it came, her fear vanished and her shoulders relaxed.

"Well, don't I feel stupid," she muttered, her cheeks pinkening.

Cain rubbed her arm. "It's all right." For a second she gripped his hand, holding his gaze, then suddenly self-conscious of their nearness, she let go and looked at the others.

"I know he's in jail, but…"

Jean Claude's expression fell. "Forgive me, Miss Phoebe." He shut off the TV.

Her gaze jerked to the chef's. "Oh Jean Claude, it's not your fault. Not at all." She waved, all bright smiles. "It's just me being a little neurotic." She released an uneasy laugh, then picked up her fork, spearing a piece of chicken.

Cain frowned. He'd never seen anyone so upset one minute, then fine the next. Or was she just smothering her anxiety for their sake? And what the hell did that bastard do to her to make her so afraid still?

"He can't hurt you here," Cain assured. "No one will."

"It's why I'm here." Phoebe shifted her gaze to his, smiling.

But Cain could tell it was forced, could see the shadows in her eyes. And right now, he wanted only to take up arms and battle her demons for her. It startled him, reminded him that it was wiser to stay clear of her. Cain didn't deserve to be around a woman like her.

Yet he stayed where he was, unable to leave.

Jean Claude went to put the loaves of bread in the pantry, and the rest of the staff departed quickly.

She looked around. "Well, I sure know how to clear a room, huh?"

"Not really. They're unaccustomed to dining with me," he confessed. "*Are* you all right?"

"Yeah sure, just great," she said cheerily, and started clearing dishes, not wanting to answer the questions she could see in his eyes. She'd been there too many times, with friends, the police, her parents. In her dreams. The fact that Kreeg could post any bail that was set and walk free never left her thoughts.

"I wouldn't do that," Cain warned, nodding toward the dishes. "You tread on sacred ground by invading his kitchen." To prove him right, Jean Claude had a fit when he came back and in thickly accented Cajun, he shooed them both out.

Cain was already at the door. "See, told you."

She mimicked him, making a face, then thanked Jean Claude and left the kitchen.

Cain was several steps ahead of her, and at the foyer, she stopped, realizing he'd just dismissed her from his mind. He confirmed it when he entered the library and closed the door. The sound echoed up the

hall, and Phoebe wondered when he'd grown so un-
feeling, then rethought that, recalling his comforting
touch in the kitchen. She could still feel the warmth
of his hand on her skin. But it felt as if he were running from her now.

What was it about her that made him so standoff-
ish and cold? Their one moment of past history? Or
was it something else? And what really made him re-
treat into Nine Oaks and never leave?

Back at his desk, Cain focused on work, making
calls to his plant and crop operations managers and
reading over a half-dozen status reports. Anything
to keep his thoughts focused when they were easily distracted. With Phoebe. Knowing she was
somewhere near.

Roaming. Being Phoebe. Driving him nuts.

Leaving his chair, he moved to the shelves of books
and selected a ledger from last year. His gaze caught
on a drawer he knew housed racks of DVDs and he
opened it, scanning them for one film he knew P.A.
DeLong had written. He popped it into the player, saw
her pen name on the credits and kept watching.

A half hour later, he was in a chair, involved in
the paranormal plot so twisted and tense, he gripped
the armrests. He glanced at the clock, then shut it off,
yet stared at the blank screen for a moment, think-

ing that maybe someone in Hollywood had put the word out that her assault was staged. Just the rumor would have been publicity enough. Or had Kreeg's lawyers done that? Phoebe's pseudonym suggested she didn't want to be known for her controversial work. She liked hiding behind it. The thought brought a smile as he returned to his desk.

But concentration eluded him. Was this to be the pattern of the next couple of weeks? He'd be bankrupt if he wasn't careful, he thought, shaking his head and plowing into work.

Sometime later, the intercom buzzed. "Sir?" Benson said. "Miss DeLongpree is outside."

Benson sounded a little tense, and Cain frowned, tapping the button. "She has free rein of the place, Benson."

"But it's dusk, sir. The dogs are out."

Cain cursed, leaving his chair, then flung open the French doors to the library and raced out onto the stone veranda. His gaze shot around the landscape.

The Dobermans were running across the side lawn at top speed with teeth bared. His attention shifted to the figure a good distance away and to his left.

He called her name, and Phoebe turned, waving. Cain ran, pushing himself faster, knowing if he didn't outdistance the dogs, the animals bred for defense would tear her to shreds.

"Phoebe, the dogs!"

She looked at the dogs running toward her and froze. Horror rocketed through him as the Dobermans leaped at her. They knocked her to the ground, pinning her.

Cain commanded the animals, but they merely hesitated, and sliding to his knees, he yanked at the dog's collars.

Then he heard Phoebe laugh and focused.

The dogs weren't attacking. They were licking her face.

She giggled. "All right, guys, you weigh a ton, back off." Still the dogs nuzzled her, tails wagging like whips in the air.

This time, Cain shouted a command at the dogs, and the pair of black Dobermans jumped back and sat still.

Instantly, he ran his hands over her damp face, shoulders, her bare legs.

"You're trying to use this as an excuse to feel me up, right?"

Braced over her, he ignored her teasing, then demanded, "They didn't bite you?"

"No. They were greeting me."

"Greeting!" he roared.

"Yeah. That and they wanted these." She held up her hand, filled with half-crushed dog biscuits. "Scooby snacks," she said, grinning.

Cain fell back on his haunches and scraped a hand through his hair. The second he caught his breath, he tore into her. "How could you be so damn stupid!"

She hitched up on her elbows. "I beg your pardon?"

"They could have torn you to pieces! They could have killed you!"

"If I ran, sure, which is why I didn't." She frowned at him. He was breathing hard and looking as if *he'd* like to chew her to shreds. "You forgot that Suzannah and I slept with these dogs when they were puppies. They remembered me."

"It's been a very long time, Phoebe," he said, pulling her off the ground as he stood. He grasped her shoulders and for a moment he simply stared down at her. *She could have been mauled,* echoed through his mind and somewhere in his chest, muscles clenched. He'd rather die than see her hurt, and without his will, his gaze lowered to her mouth. Ripe and painted rose-pink.

Tempting him.

She met his gaze and his pulse pounded. The woman had too much control over him. She made him feel like a feral animal too long in the wild and a deep, troubling hunger lanced through him, the pressure of it settling hotly in his groin. It clamored for satisfaction, for release. For her. Yet he knew without being inside her, without having tasted more than her mouth, that it wouldn't be enough. He'd never wanted a woman more.

He knew that nine years ago, *and* the instant she stepped into his domain again. Then she tipped her head back, her gaze locking with his and Cain felt himself sinking. He bent, his mouth nearing hers. They were a breath away when the impact of what he was doing hit him.

Cain let her go and stepped back. "You took a big chance that they'd remember you."

Phoebe frowned, wondering what made him stop when she wanted him to kiss her. And he wanted to do it. It was unfair, teasing her like that. "No, I didn't." She opened her palm. "These were their favorites. When 'Zannah told me the dogs were still here, I brought them with me. And I already visited them in the kennels after my swim."

"You could have warned me."

The dogs sat still, their heads tilted to the side, watching the humans.

"And when would I have the opportunity to do that? You don't come out of that cave of yours unless provoked, and its obvious that no one is welcome in there."

"I'm very busy. And we had dinner together."

"Not by choice, was it?" Phoebe clucked her

tongue and the dogs came to her, parking themselves at her feet. She tossed one biscuit to each and they snatched them out of the air. In seconds, they'd eaten the biscuits and were licking their chops. "They are a little scary."

"Their purpose."

"To keep people out?"

"Yes."

She met his gaze. "I think they're keeping you in, Cain."

His eyes narrowed, defenses rising. "My private life is not your concern."

"What private life? You have no life. You eat, sleep and work, and Mr. Dobbs said you haven't ridden a horse, sailed, even played tennis for ages. For heaven's sake, Cain, you haven't left these grounds in five years."

His eyes darkened, his expression sharpening to lethal. "Leave it alone, Phoebe." He walked away, snapping his fingers. The dogs trotted alongside him.

"Aren't you taking this seclusion too far?"

"I think I'm the best judge of my own life, don't you?"

"I hate seeing you like this."

"Then stay on your side of the house or leave."

"*My* side? You'll have to be more specific, my lord."

He turned, practically snarling at her. "I gave you the east wing, the run of the land, you can go anywhere, do anything you like. Except touch the boats."

"Don't forget except 'bother you.'" She ran after him and grabbed his arm, but he shook her loose. "Cain? Look at me!"

He did, his tone biting as he said, "I'm not your mission, Phoebe. Don't try to make me into something I'm not."

"I wouldn't dream of it."

"Excellent decision." He turned away again, determined to put more than a few yards between them and keep it that way.

"You were a selfish jerk nine years ago and apparently that hasn't changed."

He stopped and turned slowly. He had that whole intimidation thing down pat, Phoebe thought, feeling something close to pain lock inside her.

"You consider a kiss under the staircase a judgment of my character?"

"No, I consider what happened after, a fair assessment of your true self."

"And that would be?"

"Whatever Cain wants, Cain gets."

His expression was menacing for a second, then he looked at the landscape. After a moment, his shoulders drooped a little. "Phoebe," he said gently and met her gaze. "I did not intend to hurt your feelings."

"Yes, you did. You acted like we'd never kissed so I *would* go away."

Cain stared, saying nothing.

"True or not?"

"Yes. It's true."

"I'm fine with that, but what I want to know is, why?"

His gaze zeroed in on her. "Because that kiss made me see that we were incompatible."

She rolled her eyes. "Oh come off it, Blackmon. If we'd gone on for five more minutes and had privacy we'd have been in bed together. How much more compatible do you want?"

"Sex isn't a relationship, Phoebe." He'd had sex with Lily, nothing like his one kiss with Phoebe, but it wasn't enough to make their marriage work. Besides, Phoebe would have never fit into his boardroom lifestyle. She was too unconventional, too outspoken; it would have crushed her.

"I agree, but if you'd given us a chance—oh never mind." She sighed hard. "Forget it. It's past, done, over."

"Apparently not for you."

She lifted her chin, refusing to admit that she'd amused herself with thoughts of what might have been. "I don't believe in lingering in the past that long, Cain. It's a waste of energy. I can't change it, and I won't even try."

Cain wished he could change five years ago. Wished he'd simply divorced Lily instead of trying to make himself love her. She'd ended up hating him anyway. "I apologize for hurting you, Phoebe."

Phoebe frowned, wondering what mystery was hidden behind those tormented eyes of his. "Fine, I accept."

He eyed her. "I'm not convinced."

"Believe what you want. I promise to stay on my side of the house and not trespass in your office or interfere with your life. Or lack thereof."

She spun on her heels, and much to Cain's displeasure, the Dobermans, Jekyll and Hyde, followed her.

Great. His staff, and now his dogs?

He watched her stomp away, every fiber of her body shouting her anger. He didn't blame her. He'd tried to shield her from the man he'd become by staying away from her. He had to. Phoebe made him feel on edge, vulnerable, and if she knew the truth, she'd be gone by morning and never look back.

Even if he couldn't have her, he wanted her near.

On her way to her room, she passed Benson in the hall. He offered her a nightcap, but she declined.

She already knew that liquor would just make her insomnia worse unless she got completely tanked. She wasn't willing to trade a near-death experience with the porcelain god for a couple of hours of sleep. She refused to take sleeping pills, terrified she'd become addicted to the easy way out of her insomnia.

Closing the door behind herself, she glanced around the suite Cain had offered her. With a sitting area that opened to a balcony and a bathroom that would make any woman never want to leave it, it was a perfectly styled antebellum bedroom with only a few modern touches.

A fantasy in pale yellow, blue and lavender, the center was graced with an antique Rice bed, its narrow posts twisting elegantly toward the sky. The heart-shaped palm fronds of the ceiling fan waved a soft breeze on to stir the sheer drapes on the bed.

Crossing the room, she plopped down in the club chair, kicked off her shoes and propped her bare feet on the fat tucked ottoman. Picking up a book she'd been meaning to read for weeks, she opened it and skimmed a few pages. But after a few minutes, even her favorite author couldn't keep her still.

She glanced at her laptop still trapped in its case. It was a glaring reminder that she hadn't written anything worth sending out in weeks. She wasn't hurting for money, but for every five treatments or scripts she did, only one sold. It didn't pay to be a slacker. She wondered how her career would change now that the secret of her pen name had come out. She liked the anonymity of it. She was well aware she wrote weird stuff and didn't want the content to cloud people's judgment of her. Especially producers.

None of her speculation would do her any good if she couldn't come up with a single idea for her next script that was worth the postage.

She pushed out of the chair and went into the bathroom, taking a long, hot shower, pampering herself with a facial and painting her toenails, then slipping into a short chemise, robe and her fluffy slippers with bunny ears on them. The slippers always made her smile, feel silly, and she scuffed along to the French doors, pulling them open. The breeze off the river was warm and balmy, ruffling her hair, her robe.

She sat on the cushioned wicker settee on the balcony, liking that the rail was low enough to offer a view all the way to town. Lights twinkled in the distance, the moonlight glittering like fallen stars on the water. Car headlights riding over the old bridge flashed like tiny beacons. The scene reminded her that life and excitement weren't far away.

Though she'd had enough of them for a decade.

Phoebe let her mind wander, her imagination coming up with scenarios for the people she couldn't see. She was deep in a scene that was going nowhere when she heard a scuffling sound. Leaving the chair, she leaned out over the rail. The landscape was lit with floodlights in the distance, the large trunks and branches of live oaks looking like gnarled old men ready to capture wayward guests. But she didn't see anyone.

A trickle of fear crept up her spine.

Memories she'd buried surfaced. Kreeg. The strange noises she'd hear around her place and left the comfort of her little house to investigate. Only to find a trail. A rose, a note telling her he was close, but that she was his and would never see him coming.

Instantly she shut off the memories, yet a shiver prickling her skin made her reach for a potted plant, ready to drop it on whomever was lurking below. She heard the sound again, then realized where she was.

Nine Oaks. A near prison, it was so secure.

The dogs were out, she thought, releasing a long breath. They'd bark if there was anyone down there. And Kreeg was behind bars. She was almost tempted to call the police to make certain he hadn't escaped. She set the pot back down, mad at herself for being paranoid. She'd come here to get away from that, dammit. She went inside, closing the doors and climbed into bed.

She would have been surprised that within minutes, she was asleep.

Within ten, she was dreaming.

It was past midnight when Cain headed to bed, and at the top of the staircase, he paused, hearing rapid footsteps and turned. Benson rushed up the stairs behind him, looking pale.

"What's the matter, Benson?"

"It's Miss Phoebe, sir. I heard her. Through the air vents."

"Heard what?"

Then Cain knew. A scream, stifled and long, echoed through the halls.

He waved Benson back and the butler hesitated, then returned to his rooms. Cain hurried into the east wing, knowing exactly where she was, and pushed at the old-fashioned door latch. It was locked. He could hear her whimpering, begging, and threw his shoulder into the door. The latch gave and he rushed inside.

She was on the bed, curled into a tight little ball, hanging onto the bedpost as if it were the mast of a sinking ship. He hurried to the side of the bed, bending over her. Her eyes were tightly shut, her fingers white-knuckled on the post. He called her name, over and over, yet when he touched her, she clawed out at him, catching his cheek and batting at him.

"Phoebe, wake up! It's a dream. Wake up!"

Cain gripped her shoulders, pulling her from the post, and propelled her back on the bed. "Wake up." She fought him. He pressed his weight onto her, stilling her kicking legs and wild punches, then cupped her face. "It's only a dream, honey," he said softly, close to her ear. "Wake up now."

A little sound escaped her, weak and whimpering. Then suddenly, she blinked, staring at him as if he were a stranger, inhaling sharply. Cain felt his insides shift at the confusion in her eyes.

"It's me, Cain. You were dreaming."

Her lip quivered, her chest heaving to bring in needed air, and he eased off her, his hand sliding to her bare shoulder. "It's all right. It was just a dream. No one will hurt you again."

She just stared at him, tears filling her eyes, then she buried her face in his shoulder.

And she cried.

His battle with touching her was outweighed when her fingertips dug into him, and Cain wrapped his arms around her, pulling her into the curve of his body, rubbing her spine. She struggled against her tears, and Cain tightened his arms. He gazed down at her body nestled against his, the supple curves of her leg hitched over his thigh. He wanted to push her onto her back, press himself against her, yet instead, he stroked her spine and bare shoulders, hoping his own body didn't betray him. Her skin was flawless beneath his palm, and she felt so delicate against his roughness. In the silence, he sensed the tension leaving her body, in the way she softened, her curves meshing with his harder planes. Cain could spend a lifetime just like this.

After a moment, she sagged almost bonelessly.

"Sorry," she said sheepishly, and the sound was muffled against his chest.

"How long has this been going on?"

"Weeks."

"What did he do to you?"

"I'd rather not relive it again. I just had the Technicolor version."

He understood and didn't press her, watching her toy with his shirt buttons, wishing she'd yank them open and let him feel her skin against his. "Phoebe?"

"Yeah."

"You okay now?"

She looked up, searching his face. "Yeah. Just peachy." She reached out, sliding her fingers over his jaw, his lips. Cain closed his eyes briefly, smothering a moan as the walls he'd erected started to crumble. He struggled, his mind shouting reasons, flashing pictures that spilled guilt and remorse through him as he caught her hand, stopped her.

He eased back, needing to leave, wanting to stay—and each feeling clawed at him.

Her gaze locked with his. All she did was whisper his name.

Then he was sinking into her mouth.

Nine years of capped electricity connected again.

And exploded.

Four

One touch of her lips and he knew it was madness.

One taste and he was sinking into the abyss of desire.

Cain groaned darkly and gathered her closer.

And the worst happened.

She welcomed him.

Openly, devouring him, letting him taste the sweet energy that was Phoebe. He could easily become an addict. This woman had more power over him than he had over himself. Yet he thirsted for her, sliding his tongue between her lips and indulging in a long-awaited feast.

She arched her body, letting him feel all that she was under the thin cotton, ripe and curved, the plumpness of her breasts burning an imprint into his chest, through layers of cloth. He gripped her slim hips, pulling her to his groin, half crushing her into the downy mattress and still she gave back, bending her knees, wedging him between her thighs.

The heat of her center seared him.

They pawed and stroked, each touch growing more intimate, more desperate for the feel of flesh to flesh. He throbbed for completion, to slide into her body and let the sensations explode between them.

"Cain, oh my," she said against his mouth and opened like a flower again for him. "Nothing's changed, nothing."

Suddenly he jerked back, staring down at her, at the confused frown knitting her smooth forehead.

Everything *had* changed.

He wasn't worthy of this woman. He could not have her as his body demanded and Cain told himself he was stronger than temptation, than his own lust.

"I'm sorry, forgive me."

"Excuse me?"

Cain should have had a clue from her tone that something was about to explode in her as Cain slid back, sitting on the edge of the bed, his head in his hands. "I shouldn't have done that."

"You weren't alone, in case you didn't notice," she said, and he saw she was a little breathless.

Phoebe was very breathless, her body blazing hot, excitement still pouring and pulsing through her although he wasn't touching her. And she needed to be touched by him, only him as she had wanted nearly a decade ago. Yet he was doing the same thing, backing off, running. Even though he was sitting near her feet, he was already gone.

"Leave, Cain. Get out."

He snapped a look at her. It was a mistake. She looked so damn lovely, nestled in the mounds of pillows and embroidered sheets. Her face was flushed and the strap to her top had slid off her shoulder, showing him the roundness of her breasts, teasing him with her rosy beauty.

"You can't do this to me again," she said. "I won't let you."

"Be assured—" he stood "—neither will I."

Phoebe watched him walk to the door, long legs eating up the distance. He grabbed the knob, flinging it open, then went still. "Forgive me," he said without looking at her.

"Stop apologizing! Thanks for bringing me out of the nightmare. Next time, just leave me alone."

Cain felt the knife of her words and didn't blame her. He'd teased her and himself, dangling passion

between them, knowing full well it would go nowhere the instant his mouth touched hers. He
couldn't allow this to develop. Nor would he let her
suffer through another nightmare if he could help it.
He understood their torment—intimately.

"I'll have the door repaired in the morning." He
gestured to the shattered jamb, then simply stepped
out and closed the door behind himself.

Cain remained outside, stock-still, his body wanting her badly while his mind fought to convince it
otherwise. He had no right to have anything with
Phoebe. Not when the women he *should have* loved
was dead because of him.

He headed to his bedroom on the other side of the
house, resigned to a night of dreaming of what he could
not have and knowing that a dozen rooms separating
him from Phoebe truly wouldn't make a difference.

Phoebe felt her eyes water and she stared at the
closed door for a long moment, half of her wanting
to run and lock it, another part of her wishing he'd
turn around and come back in.

And finish what he started.

Damn him. She curled on her side, punching the
pillows, still smelling his aftershave on her skin. Did
he have to apologize? Twice! *Excuse me, it was
good, I liked it, but now I'm really sorry I went all
Romeo on you?*

She closed her eyes, wanting sleep, wanting him, and she drew her knees up. It did nothing to alleviate the heavy warmth between her thighs. She couldn't do this again. She couldn't fall for him and not have it returned. Though she'd like to tell herself that his ignoring her hadn't mattered, it had. She was pretty honest with herself, she thought, throwing off the covers and leaving the bed. She'd compared every man to Cain and that first kiss. As if searching for someone who'd give her the same untamed feelings, crackling heat and almost desperate hunger.

A man who'd still want her.

But no other man had compared.

She pushed open the balcony doors, stepping out into the night air. Resting her forearms on the railing, she stared out at the river, the moon's glitter on the water. The fragrance of jasmine and wisteria drifted on the breeze, reminding her of home. She'd grown up in a small town south of Nine Oaks, a dewdrop on back roads where everyone knew who she was and what she'd been up to since grade school. She never got away with anything, she thought with a smile. And oddly, that had made her more mischievous as a kid. She drove her parents crazy, always testing her boundaries, pushing to see what was over the next hill. It was half the reason she went to L.A. when she could have done her writing anywhere.

But here at Nine Oaks, the boundaries were tight, clearly marked. Cain had made that clear from the start. Yet in one instance, she thought, glancing back at the bed, he'd ripped those boundaries apart. Shredded them.

The situation made her see that Cain was a trapped man. Phoebe didn't get to where she was as a writer without doing a lot of people watching and dissecting behaviors. Cain was a surly dragon ensnared in a cave. A beast tormented by something. The memory of his late wife? He must have really loved Lily if her death sent him to this seclusion. But Phoebe had a feeling there was more to it than that. Cain never struck her as a man who did anything he didn't want, and pain and darkness were in his eyes now. He practically oozed with it.

Deciding she wouldn't figure out the mystery tonight, Phoebe turned back into the room, then grabbed a book to read. Sleep wouldn't come for her, she knew. And right now, she was glad.

She didn't want Kreeg invading her dreams again.

Cain sat at his desk, his breakfast tray untouched on the corner. He jotted notes and fielded calls all morning and was starving, but his time was in demand. Working was a good thing since if he had a spare moment, Phoebe leaped into his brain and tormented him.

He hadn't managed the latest crisis when someone rapped on the door.

"Not now, Benson."

The door opened anyway.

"Apparently I wasn't clear enough." Not looking
up, Cain scribbled notes.

"Since I'm not Benson that doesn't apply to me,
does it?"

Something inside him went still as glass. "People
do have to work for a living."

"Yeah sure, whatever."

Finally, he lifted his gaze. He saw the hollowness
in her eyes despite how sexy she looked. In curve-hugging cropped jeans and a dainty aqua sleeveless top,
she sent the control he'd fought half the night to regain right out the door. "What are you doing in here?"

"Walking, and now sitting down," she said as she
did, then set a mug of coffee and a toasted bagel on
his desk. She gestured to the breakfast tray. "You
haven't eaten?"

"Obviously not. Phoebe, I'm trying to work."

"Take a break. You've been in here since five-
thirty this morning."

If she knew that, then she'd been up all night, too,
he thought. Had that kiss haunted her as it had him?

"Did you ever get back to sleep?" He sure as hell
didn't.

"No, not really." But thinking about him meant that Phoebe wasn't thinking about her own problems. About how she had to testify; how a man she'd dated three times became so obsessed with her that he broke into her car, her house, her bedroom.

She shook the thought loose, focusing on Cain. "Are you going to spend all day in the office?" She folded her legs into the antique chair, looking right at home.

"I normally do."

"Even in the afternoon, evening? Breakfast?" She pushed the plate toward him, then tore off a piece of her bagel and popped it into her mouth.

"Often." Cain snagged a slice of toast from his own tray, biting into it.

"So, you're a recluse in your own house."

"You're on my side of it." He spread jam on the slice, eating that, then picking up his fork and attacking the still-warm eggs.

"Is there a line?" She looked around at the beautifully carpeted floor. "Be specific, Cain. I thought I had the run of the place."

"You do."

She simply arched a brow, the bagel poised for a bite. "But not here. In this room." She munched.

"I like my privacy to work and you have an entire wing for yourself."

She waved as she chewed and swallowed. "Yeah, but the fun stuff happens on your side."

Cain couldn't help but smile. "I hadn't noticed."

"You don't notice much at all, do you?" She finished off her bagel, then sipped her decaf coffee.

You, he thought, I notice you in every way. Then he said, "Sure I do, I run the place."

She rolled her eyes. "Ha. Benson runs this house, you run your companies, and I'm betting that they won't fall apart with one day's inattention."

"On the contrary, my world will crash." To make his point, the phone rang. He answered it, asking the caller to hold, then looked at her.

Phoebe sensed he was grateful for the call and stood. "Live for the moment, Cain. Hang up."

"I can't."

"Well, I'm going for a ride. Want to come with me?"

"On a horse?"

"Unless you have something else to ride." Instantly Phoebe wished the words back and tried not to blush. "Yes, a horse. Gallop, canter. You know, the four-legged things out there in the stables?"

"No, thank you."

"Fine, be the king reigning over the fiefdom. But you owe me a dinner." She headed to the door.

"I do?"

"Yes, and I'll nag you till you join me like a civilized person."

Cain pushed the hold button on the call and went after her. "Phoebe, I'd rather not—"

"I'm not listening," she said in a singsong voice, walking toward the front door. She passed Benson saying, "Two for dinner, Benson, make sure he shows up," then cast a sexy glance at him that rocked him to his heels before she disappeared out the front door.

Cain stared at the closed door, then looked at Benson standing at the base of the stairs.

"Persistent young lady," was all the butler said and marched up the stairs.

"She's a damn pest."

"Of course, sir."

"Well, she is," he muttered to himself and turned back to the library. He refused to turn on the cameras on his screens and watch her. He'd let security take care of it instead. If he began checking on her, he'd turn into a crazed voyeur and what did that say about him?

He suddenly felt like the Hunchback of Notre Dame, watching the world from afar and wishing for more.

Just as he considered joining her, his gaze landed on the picture of his late wife. Guilt set in instantly, reminding him that he'd ruined her life because he couldn't love her. He lusted after Phoebe and even if that were satisfied, he'd ruin her, too. He smacked the photo facedown on the desk.

Yet an hour later, he was walking through the house toward the rear, stepping out on the veranda in time to see Phoebe gallop across the lawn at full speed on his finest mare. Given her personality, he would have expected her to take the stallion, but Mr. Dobbs had more sense than to let her ride the mean-spirited horse.

She threw her arms out wide, letting go of the reins and riding the chestnut horse with the strength of her knees. He watched her, her laughter pinging through the warm air and sliding over Cain like a cloak. It had been a very long time since a woman had laughed in this house, he thought, then turned away from the sight of her.

For Cain, the temptation of Phoebe DeLongpree was more than he could handle.

Cajun music was rocking the kitchen as Phoebe swept the mop over the kitchen floor. Willis was at the long worktable, polishing silver that didn't need polishing while a male servant ironed napkins and a tablecloth at the other end. She was here because she was already tired of being alone to amuse herself, and Willis was a fun person to be around. He joked easily as he did his work, which in her opinion was busywork. Without guests in the house and few to cook for and look after, the servants were as bored as she was.

Jean Claude was singing along, sounding rather good as he punched dough for bread.

"Willis, lift your feet."

"Oh yeah sure, like there is an inch that you didn't already get, Miss Phoebe?"

"Do a job well and you won't have to do it twice."

"How much caffeine have you had this morning, *bébé*?" Jean Claude said, chuckling as she rinsed the mop and attacked the floor again.

Before she could answer, a deep voice cut through the noise like the crack of lightning. "What the hell are you doing?"

Phoebe whipped around. Cain loomed in the doorway, and the room instantly quieted. Jean Claude shut off the radio.

Oh hell. He looks furious, she thought, not willing to bow to his bluster. "You're smart, figure it out," she said and heard several indrawn breaths.

"You're mopping the floor?" he said, louder than necessary.

"See, I knew you were smart."

"Put that mop down and let the servants do their jobs, Phoebe."

Phoebe glanced around at the stoic faces, then leaned the mop against the counter and marched right up to Cain. "Excuse me?"

"I said—"

"I heard you. Are you giving me orders, Cain Blackmon?"

"I'm warning you not to bother my employees in their jobs."

"Or else? Or you'll what? Toss me out? Be grouchier than you already are?" She poked at his chest as she spoke. "Well, let me tell you, Augustus Cain Blackmon the fourth, I don't take kindly to you growling at me." The more she poked, the farther Cain stepped back out of the kitchen. "You can hand that ogre-in-the-castle stuff to everyone else, but not me. Got that?"

"You're interfering with the workings of this house!"

"Really, show me then?" She gestured around herself. "There is nothing to do. You don't use most of the house. The flowers are in bloom in the solarium, did you know that? The furniture in there still has the packaging from the store on it. Heck, there's enough groceries in that kitchen to feed a battalion of Marines, and enough rooms in here to house them all. But it's just you, Cain, no one else. It's a waste. All these people around for *your* beck and call? Honestly, fend for yourself once and—"

"And you're changing the subject," he butted in.

She looked away, then back and muttered, "Yeah well, it seemed like a good idea at the time."

Cain stared down at her, liking the spark of anger in her eyes. She wasn't the least bit intimidated by him when most people ran for cover. Part of him wondered if he was just looking for an excuse to growl when she was having a good time with the servants because Lily barely spoke to them except to give orders. Comparing the women made him angry again, and as if she could tell, she backed up.

"Regardless of what is used or wasted, it's my decision and I'm asking you to leave them to their jobs."

"No."

His eyes narrowed. "I beg your pardon?"

Hers narrowed right back. "They're my friends and I won't stop speaking to them because you demand it. And because they are all working like nuts for you, the only time I can is while they are at their jobs. So no. I won't leave them be."

Cain gritted his teeth, wanting to shake her. Or kiss her.

And when she spoke, her voice was lower, softer. "Your staff are grateful for the jobs, but I don't think they like you very much. Do you want to live like that? Intimidating everyone?"

No, he didn't. It was five years of loneliness that made him feel so on edge. Or was it just that she was near, tempting him? "Except you?"

"I don't have a stake in ticking you off. They do." She gazed up into his dark eyes. "Life would be more pleasant around here if you didn't snap at everyone. These people practically fear you!"

He arched a brow, a look that said it wasn't a concern.

Her gaze thinned.

Cain felt inspected and found lacking.

"I don't like you right now."

"Really?"

"No, not at all." She marched back into the kitchen, apologizing to the staff for *his* behavior, then walked past him without a glance and down the long hall.

"Phoebe," he called.

She just put her hand up behind her head, waved him off and kept going. When she was out of sight, Cain stared at the floor, his polished shoes, the pristine floor, then lifted his gaze to the immaculate house— not a speck of dust, not a thing out of its precise place.

He almost, in that moment, wished for messy, for lived-in, for the sound of voices and laughter he'd heard just moments ago. She was right, it was as if no one lived here. Like a museum of fine things no one appreciated. Or used.

Cain pushed his fingers through his hair and let out a long-suffering sigh. He stepped into the kitchen, apologized, then went to his office, suddenly hating the four walls and himself.

That evening, Cain sat at the table in the formal dining room, waiting.

She didn't arrive.

But Benson did.

"Well? She demanded this meal with me, where is she?"

Benson cleared his throat uncomfortably. "Miss Phoebe has decided to dine in her room, sir."

Cain hated the pity in Benson's eyes, though he'd never let it show in his face.

"She did have a message for you."

"I'll bet. Well, what is it?"

"She agrees to stay on her side of the house, sir. With pleasure."

Cain's features pulled taut. He stood, leaving the aromatic meal behind and headed back to his office.

He didn't make it, glancing up the staircase and shaking his head. The woman wasn't even around and she was turning him inside out.

"Shall I bring your dinner into the office, sir," Benson said.

"No, thank you."

Cain started to walk away, then said, "Wait, I'll take that." Cain gathered the plate, napkin and utensils from the tray Benson held.

"Sir?"

"Go relax, Benson. Take a break." The butler's brows shot up. "I'm fine," Cain assured him, suddenly realizing that he let Benson cater to him and had gotten too used to the fact. But then, Benson was his only company.

Cain walked to the solarium, stepped inside, then set the plate down before he stripped the plastic off the new furniture.

He sat at the little bistro table in the corner, his feet propped on another chair, eating alone, staring at the abundance of color bursting in the sunny room. The paddle fan overhead moved the sweet fragrances around him.

This was his mother's favorite room. She swore to all, she'd married his father just so she could enjoy it. And halfway through his dinner, Cain faced the fact that Phoebe was right. Damn it. He hadn't enjoyed his own house. Even after he'd spent a fortune restoring it.

Good God. There would be no living with her now.

That was *if* she decided to speak with him again.

Five

Cain pulled at the sash to his robe and paused at the top of the staircase, looking toward the opposite wing, knowing Phoebe was there somewhere down that long hall.

He hadn't seen her in two days. Good to her word, she'd kept to the east wing. Once in awhile he'd hear her voice, drawn by it, but when he looked, she was gone, off doing God knew what, far from him.

She was like a mystical being, darting off into the forest when the evil human came near.

It made his isolation feel more pronounced than it was before she arrived. It shouldn't matter, he told himself, but he didn't like knowing that she was mad at him.

Nor did he like how he'd treated her. He wanted to apologize, but seeking her was out of the question. Alone with Phoebe was not a good thing.

Especially at night.

He descended the stairs, intent on the kitchen and something to quiet the growling in his stomach and perhaps make him sleep. Her insomnia was catching, he thought. He knew of it because Benson reported that she prowled the house at odd hours or that the lights were on in her suite nearly constantly.

Cain wondered if he was here because he hoped to run into her. And what kept her from sleeping? Her attacker was in jail, and the trial was set for a couple of weeks from now. Was she still afraid? She'd nothing to fear here at Nine Oaks, that was for certain.

He stepped into the kitchen, reaching for the switch when he saw a figure sitting on the worktable. The light over the range glowed enough for him to recognize her. She looked over her shoulder toward him, but he couldn't see her face. Then she turned away quickly and Cain could swear she was wiping at her eyes.

"Phoebe, are you okay?"

If okay meant being woken by nightmares,

Phoebe thought. She was actually relieved he'd interrupted her. The pity party was getting really pathetic. "Sure I am. Come in, I won't bite."

"Just as well, I'm in no mood to battle."

"Like that would matter to me?"

Cain smirked to himself and moved into the kitchen, flipping on another light.

She immediately closed her robe a little tighter, suddenly aware they were both in pajamas.

He looked at her snack selection. "Ice cream? At this hour?"

"Anytime is good for Rocky Road." She shoved a scoop into her mouth and smiled hugely.

He sensed it was forced, noticing the redness in her eyes, but he didn't pry. He opened the refrigerator, staring into it, then gathered the makings of a sandwich and set it on the worktable near her. He went for bread and a cutting board and then started slicing.

"Benson said you've been up late a lot. Do you even try to sleep?" he asked.

She dug into the tub of ice cream. "Sure. Count sheep, imagine a white room, clear my thoughts with meditation. Nothing works. Drugs are just too easy to get dependent on."

"You keep thinking of him, don't you?"

Her head snapped up, her expression sharp.

"Yeah, some." She deflated, like a barrier sliding away. "Rational thought tells me he's locked up, but I can't help the feeling that—" her shoulders moved restlessly "—that he's behind me, watching."

"He isn't."

"But he's rich enough to get out on bail, Cain. His lawyers have already smeared my reputation and warned me that I couldn't put him away." She clamped her lips shut, fighting the wave of fear that came.

"He will go to jail." Cain sliced roast beef, waiting till she gathered her composure, though his arms ached to comfort her. "What did he do to you?"

She hopped off the table and put the ice cream back in the freezer. "He taunted me," she said carelessly, but Cain heard the fear still lingering in her tone. "I don't want to talk about it."

"Fine. Sandwich?"

She shook her head, but snatched a slice of meat anyway.

Cain was surprised she didn't rush off, but stayed near, watching him, then lifted her gaze to his face. He didn't have to make eye contact to know it. He could feel it on his skin. It raised the tension in the large room, narrowing the space around them. He felt charged, crackling with her energy. Cain could smell her perfume, sense the cloth lying against her skin, the soundless slide of silk. And the memory of kissing her so wildly poured through his brain and doused his body with desire.

He swallowed hard and lifted his gaze to hers. "I'm sorry, Phoebe."

"Since we exchanged some nasty words, I'll ask for what?"

"For all of it, for the way I spoke to you, treated you the other day."

She met his gaze. "I forgive you."

His brow shot up.

She smiled. "I'm not as hard-nosed as you think, Cain. Don't give me orders again, though."

"I should have remembered that you never did like restrictions."

"That's from a childhood of everyone knowing what I was up to and squealing to my parents. Which got me grounded and watched even harder."

"I know the feeling. I had a houseful of people that knew what I was up to constantly."

"Yeah, but you were the boss."

"Not always."

She rolled her eyes. "Get real. Might as well have been. No one is going to stop the prince of Nine Oaks from doing what he wants."

He spread mayo on the bread and slapped together a sandwich. "Are you saying I'm spoiled?"

Phoebe fetched him a plate. "Yes, of course you are."

He didn't use it, cutting the sandwich and eating it off the table. "Good God, you are blunt. Why do I feel a lecture coming?" he said, then bit into the sandwich.

She nipped a pickle from the pile he'd sliced. "Want one? I hate being lectured. But now that you asked…"

He swallowed fast to defend himself. "I didn't."

"Coward."

That brow shot up, looking more darling to her than menacing. She didn't think he'd want to hear that observation. "You're used to everyone jumping to your tune."

Except her. She danced to her own music. He liked that about her, but felt the need to put in his two cents. "How about you? You want everyone to be on the same tempo—*yours.* Which is high-octane and in fast-forward."

"True," she admitted, shocking him. She started putting away the food. "But life is too short to waste it on anything, except doing what you want."

"But you're not doing what you want. You're here, hiding out."

"From the press and phone calls. And hello? Don't throw stones, Blackmon. Why have you refused to leave this place in five years?"

Instantly his mood changed. Phoebe felt it as if a

door slammed somewhere. His body tensed, eyes shuttered. "Don't dissect me."

Slowly she set down a jar and inched closer, forcing him to look at her. He was so darkly handsome, she thought, dressed in rich satins, looking very powerful and wealthy. And incredibly sad.

"You opened this subject, Cain."

Her voice was so gentle Cain felt an ache burst in his chest. He set the last half of the sandwich down, pushing away the plate. "I'm sorry I did."

"You loved her that much?"

His head snapped up, his gaze sharp and suddenly icy.

"Your wife, Lily. She must have been a wonderful person."

"Is that what you think? That I'm mourning her?" Oh for pity sake, Cain thought. The rest of the world thought that, but he didn't want Phoebe believing the lie. Yet he wouldn't tell her the truth, either.

"Well, yes...no, I mean, my mind doesn't sit still so I can think of all sorts of reasons, but Suzannah believes—"

"Suzannah hasn't a clue."

"Because you won't confide in her."

"She doesn't need to know and neither do you."

She reared back for a second, hurt by the razor bite in his tone. For a moment, he looked so tortured and ashamed that she knew she had to be misreading the look.

"Cain? Look at me."

He didn't, closing jars and wrapping food instead. "Don't think I'm so noble, Phoebe. You'll be sorely disappointed."

He strode out abruptly, leaving her feeling suddenly cold and unprotected. She stared at the empty doorway for a moment, then finished cleaning up the mess. She stopped to eat the untouched half of his sandwich and as she munched, one thing stuck in her thoughts: he wasn't mourning Lily. So why on earth was he torturing himself with hiding away here?

"Don't look at me like that, Benson," Phoebe said. "He'll do it."

Benson's stoic expression spoke his doubt. "I wish only to spare you heartache, Miss Phoebe." The butler handed her the picnic basket and draped the blanket over her arm. "He will not join you."

"Doesn't hurt to try, does it?"

Phoebe understood his concern and she was touched, since a wiser, more sensible part of herself agreed with him, and warned her to leave Cain alone, mind her own business and enjoy the estate.

Yet another part of her ached for the man he'd become. The one she saw last night. Gone were the easy smiles, the charm from years ago. Though his mere presence still set her heart pounding and her body—well…on fire, it was her soul that cried for him.

Like I've known him for centuries, she thought again.

She ignored the fact that by focusing on him she didn't have time to think about Kreeg and his band of lawyers and what else she'd lose. Those problems seemed so trivial right now. The wiser part of her lost. Easily.

It was her nature to interfere.

Especially when Benson told her that although they'd argued, Cain waited for her in the dining room to join her for dinner. As far as she was concerned, she owed him a meal.

She walked briskly out the front door, then around the west wing toward the veranda outside the library. The best way to get him to come with her would be to coax him out on this beautiful day. Which he could see from his cave.

Tempt him with food, she thought, and rapped on the glass door, waiting, her stomach in knots.

Cain left his chair, frowning and wondering who the hell was disturbing him from the patio. When he flung open the door, he was struck first by how beautiful she was in the afternoon light, the sun gleaming off her hair blowing in the breeze, the bright smile she offered despite how he'd snapped at her last night. When he finally dragged his gaze from her compact body in shorts and a simple T-shirt, and those incredible legs, he saw the basket on her arm.

"No."

Her smile melted, and he hated himself for it.

"But you haven't heard my proposition."

"It's rather obvious, Phoebe."

"Aren't you hungry? Wouldn't you like a break from that dark dismal room with all those computers and phone calls and people bugging you?"

"Does that include you?"

"Of course not," she said with an easy smile. If she had to use force, she would, and she grabbed his arm, pulling him toward her and out into the sun. He actually squinted against the brightness, and Phoebe knew she was doing the right thing.

"It's gorgeous, breezy and just look at the million-dollar view." She gestured to the flowers blooming, the live oaks elegantly festooned with Spanish moss. "Come on. Play with me."

The implication shot through him like a crack of lightning, and Cain stiffened. Her look dared him, invited him. Hell. He wanted to do much more than play with her. And he couldn't. Not with Phoebe. He'd be consumed whole if he let himself indulge in her, even if she was only suggesting a picnic. God help him, he didn't want to hurt this woman. And he knew, eventually, he would.

"Phoebe, I know you mean well and you think you're trying to help, but I do not want it."

"Help with what?"

"Me. My life."

She gave him a long look up and down that ignited his blood, then said, "You're a grown man, and don't need my help. Whatever reasons that you've made yourself a recluse, it's your business. I'm bored and while I enjoy my own company, I want to have a picnic and I'd love for you to join me."

"You aren't giving up on this, are you?"

"Nope. Face it. I'll be a nuisance."

She got behind him, giving him a push, and Cain smiled when he didn't move. She kept trying like a kid who wanted someone to ride the roller coaster with her and could find no takers.

"I have work to do."

"You're the boss, take a day off. And if you say your company can't stand the inattention, then you're not that good at running it."

He twisted to look at her. "That's a gauntlet you've thrown down, m'lady."

"Then pick it up, m'lord." She winked. "Take the challenge."

Cain wanted to go, he truly did. Spending a couple of hours with her was like drinking in sunshine. And she was her usual energetic and impatient self. It was addicting.

"All right, but let me change."

"Oh no," she said, pushing him toward the stone path. "It's a 'Come as you are' party. You're not getting a chance to talk yourself out of this."

"God, you're an imp." And a delight, he thought.

"So what else is new?" She flashed him that smile, and Cain felt a renewing feeling race through him when he saw it.

He took the basket from her. "Good grief, what's in here?"

"Jean Claude's Cajun fried chicken…"

"For an army?"

"Oh, there's more, but it's a surprise." They walked toward the shore.

Cain felt apprehension creep up his spine. He hadn't been near the water in a long time.

"Want to take a boat ride?"

"No." And he didn't want her to take one, either.

"Okay, fine. The docks then."

"I'd rather not."

"Be brave, I'll protect you," she said, already walking briskly toward the pier.

Cain watched her go, his hands on his hips. The

woman was rather comfortable with her own stubbornness. She headed toward the open-air gazebo at the end of one dock. It was more of a place to sit and relax while watching the movement on the river than to dock the boats. Cain hadn't been here in five years.

As thoughts of Lily and her death started to crowd his mind, Cain shook them loose and started walking.

When he caught the scent of the bug fogger and noticed the area was swept clean of debris, he realized she had a conspirator. Yet instead of sitting in the loungers, she went right to the edge of the pier, spread out the blanket and relaxed.

Phoebe glanced over her shoulder, wondering why he looked so apprehensive just then. "Come, sit." She patted the space near her, and when he set the basket down, she opened it.

Cain realized this would be an old-fashioned picnic in more ways than just sitting on the docks with a pretty girl when she lifted out bowls and plates wrapped in cloth and tied with ribbon.

He was touched beyond measure. She'd planned this carefully, so determined that he join her. He felt honored. He took off his shoes and socks, and her gaze followed him as he lowered himself to the decking.

"See. That wasn't so hard, was it?"

"Painful. I have ugly feet."

She glanced. "You have big feet," she teased, her eyes twinkling as she dipped her foot in the water, swishing while she unwrapped food and served up two plates.

"There's something about eating outside that makes you take your time, enjoy the view and the tastes."

"Are you making excuses for bullying me?"

"Bullying you? Ha." She poured sweet raspberry iced tea into thick glasses and handed him one. "You needed to get out or you would have barked and growled and crawled back into your cave."

"I think I resent that description."

Her gaze sparked with a challenge. "Deny it, I dare you."

His lips curved as he met her gaze over the rim of the glass. "Never. You'd gloat." He sipped once, then bit into a chicken leg and moaned at the explosion of flavors.

"See, wasn't it worth Jean Claude's talent?"

He merely nodded, hungrier than he'd thought as he finished off the chicken and reached for something else to try. Then suddenly he fingered the edge of the quilt, smiling to himself. "My grandmother's mother made this."

She looked startled at the red, white and blue

quilt. "Oh no. Maybe we shouldn't use it. Benson gave it to me."

He waved that off. "No, no, she always said things were made to be used and not viewed from afar."

"Sounds like my mom. There wasn't much in our house that didn't have a practical use."

He stared out over the water. "I used to love sitting out here when I was a kid, fishing and never catching a thing. Just thinking."

"Alone time. I do that a lot."

"I watched one of your movies."

She looked up, chewing. "Really? I just write the stories. Once I sell them, I don't have any more to say about who plays the roles or what the directors change. I've only been hired to do the on-site writes once."

"Just the same, you have an amazing talent."

She blushed.

"And a twisted mind."

"Rest assured, it's all fictitious."

"Good, you had me worried."

She smiled and nipped a spoonful of shrimp salad. "I would be huge if I ate like this all the time. Jean Claude has my undying love and admiration."

"Can't cook?"

"Sure I can. Open the package, set the timer, nuke it." He chuckled and his smile changed his whole appearance, Phoebe thought. Now that's the man she remembered.

"Even I have more talent than that."

"Some people are good at some things, some at others. I don't cook." She glanced up as she said, "Only because I never really had to do it, but I'm more than willing to pay those with the talent for their wares." She shrugged as if that made perfect sense and dug into the fruit compote and sweet cream.

"I went into the solarium," he said suddenly.

She met his gaze. "Oh yeah?"

She licked cream off her upper lip, and he was enthralled with her tongue passing over that lush mouth. "You were right, there are a lot of rooms no one uses, least of all me."

"It's lovely in there. I think it's my favorite room."

"Have you ever seen the whole house?"

She rolled her eyes, lifting a spoon of shrimp salad for him. "You should taste this."

He caught her hand and brought it to his mouth. He ate off her spoon and something shattered between them, a barrier, a wall, he didn't know what. "So have you seen the whole plantation?"

He was closer now, close enough that she could see the sparkle of gold in his eyes. Sexy, restrained power.

"Yeah, except your bedroom."

"That can be arranged," he said in a heavy voice.

Awareness simmered between them. "Is that an invitation?" She arched a tapered brow.

His body clenched at the thought. "For a tour," he clarified wisely, yet the image of her in his bed sent his mind off to a place he shouldn't go.

"Oh, well. How about showing me all of the secret passages?"

"'Zannah told you," he muttered dryly, then dipped his spoon into her shrimp salad. "When?"

"Years ago," she said with feeling. "How do you think we skipped out of here so often?"

He shrugged. "Conning Benson."

"I adore him, but no. He'd tell if we'd really misbehaved."

He was eating off her plate, she off his, tasting and sharing, so that neither realized the time passing. For long moments, Cain listened to her chat about her family. Phoebe had a sister and brother, both married with children and living on another coast. Cain's parents were off on a summer tour of Europe.

"I'd have thought you'd be married with kids by now, Phoebe."

She groaned. "You sound like my mother."

He made a rolling motion for her to keep going.

"Yes, I want all those girlie dreams, marriage, kids…someday I'll have a house full of children."

She got a faraway look that pricked his heart. "You certainly have the energy to chase after them."

She smiled. "They're such fun. Everything is new to them. Makes you look at the world differently. I think people make the mistake of thinking that once they can talk, they can also understand."

Cain drew up his knee and leaned his back against the post. He wasn't interested in eating or the view, but in listening to her, watching her. She sat with one leg bent, the other swinging slowly in the water as she hovered over the meal. Her appetite was nothing short of startling for one so small. Her petite size made him feel so gargantuan near her. Protective.

Thoughts of Kreeg and what he might have done to her crept into his mind, and he bit back the questions that plagued him. He didn't want to ruin this peaceful moment with her. He was deep in his own thoughts and didn't notice she was standing till she brushed him. He looked up.

"I want to move this back from the sun," she said, and he stood to help her tug the quilt farther under the shade.

She was on the edge, reaching for his tea glass when Cain twisted to take it from her. She turned at the same time, and he bumped her.

He heard her indrawn breath and stared, horrified

as she lost her footing, then dropped backward into the water.

"Phoebe!" He scrambled to the edge, kneeling, impatient for her to surface. "Phoebe!" Oh God. He drove his hand under the water and felt nothing. Memories of Lily crowded rational thought, his heartbeat escalating out of control.

Phoebe popped up, pushing her hair out of her face and laughing hysterically. "Oh, for pity sake."

"Give me your hand!" He reached out.

"It's okay." She treaded water. "I'm fine." She dived under, then came up closer to him. Instantly, he scooped her under the arms and lifted her out of the water and onto the dock. Then she was in his arms, his strength crushing her to his body. He buried his face in the curve of her neck, his breathing fast and harsh.

Something's very wrong, Phoebe thought. "You're getting wet."

"I don't care."

Then she realized he was trembling. She eased back to look at him, and brushed his hair off his face, cupped his lean jaw. Then she remembered his wife had died from drowning.

"Cain, talk to me. I was on a swim team, remember? You don't have to worry."

But he was in another place, in darkness and pain

and guilt. She could see it in his eyes, in the way his gaze scraped over her features.

"Phoebe," he whispered, passing his hand over her wet hair. Then smoothly he lowered his head, his mouth capturing hers, fusing her with the mind-blowing heat that always bubbled between them.

It needed only a spark to make it flame, she thought.

And this was it.

Six

If passion had a sound, it was a deep ripping tear. If it could be seen, it was hissing steam vented between them, sliding and pouring over her.

Her feet left the ground as he stepped back from the edge. But that didn't stop his consuming kiss, the power grinding through her with nearly painful clarity. She could barely draw a breath his embrace was so tight, his hands fisting in her wet clothes as if to drive her into him.

She felt gloriously smothered and devoured and wanted.

And she let go. Of her emotions, her desire. His

body hardened against her, thrilling her, and her hands climbed up his chest, wrapping his neck.

Cain groaned and kept kissing, unwilling to break it off, unwilling to give in to the denial in his mind. His hands charged a wild ride over her body, and as if he couldn't stand on his own power, he fell back against the support post.

Phoebe went with him, wedged to him and when he cupped her breast, she thought she'd disintegrate. When he thumbed her nipple, she knew she would.

She pushed into his touch, letting him know it was okay, that she wanted him, too. Yet she could feel something inside him battling with his need. She hoped he fought it. He broke the kiss only to draw in more air, then devoured her mouth again, moaning deeply when her hands shaped the contours of his chest, and lower.

She was bold and provocative, and Cain hungered for it, for the womanly sounds, for the feel of her flesh melting with his. He wanted her now, right now, and he tore his mouth from hers, but couldn't stop as he nibbled her jaw, her throat.

"Phoebe, you make me crazy."

"Oh yeah, same here," she whispered, sliding her hand down and letting her fingers slip over his erection.

The sound he made was part pain and part pleasure and she wanted to be naked and warm with him, wanted the freedom to experience, and explore what had haunted her for years.

He leaned his head back, his lungs laboring. "I'm a basket case around you," he said, and the hint of regret made her touch his jaw and force him to meet her gaze.

"Don't you dare apologize." She nipped at his mouth.

"I wasn't planning on it."

She searched his handsome face for a moment. "You were scared."

His features tightened. "Out of my mind."

"I can swim, Cain, rather well. I'll show you the awards for it, if you want?"

His lips quirked. "Not necessary."

"I like that you were, though."

"Say again?"

"Not because of Lily, but that you cared enough."

"Oh man, Phoebe. Don't you get it? I want you like breathing."

"And then what?"

"Huh?"

"After having me, then what?"

He said nothing, and she could see the openness she'd just shared with him dissolve a little.

She stepped back out of his arms, her body still tingling, still hungering. "I see."

"Phoebe." He tried to grab her back.

"I'm a fantasy, I get it. That's okay. I've never been the fantasy of a recluse before."

He didn't think she was okay with it at all, or she wouldn't be miffed, and part of him was screaming for joy over it. Yet reality had a way of crashing in and he said, "Yes, I am a recluse, but now, so are you." He caught her by the arms, turning so her back was to the gazebo railing.

She frowned up at him. "What are you doing?"

"Look beyond me, near the fence line."

She peered around him, to the woods separating the land from the road and saw a white news van.

"We both have good reasons."

There were photographers in there, she knew. And he was shielding her.

"Oh no." Her gaze snapped to his. "Do you think they photographed us?"

"If they have a long-range lens, yes. Probably."

"Great." Her shoulders drooped.

"Ashamed?"

"No. You?" He shook his head, his gaze intense and scrutinizing. "I'm thinking of what the press will do with more pictures. It could hurt you."

Though he didn't care what happened to him, he was moved by the thought. "They've been using me for fodder for years, Phoebe, I don't care."

"But you knew they were there?"

"They've pretty much camped out there since you drove through the gates."

"I'll have to remember that." She glanced at him under a lock of deep red hair, smiling devilishly. If those idiots weren't in the van, she'd have stripped for Cain and played with him right here, right now.

As if he could understand her thoughts, his expression grew darker, his eyes smoky-brown and sultry. She glanced to the left toward the van they could barely see. Then she ducked low. When he stared down at her frowning, she pulled him to the deck.

"I say we hide from them." She started stuffing the picnic lunch back in the basket.

"I beg your pardon?"

"Let's run. We'll see if they are really watching."

"Phoebe, we don't have to. Who cares what they want?"

"I know." She looked up and the delightful gleam in her eyes caught him in the heart. "It's the principle of it."

She was daring him and Cain felt as if he hovered on the edge of fun. He wanted badly to jump in. "Leave that," he said suddenly, taking her hand and pulling her from the dock. "We can get it later." He looked toward the property line and could see figures moving toward a break in the trees. "Run."

Phoebe didn't have to be told twice and barefoot and wet they took off down the dock. Cain's legs were twice as long, and Phoebe tried to keep up as they raced across the lawn toward the east of the house. The mansion was on a small jut in the land, and they hurried across the curve toward the rear where the pool and stables were located.

She couldn't keep up. "Cain," she said and he paused, glanced, then scooped her up, darting around the edge of the house, then flattening against the wall. She laughed as he lowered her feet to the ground. He kept her close as he peered around the edge.

"The little fools are moving. I'm betting they'll try to get near the east orchard." He shifted back and grinned down at her.

Her breath caught hard.

Everything around her faded at the sight of his handsome face lit up with delight. Her throat tightened and she smiled back, absorbing it. What woman could resist this man when he smiled like that?

A few yards from them, a groundskeeper paused in pruning bushes, and started moving toward them. "Mr. Blackmon, you all right, sir?"

"Fine ah…"

"Mark," Phoebe supplied softly.

"We're fine, Mark. Thanks."

The man nodded, not convinced, yet went back to work.

Cain looked down at her, surprised. "You knew his name?"

"Yeah, *I* pay attention." She nudged him.

Overhead the sky darkened, rain threatening and she looked up. "Oh no, the quilt!"

"It's been left in the rain before and it's under the gazebo." He looked around the edge of the wall again.

"Think we lost them?"

"Don't count on it. I suspect the instant they knew I had a houseguest, they beefed up their spying techniques." He gestured toward the house and they started walking.

"Sorry about that."

"I'm used to it."

"I'm not."

"From what I've read, they haven't been kind to you."

Her expression saddened. "They've single-handedly destroyed my reputation, too."

"I think you'll be more in demand, especially when Kreeg is behind bars for good."

"I doubt it. He's got money and power and that makes people do what the rest of us can't."

He heard a bit of chastising in her tone but let it go. "Such as?"

"Making certain their side of the story is told and not the real one."

"I know he's lying, Phoebe."

"So do I, but the jurors might not, and might think I'm nothing but a gold digger or something."

"What does your lawyer think?"

"That he might get off with a slap on the wrist and a restraining order."

No wonder she was scared he'd come after her. "Then you need a new lawyer."

"I can barely afford the one I have."

"We'll see about that."

She stopped walking, and droplets of rain pelted her upturned face. "What do you mean?"

"I'll make certain you have the best."

"No."

He scowled. "Why not?"

"I don't want charity and I don't want you dragged into this. It's bad enough that I have to hide in the first place, but I won't have your name dragged in the mud with mine."

Cain's gaze sketched her features, his expression hardening. "Do you want him to pay for his crime?"

"Of course."

"Then you have to fight fire with fire. Not with a match."

She opened her mouth to object and Cain gathered

her in his arms, the rain coming harder now. "Let me do this. I can and I want to." He needed to protect her from Kreeg. Or maybe from himself. She was alone in her battle and she didn't need to be.

"Please, Phoebe, I have the resources."

Phoebe nodded finally and Cain pressed his lips to her forehead. The clouds unleashed and they stood there in each other's arms, feeling something weave around them and bind them. Fear eased, loneliness receded.

Cain wondered how he'd handle those feelings when they came back. When she was gone.

Yet all Phoebe knew was, for now, she had a true champion.

Several moments later, Benson appeared at their side, holding an umbrella. "I beg your pardon, sir, but did you by chance notice it was raining?"

They looked at him, then at each other and laughed.

"Really?" Cain said and, dismissing the offer of the umbrella, they headed toward the house. The rain fell suddenly harder, lightning cracking overhead, and they ran, ducking inside.

Cain shook his head like a dog, then looked at her. She was plucking at her shirt molded to her body and showing him the shape and curves beneath. In a flour sack, she'd still be sexy as hell, he thought. A servant showed up with towels, and handed them each one.

Cain toweled her hair, then wrapped her in the terry cloth blanket.

"You'll catch a cold."

"I have a great immune system."

"Go change before Benson goes all nursemaid on you."

Benson made a face as if that behavior was beyond him.

She nodded and started to walk away, then turned, walking backward. "Cain."

He glanced up from rubbing the towel over his hair. "Yes?"

"Sometimes you surprise me."

He smiled gently. "You always surprise me, Phoebe."

She turned away, heading to her room, leaving wet footprints on the wood floor.

Cain looked at Benson, smiling sheepishly, then told him they left the picnic at the gazebo. But Benson simply stared, looking a little stunned.

"What's the matter?" Cain asked.

"It's been years since I've seen you smile, sir."

His expression fell a little and Cain glanced to where Phoebe had disappeared. "Yes, I know. Get it while it lasts." Because when she learns the truth, she'll be gone.

Cain had a taste of what life would be like with her and the bittersweet knowledge that he'd never have more was slowly killing him inside.

An hour later, Cain was in the library, shaking things up. First, he'd called Phoebe's lawyer and wasn't impressed. The man was either not good enough to represent her side or was simply too inexperienced to handle Kreeg's fleet of attorneys.

So Cain called his own, who enlisted the best criminal lawyer in the state. After half an hour on the phone, he was satisfied that Phoebe was represented fairly. He called his broker next.

"Sell all of my Kreeg CGI stock."

"I wouldn't advise that, Mr. Blackmon. It's making you a fortune."

"I already have a fortune. Sell it and then buy up the competitor." He glanced at his notes. "Dream Images."

The broker grumbled, but Cain wasn't budging. He wasn't intent on ruining Kreeg, but he wasn't going to back a company whose CEO stalked and attacked women.

He cut the call and dialed a private investigator. Now that he had Phoebe's consent, he took control.

* * *

Phoebe knocked on the door, then peered around the edge. Cain was on the phone and looked more than a little irritated with the caller.

"If he's done this once, there is reason to believe he's done it before." He listened to the caller for a moment. "I'm betting there are more women out there, so find them. Fine, good." He hung up and looked at her. His expression softened.

"Thank you," she said.

"I haven't done anything yet."

"Yes, you have. You've given Kreeg a reason to be nervous. I take it this is all anonymous?"

"For anyone but my attorneys, yes. It has to be, for your sake. My name has mud on it, too."

Phoebe disagreed, but she wasn't going to try to persuade him otherwise. His name had fear on it. She wasn't surprised; he could be rather intimidating when he wanted to and on the phone with whoever that was, she could see he wasn't taking "I'll try my best," for an answer.

Phoebe admired someone so determined. But it made her wonder again, why, with all he had, he wouldn't face the world beyond Nine Oaks' walls. She was confident he'd trust her enough to tell her someday and she didn't want to press it. She'd seen the side of Cain she remembered and wanted to keep that close for as long as she could.

The thought made her realize that despite his life-style and that annoying way he could shut off his emotions, she was starting to fall for him again.

"So what are you up to now that it's raining?" he said.

A summer storm raged outside but they could barely hear it.

She shrugged, adjusting her V-neck top. She felt sluggish since she'd showered and slipped into soft jersey slacks and a top. "A feeble attempt at reading." She moved to leave. "I'll let you get back to work."

"Wait." Cain went to the antique sideboard and poured brandy into a snifter, then set it on the warmer.

Her brows knit as he waited for it to reach the per-fect temperature. "Don't leave."

Phoebe's heart leaped. He was usually telling her to get lost. "If that's for me, Cain, I don't need it."

"It's just a little brandy." He came to her. "Have a seat."

She dropped to the cushy sofa and he handed it to her. Then he knelt, his hands on either side of her hips on the cushion. "Your fear makes you so rest-less. Try sleeping. You look exhausted."

Three days here and she still hadn't slept, he

thought. What good was this fortress if she still didn't feel protected?

"I know," she said, "but I can't seem to rest for long."

"Try." He tipped the snifter to her lips and she sipped. "You're safe here. I won't let him touch you again. And in your dreams, he can't hurt you."

"But he does," she said weakly, her eyes tearing, her wounds showing so clearly, Cain's heart fractured a little.

"You give him power when you let him torment you," he said, brushing layers of hair off her forehead.

Phoebe fought the urge to turn her face into his palm. "I know." She sipped again, feeling the warm liquor soften her limbs. "I'd better leave you alone to work."

Her lids felt heavy.

She started to get up, but he kept her there, adjusting the pillows, then taking the finished brandy and easing her to lie down. "You'll wake up too much if you have to walk upstairs, so sleep right here."

"But you're working."

He pulled off her sandals, then grabbed an afghan from an old trunk to cover her. "It's all right," he said gently. "Close your eyes."

"Yes, m'lord." She obeyed.

He smiled with tender humor. "Imp."

"Ogre," she muttered, then sighed into the cushions.

Cain ached to touch her, to kiss her, but instead he stood, moving to sit behind his desk. He didn't make a sound, watching her. She looked so tiny on the long sofa. Despite her zest and energy, she was still hurting inside, still tormented. He could learn what Kreeg had done to her from the detectives and lawyers, but it was her private business. He'd wait in the hopes that she'd trust him and tell him herself.

He didn't even consider telling her about Lily. It was not the same. Phoebe was innocent. Cain was not.

He focused on work, routing all his calls to a machine. Occasionally he looked up, and was relieved that she was in a deep sleep.

After a while, he left her alone to rest. He met Benson in the hall, looking panicked.

"Sir, I can't find Miss Phoebe."

"She's sleeping." He inclined his head to the library.

Benson's brows shot up.

Cain ignored his shock. He was well aware that it was not his normal behavior to have anyone that close. "See that no one disturbs her till she wants to be."

Benson nodded, his stoic expression melting into a smile as he walked off.

* * *

It was near midnight when Cain scooped Phoebe up off the sofa and carried her upstairs. Her compact body felt fragile in his arms and the fact that she didn't stir much told him she was finally sleeping peacefully. He entered her suite where the bed was already turned down and laid her in the center, then drew the coverlet over her.

For her peace of mind, he locked the balcony doors, and windows, and he was tempted to post one of dogs at the foot of the bed, but didn't. He started to leave, then turned back, suddenly beside the bed, gazing down at her.

She stirs up a lot of trouble for someone so small, he thought. Then admitted he liked it. A lot more than he should. She brought life to this old house, and he'd missed that.

Without will he bent, and kissed her soft mouth. That she responded in her sleep stirred something deep in his heart.

That she whispered his name—touched his soul.

Seven

Cain asked himself what he was doing when he left the library for the third time in a day.

But he knew.

A dozen reasons to stay locked in his cave, as Phoebe called it, trotted through his mind. He'd tried to ignore the noise that broke his concentration, yet knowing she was near, bringing laughter to the dark lonely house, pushed him beyond the warnings.

A part of him hoped he didn't find her.

But he did, chatting in the solarium with Willis. The young man was laying out a lunch for her as

Phoebe sat on the garden sofa, her feet propped on the coffee table, a book on her lap. Her voice was animated as she talked to the young man, but Cain couldn't hear her clearly. Leaning his shoulder against the wide French doors, he simply watched her interact. It was truly pitiful that he was so fascinated by her expressive face.

Willis stepped back, talking softly as she teased him that Jean Claude obviously thought she was too thin if he expected her to eat all that food. Willis laughed, she smiled, and the entire room lit a little brighter.

Willis was enamored with her, and while jealousy pricked Cain, he also admired how Phoebe could put anyone at ease.

Then her gaze strayed past the young man and her smile widened. "I know your mama taught you that eavesdropping was impolite."

"Yes ma'am, she did."

Willis turned sharply, his posture stiffening, his gaze nervously shooting between Phoebe and his employer. Cain frowned, realizing again that the people who worked for him feared him. It made him more aware that, in the last years, he'd become a demanding taskmaster with little patience for anyone. These people didn't deserve it. Especially when his wrath was directed at himself.

He looked at the servant. "Relax, Willis," Cain said softly. "Why don't you take a break for a while." He stepped into the large room.

Willis's eyes rounded. "Sir?"

"Take off for the day. I'm sure we can fend for ourselves." He glanced at Phoebe and her smile was so dazzling, Cain swore nothing else was more beautiful.

"I beg your pardon, sir, and I don't mean to sound ungrateful, but Benson sets my duties and he might not like that."

Cain walked to the intercom and depressed the button, calling for Benson.

"Yes, sir."

"Give Willis the day off." The lad smiled. "In fact, give the entire staff the day off. With pay."

"I beg your pardon, sir?"

"Is there anything that can't be taken care of tomorrow?"

"Dinner, sir."

He glanced at Phoebe and winked. "We can manage. Anything else?"

"No sir, but…"

"Good lord, do I have to shove you people out the door?"

Willis snickered under his breath.

"Apparently, sir." Benson's voice came through

the speaker, clear with a touch of humor. "Very well, sir. Have a pleasant afternoon."

Cain bid him the same and clicked off the intercom. Willis nodded and left in a hurry, already pulling at his tie. Cain turned his gaze on Phoebe. She swung her legs off the coffee table and just stared at him.

"Bravo," she said softly. "I'm impressed."

That he hadn't paid attention to his staff's fear, or the busywork they did to keep themselves occupied, embarrassed Cain. "They hover," he said, as if that was the reason he wanted them gone.

"Come sit." She patted the space beside her. "Share this with me." She pointed to the tray of food. He moved toward her almost gracefully and settled beside her.

"No pressing work?"

"No, it's all done." It was a white lie, he always had work to do, but nothing that couldn't wait. "I'm a genius, didn't you know that?" he teased.

His playfulness wasn't as much of a shock as it was a few days ago. But Phoebe loved seeing it just the same. "I knew that years ago."

She split her sandwich and handed him half, then curled her legs on the sofa and took a bite. Cain set the plate between them, snatching at her chips, tasting the crab salad.

"So why'd you leave the cave?"

Only his eyes shifted to lock with hers. "I think you know why."

"Nope, I don't. If you mean to say you did it for me, I don't believe you."

"Why?"

"Because it was like pulling teeth to get you on the picnic."

Cain shrugged, unable to answer with anything that wouldn't open a door too wide. He thought about what he wanted, what he was keeping at bay. He wanted Phoebe and he needed his past to stay out of it.

If she knew, she'd leave instantly and he couldn't bear that.

"You're in here a lot."

She looked toward the ceiling, the tempered glass showing the afternoon sky. A paddle fan pushed the cooled air around the large room, swaying the flowers, surrounding them with fragrance. Beyond the glass, rain fell.

"It's like being outside without all the ick."

He arched a brow. "Gnats, the oppressive heat?"

"Nosy reporters sitting at the fence with long-range cameras."

Cain scowled and started to get up to see to the matter when she grabbed his hand.

"Let it go. It won't do any good. They'll just find another way."

Cain begged to differ, yet he eased back into the seat, finishing off the sandwich and looking for more.

She offered him hers. He shook his head.

"You want it," she teased, "you know you do." She held it closer.

"There are other things I want more."

"Oh?" she said, suddenly breathless and reading the velvety look in his eyes.

"Yeah, your chips." As he said that, he munched into one.

She grinned, then ate the sandwich in record time.

He blinked. "Glad I didn't really want more."

"Hey, you had your chance."

"You have mayonnaise on your mouth."

She licked her lip and the slow slide of her tongue over her lips felt like a charge to Cain. The woman was too deliciously sexy and when she reached for a napkin, Cain leaned forward, swift and stark like a hunter seeking its prey.

"I'll take care of that," he murmured, then kissed her.

Phoebe melted, instantly, completely. His tongue snaked over her lips, outlining them so provocatively she felt at once unhinged and desperate for more. He tasted her, and she savored each nuance of the kiss—the way his lips worked over her, his rushed breathing—and when he applied pressure she leaned back, pulling him on the sofa with her.

He deepened his kiss, taking it from the soft, erotic exploration to total possession. His mouth moved heavily, passion rising swiftly through her until she couldn't contain it.

His hand slid under her, lifting her hips to his, his erection pressing deeply and eliciting a moan for more. Yes, she thought, more. She wanted him, and her response left no question between them. She'd wanted this for years, aching in her soul to know if passion was all they had, and Phoebe knew, even as her heart tumbled, even as his hands swept her body to cup her breast, this was the passion of a lifetime.

She clawed at his shoulders, urging him yet feeling his resistance, and when he broke the kiss, staring down at her, Phoebe wondered what was going on in his mind.

Then she knew.

"I want to touch you. No, I need to," he said, nipping at her mouth, her throat and lower. "You excite me more than anything."

"That's a good thing then," she said, smiling and tipping her head back as he nibbled his way lower.

"I didn't think anything would stir you from that place you keep yourself in."

Instantly she regretted the comment when his gaze flashed up and she saw it again, that self-recrimination. A dark burden, like a demon looming ready to pounce, and she leaned up and kissed him, forcing it from his mind, drawing him back to the moment, the passion bubbling between them.

Cain went willingly, eager for anything to keep guilt at bay and indulge in her. He never broke the kiss, making her breathless, stealing her will as she stole his.

His hand crept under her shirt, a finger hooking the edge of her bra and pulling.

Phoebe was more than eager, and pulled her shirt up, letting him unhook her. His hand played over her breast, pushing the bra aside and he savored the feel of her smooth skin beneath his palms.

When his lips closed over her nipple, she made a little sound and arched into him. He shifted, pulling her onto his lap, then spreading her thighs so she straddled him. She smiled at him and he stripped off her shirt, the bra. His mouth was on her, laving her flesh. He suckled and massaged and she arched back, gripping his shoulder and Cain watched her passion rise, stroked her smooth skin, feeling the weight of her breast so warm in his hands. His fingers trailed lower and he dipped below the waistband of her thin jersey slacks. Her muscles contracted and she straightened, meeting his gaze.

"Can I touch you?"

Phoebe was incredibly moved by that, the trickle of fear in his voice, that she might turn him away. "I wish you would."

His lips quirked, half arrogant half delighted and he shifted his hand, his fingertip stroking her soft center through her panties. Her breath rushed in sharply and she whispered, "More," then kissed him.

Cain devoured her sweet mouth as he dipped his hand under the band of her panties and touched her heat. His fingertips slid wetly over her delicate flesh and she shivered in his arms, made a tight little sound and flexed her hips.

Then he plunged a finger inside her. She inhaled and cupped his face, staring into his eyes as he explored and teased. "Cain, oh Cain."

"You have to let me see it. It's been haunting me for years, Phoebe." He didn't give her a choice and withdrew and plunged, feeling vulnerable himself as he touched her, scented her like a stag on the prowl. Her passion was overpowering, her slick body throbbing against his touch and when he circled the delicate pearl of her sex, she thrust hard against him.

He gave her what she wanted, what he needed to

see, to experience. It was as if this were a little flash
of light in a dark tunnel. His own body was hard and
ready; it would be so easy to open his trousers and
drive into her. He throbbed to do it. To be primal and
raw with her. To feel her lush body grasp him, take
him. He wanted her so much that when he felt her
tensing, he nearly climaxed.

He plunged and flicked, and stroked, aware of her
every quiver, her staggered breath. Wet heat coated
him. It was as if he'd known the workings of her body
for years and how to pull the sensations from her. She
was wild in his arms, flexing in erotic rhythm to his
touch.

And then she found it, capturing his soul as she
contracted and shivered in his arms. Her scattered
breaths sounded in his ear, and he knew he'd never
forget it, never banish this from his mind for it felt
as if he were holding daylight. She tensed hard, then
collapsed against him, and Cain could only gather
her tightly and feel the shudders of her desire fold
around his heart and take him prisoner.

Phoebe tried to catch her breath, tried to find logic
and reason why he wanted to do that to her so badly,
then just gave up and accepted it.

After a long moment, she lifted her head and met
his gaze.

He arched a brow, a bit of arrogant pleasure in his soft smile.

"Is that why you sent everyone away?"

His smile dropped a little. "No." He removed his hand, smoothing her spine. "Though the thought had crossed my mind."

She smiled widely and bent to kiss him. As if they'd never touched, the fire sparked. Like wind on flames, it grew and Phoebe slipped her hand between them molding his erection pushing against his tailored slacks.

Cain groaned and held her back. "Phoebe, don't."

"Why?"

"I'm about to explode and as much as I want to have you, we cannot go further."

She blinked. "Excuse me?"

He didn't like the anger in her eyes, didn't want to be the cause of it.

"Was that just satisfying your curiosity? Don't answer, forget I said that." She shifted off his lap, snatched up her clothes and dressed.

"You're angry with me."

"No, I'm hurt."

"Didn't you like it? I did."

She cast a glance over her shoulder. "Didn't I look like I enjoyed that? I am, however, feeling like a plaything right now."

She stood and started to leave. Cain shot off the sofa and grabbed her hand, ignoring the intense pain and hardness in his body and turning her toward him.

"You would never be a plaything to me, Phoebe. You have to know that. Tell me you know."

Phoebe sighed, not wanting to end this with a fight, not wanting to really dig deep into his mind when she didn't want anyone digging into hers. Then she noticed the torn look in his dark eyes, in his expression. Something was eating him. It made him look raw and desolate as he waited for her answer.

"Maybe without meaning to."

"There are no maybes about it."

"But then where will this go? Moments for a couple of weeks? Is that it?"

His gaze thinned and she knew she'd just touched a nerve.

"I understand now. You won't *allow* yourself to have more, with me, or anyone and I'm not just talking sex."

His expression went shuttered.

That he did it so often she could recognize it angered her. "Don't do that! Don't leave me out in the cold. Can't we just take this new stage one day at a time?"

Cain went still, a battle waging inside him—push the door a little wider open or pull it closed. Yet he knew one thing—with Phoebe, he had little choice. She was an energy he couldn't ignore.

He forced a smile, pulling her close, and smoothing her wild hair out of her eyes.

"One day at a time then." He didn't say it would go no further than her stay here at Nine Oaks until the trial. That, he knew, was enough heartache for the both of them.

Oblivious to his thoughts, Phoebe smiled widely and pecked a kiss to his mouth. "I won't even expect a miracle, I swear."

That, Cain thought, was what he needed—and did not deserve.

Something had changed between them. Neither one spoke of it, but Phoebe could feel it. His guard was down a little further. A line blurred when he cooked for her. It faded when he smiled and laughed and teased like the man she remembered.

"You didn't want to take over for your father?"

"Not really. It was always expected of me, but I would've liked to have made another choice."

"Such as?

He shrugged, sitting in the lounge chair on the balcony, watching the mist of the evening roll over the river. Cain turned his gaze from it, the scenery too much like the night Lily died.

"I'm not sure."

"Well, if you don't have a choice waiting, and I'm not saying you have to, then keep running the family companies. You're great at what you do, Cain."

"And you know this how?"

"I bought stock in your company."

He frowned. "I'll have to check the stockholders' list."

"I'm small potatoes." She sipped a mimosa and stretched on the lounge. The sounds of the night approached—music for them—and Phoebe looked over at him and found him staring.

He was trying not to be obvious but she could tell. He seemed to be comparing her to something when he looked at her. Then she remembered what he'd said that night in the kitchen. Not to think he was so noble that he was mourning his dead wife, that she'd be disappointed.

"Did you love Lily?"

His gaze snapped to hers. He hesitated before answering. "No. Barely."

She sat up a little straighter. "Then why did you marry her?"

"She was pregnant with my child."

"Oh."

"She miscarried a couple of weeks after we married."

"I'm so sorry. Did that happen when she died?"

"No. Do we have to discuss her?" He said *her* as if it tasted foul.

"I'm trying to understand you better. You're not making it easy, you know." He scowled and she took another avenue. "I, on the other hand, am an open book."

He chuckled, but it held little humor. "You have your secrets, too, pixie."

She flashed him a smile and lay back, drawing her leg up and resting her glass there. "What do you want to know?"

"What gives you nightmares?"

He saw her fingers grip the glass a little tighter and she took a huge sip. "I've been loud again?"

"I'm afraid so." He'd come into her room the night before when he'd heard her cry out with such fear it left a mark in his heart. Despite her brave front, the dreams tormented her nearly every night.

She groaned, and put the glass down, then rubbed her face. Cain left his chair and went to her, nudging her legs aside and sat on the end of the lounge.

She wouldn't look at him, and he touched beneath her chin and forced her to meet his gaze. "It's not my business, so don't think you must tell me a thing." But Cain could see the memories clouding her eyes and prepared himself.

She took a deep breath, then let it out and when she spoke, her voice was dry and monotone, as if she had told this story many times before. He suspected she had. "Randall and I dated a few times and he was nice enough, spending way too much money on the dates, but there was something about him that gave me the creeps. I couldn't point a finger at it, but it was there. So I broke it off and everything changed."

"He stalked you."

"No, not at first. He'd show up at my place and want to come in. Then he'd appear at the strangest places, and since we knew some of the same people, I couldn't attribute it to stalking." She sat up, drawing her legs cross-legged. "But he'd butt into conversations, touch me. You know, behaving like the boyfriend, and of course, no one would say anything to him because he was popular, and admired and rich." She turned her gaze to the water. "I went to his place to tell him to back off and he had pictures of me all over the place."

"Good God."

"Yeah. Beautifully framed, I might add. That's when I knew for sure he was dangerous."

She fidgeted and Cain grasped her hand. She gripped back and met his gaze. Tears wet her eyes but never fell.

"I called the police but since he hadn't hurt me,

they couldn't do much." She swallowed, the memories crowding in on her and she moistened her lips. "He grew bolder, more arrogant, as if nothing could touch him."

"How so?"

"He left a rose on my car seat, yet my car had been locked. The alarm didn't go off, either. The police suspected he took my keys and made copies."

She pulled free and ran her fingers through her hair. Cain could feel the tension rising in her and wanted to stop her, but she kept going.

"Then I heard sounds. At night. I would get up to investigate and find a window open when I knew I'd locked it. It was stuff like that for a while, then one night, he was in my bedroom."

Cain stiffened. "Excuse me?"

His tone went suddenly dangerous, cutting, and she met his gaze. "I woke in the middle of the night and he was standing over my bed."

"My God, Phoebe, what did you do?"

"I screamed, and he bailed out the window. The police found footprints outside. He'd been there for a while, watching me." The fear that he'd get out and start again had kept her awake nights.

"Why didn't they arrest him?"

"I didn't get a clear look at his face in the dark so I couldn't say it was him for sure."

She shivered, despite the warm evening and Cain shifted closer and rubbed her arms and shoulders. "But you knew it was."

She went into his arms without missing a beat.

"I changed the locks, and my phone number, and signed a restraining order, but when I stepped out of the shower, he was there. He said he belonged there. That I belonged to him."

"Did he touch you?"

Suddenly Phoebe had a death grip on his arm, and Cain pulled her across his lap, holding her tightly. "Phoebe?"

"Yes, yes! All over." Phoebe closed her eyes, trying to banish the memory of that man's hands on her skin, the ugly way he groped her. "He would have done…more if I hadn't fought him. He ran from the house and I called the police, but Randall had worked up a nice alibi and it couldn't be disputed right away." She was hoping her lawyer could do that at the trial. "I looked like a neurotic paranoid fool after that. I felt like I was the criminal. They had a cruiser drive by at night, but I was so scared I couldn't sleep at all." Her voice wavered and Cain felt immersed in her emotions. "Thank God one of the detectives believed me, and on his own time he sat outside my place."

"When did they catch him?"

She stared at her fingers, one of his making slow circles on the back of her hand. It was so incredibly soothing, she thought, and the words came easily.

"When he held a knife to my throat." Cain tensed against her and she could feel his anger rising. She met his gaze. "He was outside in the dark when I went to put out the trash one night. He said if he couldn't have me, no one would." She let out a slow trembling breath. "Then he forced me back inside. The police were there, watching, and I didn't think they'd get inside in time. They did, but not before he cut me." She flicked at the curls on her neck to show him the scar.

Good God, it was at her jugular.

Cain bent and kissed it, then sheltered her in his arms. Phoebe inhaled his scent, curled into him and her fear began to slide away.

"He's going to jail," Cain murmured, wanting Kreeg to pay dearly for this.

"Don't talk about that. I don't want to, not anymore. Kiss me, Cain, I need you."

He did.

Deeply, hotly. And she curled into his body, loving when his hands rode up her thighs, her hips, then under her shirt. He cupped her breasts, his fingertips smoothing the delicate lace of her bra and his kiss grew stronger. The skies unleashed, water drenching them in seconds, yet his hand slipped between her thighs. She pressed him to her warm center and he rubbed, aching to have her bare beneath his touch again, to hear her cries when she climaxed for him.

"Oh, Cain."

"I want you." Madly, desperately, he thought.

"Me, too. I have for nine years."

He hesitated. "I'm not the same man."

"That's a good thing," she whispered, smiling, and wanted to be lying with him not across his lap.

Cain didn't think so, and with her cradled in his arms, he stood and walked with her through the silent house.

"Are we going where I think we are?" she said, and he liked the lightness in her tone, but couldn't allow himself to fall for it.

"No. You're going to bed." She made a face, looping her arms around his neck.

He entered her suite and laid her on the center of the bed, covering her.

"Alone?"

Good grief, the woman could tempt a saint and Cain wondered when his resolve would shatter. "Sleep, Phoebe, you've had enough for one night."

"You're babying me."

"I want to, let me. Sleep, no one will hurt you. I'll be right here." He pulled a chair close and sat.

"You could be right here," she said, yawning hugely and plucking at the bedsheets.

He gnashed his teeth, thinking he was damn noble, and wished she'd just conk out before he got stupid.

Like a charm, the earlier cocktail sent her into sleep quickly, and Cain stretched his long frame out in the chair that was too delicate for his size.

As if waiting till she was most vulnerable, Kreeg invaded her dreams. She twisted, again trying to crawl away. Then she kicked out violently, flinched and gasped, and Cain could only imagine the details of her trauma as he quickly came to her, braving her flailing fists to gather her in his arms. She made a pitiful, angry sound and he whispered her name and how he'd never let anyone hurt her again. She didn't wake, yet a tear slid down her cheek. He drew her into the curve of his body, his arms wrapped tightly as he lay down on the bed. After a moment she settled, calling his name in a whimper that cut through to his bones.

Cain squeezed his eyes shut, hurting for her, and offered her the only thing he could: soft whispers and his strength. When he wanted to give her the world.

Eight

Phoebe was descending the stairs, dressed in Suzannah's old riding habit when she saw Cain.

She smiled, her heart doing a little dance as she neared. Nobody made her feel the way he did. His dark looks and angled features were to die for, but it was his soulful eyes that got to her. They seemed to dig into her heart and make a home there, and beg her to set him free from this self-imposed prison.

Last night, he'd held her through her dreams, keeping her safe from them, and she'd never felt so protected and cherished. He'd become her port in her private storm. She wished she could be that for him.

"Out again?" he said, leaning on the banister and looking more relaxed than ever.

"I have at least five acres I haven't seen yet."

"It's just fields."

"I know, but it's neat to see them filled with crops." He made a sour face, and she gave him a playful shove. "You've been around it all your life, you take it for granted. But the food and textiles have grown here on the same land for hundreds of years. Sort of unusual nowadays."

He stared thoughtfully. "The strangest things amuse you."

"I know. I'm a cheap date." She stopped on the last step at his eye level and met his gaze. Her entire body ached for him, her mouth tingling to be kissed. "Join me?" She'd asked before, but he never had.

Cain thought for a second, the temptation of being alone with her far outweighing the reasons he shouldn't. "In about a half hour?" He flicked at the sheaf of papers he held.

Her expression lit with excitement, making her eyes bright. "Really? I'll ask Mr. Dobbs to saddle Pegasus. Shall I wait or meet you?"

"By the stream. It's going to rain again, though, so we won't have a long ride."

"I'll take what I can get." She leaned and kissed him softly.

Cain's hand immediately gripped her waist and pulled her off the last step and into his arms. The papers fell to the floor as Phoebe sank into him. His mouth moved heavily over hers, his hands expressing his banked passion as they slid up her rib cage, her back and pressed her ever harder.

Phoebe wanted to drag him into the nearest room and explore this with him.

Then someone cleared his throat.

Cain drew back slowly, his breathing labored, and he loved that she didn't open her eyes right away, as if savoring the sensations that exploded between them.

Then they both looked toward the sound.

Benson stood near the door, actually smiling, a riding helmet in his hand.

Phoebe didn't say a word except to brush her lipstick off his lips, then went to Benson, taking the helmet.

"I'll be waiting," she said with a glance back, her eyes begging him not to disappoint her.

Cain wouldn't.

Or at least he didn't mean to, but a half hour later, he walked to the stable in time to see her riderless horse trot toward him.

He groaned. She was going to be mad, he thought, grabbing the mount's reins. Dobbs rushed out to take the animal, and then looked around.

"Where's Miss Phoebe, sir?"

Cain's gaze shot to the saddled horse, the stables, then to Dobbs. "She's not here already?" Cain asked carefully, his heartbeat skipping when he realized the mount was winded.

"You saw, sir. The horse came back without her."

"Oh, God." Cain ran into the stable and was astride his stallion and leaping out the exit before Dobbs could say more. At breakneck speed, he headed to the stream, panic racing harder with the pounding of the horse's hooves. His imagination tortured him with a short burst of dangerous pictures as he rounded a curve, branches swiping at his clothes.

Overhead the black clouds formed and collided, threatening to unleash their wrath before he found her.

Then he did, on her back under a tree, and his heart tumbled to his stomach as he yanked back on the reins. The horse reared, pawed the air, then dropped its hooves to the ground with a hard thump as Cain threw himself off and raced to her.

"Phoebe!" He grabbed her up in his arms. "Are you all right? Are you hurt?"

"No. I'm fine. My dignity's bruised, though."

Cain let out a long breath, clutching her tightly, realizing exactly how terrified he was, how much she meant to him. Then he showed her, cupping her face and kissing her wildly.

She responded instantly, and the power of his kiss drove her head back, her body arching into his. Heat bubbled and flowed between them, the wind doing nothing to cool the passion that boiled over and took them with it. Cain tasted her like a madman, a starved man, and he knew he was. She was an addiction, a deep need in his heart that cried out to be satisfied. Having more of her would never be enough, yet his mind warned him that the tempest would erupt and there would be no stopping it.

"You've scared the life out of me three times," he said fiercely against her mouth, then kissed her again.

The dogs, at the river, and now this, she thought. "Yeah, I know."

He cupped her jaw and met her gaze. *"Stop it."*

Phoebe saw real fear for her in his eyes. "I'm sorry. It wasn't intentional."

"I know. I know… What happened?"

"A branch knocked me back and I lost my seat."

He peppered her face with kisses, wanting to take her to the ground and have her now. "Thank God, you weren't thrown."

"Tell that to my butt."

He smiled against her mouth. "Want me to rub it?"

"Oh yes, please." His gaze slid to hers and her expression went sly and sexy. "Never offer if you aren't ready to do it."

He hands slid from her waist, cupped her behind, and massaged gently.

"Oh man," she said, and he groaned with her. She wiggled against him, wanting to stay right there.

"This opens a door, Phoeb."

She framed his face in her tiny hands. "Been open for a long time, Cain." Her tongue snaked out to lick his lips. "Stop knocking and walk through." The challenge turned her green eyes smoky.

"Good God, I didn't need to hear that," he said, but the temptation of Phoebe DeLongpree was more than any man should have to suffer. He ducked his head, and laid his mouth luxuriously over hers again. Overhead, the sky darkened, and storm clouds rumbled inland from the river as he tasted her.

Rain fell. Lightning cracked and she flinched. Cain dragged himself from her arms and went to the horse, climbing up, then tipped his booted foot out. She placed hers on his instep and he leaned, slipped his arm around her waist, and hoisted her up to deposit her on his lap, side saddle.

"So gallant," she said, and shivered dramatically.

"We're going to get drenched again," he murmured against her lips, then drank her in again.

She nipped at his lower lip, her desire for him pounding with the thunder. "It's just water."

Things were so simple for her, he thought as he nudged the horse toward home.

But the motion of the horse ground her behind into his groin. Cain shifted her, mumbling under his breath.

"I'm too heavy."

"No, you're making me...insane."

"Yeah, I can feel it," she teased, and his eyes darkened, the strain showing in his features. "You'll be ready for the loony bin soon."

Rain splashed over them, water dripping down his handsome face. His gaze was coal-black and intense, and Phoebe felt a tidal wave of emotions at the powerful stare. He seemed on the brink of something, his body tense, edgy.

"Save me then," he said. More than just teasing, more than a consent between them, his words held a desperate plea for her. He'd denied himself the pleasures of people, of simple delights, and while Phoebe wanted to solve the reasons, she simply kissed him.

And he possessed her. The passion they'd shared before rose fast and furiously to a new height, a new place and Phoebe felt swallowed whole and consumed down to her heels.

He stretched her across his lap, his hand hurriedly

mapping her curves, dipping between her thighs to rub and tease. Rain melted over them, into their kiss and Phoebe drove her fingers into his hair and held him, telling him she wanted more, wanted anything he did. And in the kiss, she let all her doubts fall away and soak into the ground with the falling rain.

She hungered for him, and while she knew in her heart her own feelings, she didn't dare bring them out. He would hurt her again and she asked herself, "Will you risk hurt for him?" And her heart shouted, "Yes."

Cain let go of the reins to hold her, his hands skimming her impatiently from breast to thigh and back again. Phoebe arched in his embrace, the horse jolted and Cain gripped her, laughing and curling her around him.

"Good God, we'll end up in the mud."

"Hmm…kinky."

He chuckled darkly and laid his mouth over hers again, his tongue slipping between her lips and teasing her with the motion. Near the stable, the horse quickened its pace and Cain tore his mouth from hers and drew on the reins.

In the pouring rain, he met her gaze, and she could see the question in his eyes. Did she want to take this further?

She touched his jaw and in a single kiss answered, begged to be fulfilled. Right now.

He eased her down, then hopped off as Dobbs rushed out.

"Oh, thank the lord you're all right, Miss Phoebe."

She glanced at the man, smiled. "I am, Mr. Dobbs, thank you."

Quickly, Cain positioned her in front of him. "Please don't move."

She twisted a look at Cain, amused, and feeling the evidence of their playing pressing warmly to her behind. "Now would I do that to my rescuer?"

"You'd do anything to tease me."

Oblivious, Dobbs took the reins and led the horse away, saying, "Gonna be a big storm. Best get out of it and them wet clothes before y'all get sick."

Cain winked at her. "Yes, we best."

She grinned. "Race yah," she said and she shot toward the house.

Cain blinked, staring after her, then chased her down. He caught her in the mudroom, snagging her around the waist, and went crazy kissing her.

"Here? Oh fun," she said, working off her muddy boots.

"Hell no, but I have to touch you. Everywhere."

Excitement coursed through her as Cain toed off his boots, then grasped her hand, pulling her into the house. He paused in the back hall, looking around.

"You're sparing my reputation, how sweet."

He glanced. "I should send them all home."

"Do." She slid her hand provocatively over his flat stomach, her fingertips grazing his erection. "I plan to be vocal."

"Oh God," Cain groaned and swept her up in his arms, bolting toward the staircase and taking the steps two at a time.

Phoebe laughed at his enthusiasm and he silenced her with a kiss at the top of the stairs, then let her legs go. She stood on her toes, her body pressed against his, his back to the wall. His hands were busy rediscovering her contours, enfolding her breasts to thumb her nipples in deep circles through her wet shirt. She whimpered and leaned into his touch, yanking his shirt from his trousers, and driving her hands up his bare chest. He made a growling sound of such dark hunger, Phoebe felt empowered.

Then the sound of voices floated up from downstairs.

"Oh no, spies," he whispered, then wiggled his brows.

Phoebe was captivated by the freedom in his smile, and when he pulled her toward the west wing and the wide double doors of the master suite, she didn't hesitate. The antiques, and the opulent decor blurred around her. All she saw was Cain. How, in his own way, he cared deeply for her. He'd limited himself for five years, but now, he wasn't. Then outside the doors, he stopped and looked at her intently.

"Are you sure? Nothing will be the same."

She gazed up at him, seeing how greedy he was for her and knew it mirrored her own passion. If nothing came of this beyond one night, she told herself, it was a precious moment in time she would cherish and accept.

"I'm sure, Cain. Are you?"

"I don't think there is a question in my mind that I couldn't reason away, but God help me, I want you so badly." At the last word, his mouth came down on hers and he backed up and nudged the door open, then maneuvered her inside.

He kicked the door closed behind them, drawing back to look her in the eye. Something had changed. Phoebe felt him quake, the restrained power in his tall body, and it thrilled her. She touched the side of his face, her feelings and her desire for him overwhelming her. He was so handsome, and so different right now. His damp hair was wildly mussed, far from the well-manicured way he'd looked when she'd first seen him. His clothing was wet and muddy, and he appeared more rugged than elegant, more real than the fearsome beast she'd met two weeks ago.

"I like you like this," she said, gripping his belt and tugging him near. "Messy, relaxed."

"I'm far from relaxed."

"Oh?" She opened the buckle.

"I feel like I'm about to crack in half." He smoothed his hands over her hair and cradled her face. "I'm almost afraid to let go."

Something tightened around her heart, clamping down hard and squeezing her breathless.

"I don't want to hurt you."

But you will, she thought. *You won't leave Nine Oaks and that hurts me. Hurts us.*

Yet she said nothing, leaning into his body, and he snatched her up, kissing her madly, the force of it bending her back over his arm.

"You taste so good," he murmured. "I can't wait. I can't."

His gaze traveled over her as she stood stretched out to him, nearly limp under his touch, and his hand moved up to her waist, savoring the feel of her cool damp skin before he slipped under her shirt and filled his palm with her breast. She made a sweet sound and he pushed the wet shirt and bra upward, baring her to the heat of his mouth. Warm lips met her cool flesh and she shrieked at the contact, then moaned as he laved, his lips tugging at her nipple, sending tight clawing desire spiraling outward.

He kept tasting and the feelings magnified and blossomed.

She let him have what he wanted, loving the fierceness of his touch, the gentleness of his embrace. She crossed her arms, pulling her shirt off and dropping it to the floor. The bra followed. She straightened and worked her slacks off.

Cain was treated to the erotic sight of peeling fabric and flawless flesh. It left him incapable of moving, his gaze ripping over her. She wore only a black thong. She moved closer, unfastening his shirt buttons, but Cain couldn't be bothered and tore off his shirt, popping buttons in his eagerness to feel her skin next to his.

Phoebe was almost stunned by the sight of his body. The muscles molded his frame like sculptured ropes of power, flexing as he tossed aside the shirt.

"What?" he said when she stared.

"You don't sit behind a desk all the time."

"I have a lot of time on my hands."

Now he was hers. He was her prisoner, and she explored him, her hands gliding delicately over his skin. The simple act tightened his grip on her waist. Then she slicked her tongue across his nipple and he trembled for her.

She pulled his belt free, swinging it once before she dropped it, then sent his zipper down. His hands curled into fists, knuckles popping, and she could taste the tension in him, see it in the flex of his jaw. He was hard perfection and this would be fast and heated, she knew. There was nothing stopping their first taste of each other and she planned on it going on for a while.

Forever, if she had a choice. The thought made her still for a second.

"Phoebe."

"There are no rules, Cain. Not with us."

Then her hand dipped inside his trousers, and she enfolded him. He slammed his eyes shut, throwing his head back with a deep growl of male pleasure. His throat worked, his arousal flexed in her hand.

She stroked him, pushing his trousers down and he looked at her, pulling her hand free.

"I won't make it," he said honestly and was surprised he had any control left.

He kissed her, his hands sweeping her ripe body, teasing her with a dip and stroke, then slipping inside her panties and toying with her center. Her breathing increased, and Cain wanted more of her, needed her so desperately and for a moment, he wondered how he'd survived all these years without her.

Then he gripped the delicate thong, and tugged. It popped and he tossed it aside.

"Oh, you enjoyed that."

"Every man's fantasy? You betcha."

He moved forward till her back was braced on the bedpost, the giant Rice bed looming beyond, tempting them with wild play. But Cain wanted to have his fantasy with Phoebe, to play out the dreams that had been torturing him since she walked through the door again. His hands on her waist slid upward, coasting under her arms and pushing them high. Then he wrapped her hands around the carved post. "Hold on."

"I'll need to?"

"Yeah." His look was savagely erotic with promise. "Don't let go."

She smiled, and he bent and took her nipple deep into the hot suck of his mouth. She inhaled and moaned, arching and with his knee, he spread her thighs, his fingers sliding warmly and smoothly, teasing her with light pressure. She was vocal, telling him how good that felt, wanting more, deeper, longer strokes, and her hips thrust into his touch. But he wouldn't give her what she wanted, not enough to satisfy her, and she was panting, begging him.

It was exactly what he wanted. She was a strong woman, candid and outspoken, and Cain had little power. Here he did.

He discovered her, what made her squirm, what brought her closer to the edge of a climax. His mouth found the sweet under-curve of her breast, the ticklish spot on her ribs, and he heard her gasp when he dragged his tongue down the line of muscle to her navel.

He swirled and licked, and her legs softened. She gripped the post. "Cain. Oh Cain."

He ran his hand over her behind, pausing to dip into her and stroke her liquid center, then he curled his long fingers around her knee, and lifted it to his shoulder.

"Oh my sweet heaven," she gasped.

He left nothing to chance, no inch of her delectable skin untouched. His broad hands splayed her hips, thumbs teasing her center. He looked up, met her stormy gaze, then peeled her open.

He tasted her.

She slammed her eyes shut, her breath tumbling as he pleasured her. Years alone had not dimmed his expertise, but made him precise and intense. In seconds, she was close, and he possessed the bead of her sex in every way. He brought her near and receded, chuckling when she demanded, when she told him this was divine and he'd get his.

"You first," he growled when she was shivering, till her breathing was fast and hot. Till her body glistened with sweat.

Then he plunged two fingers inside and pushed her over the edge of rapture.

She climaxed beautifully, a ribbon of femininity bending, her body flexing and pawing beneath his touch.

"Cain. Cain!"

He didn't answer, silent in his assault, loving how she spoke of her feelings, of what he did to her body, her heart. And the cries, oh yes, the cries were like music to his ears.

She'd yet to settle past the pulse of her climax, was still in the throes of it when Cain stood, sweeping an arm around her and pulling her with him onto the bed. He shucked his trousers, his erection fiercely hard, and she curled toward him, her hand sliding over his body, pulling him onto her.

"Cain. Now."

He produced a condom and she applied it deftly, quickly, watching his eyes flare, feeling him elongate for her. Her throat went tight again, and she kissed him.

"Now," she said. "Please."

"Yes, now." He plunged deeply, filling her in one smooth stroke.

She felt his trembling all the way to her spine.

He slammed his eyes shut, the pulse of her body trapping him more than he could bear.

When he opened his eyes she was staring at him, then pressed her forehead to his, rasping her thumb over his lips as she said, "I feel like I've waited an eternity for this."

Shock and pleasure riddled him. "Me, too."

The need to move took them, stole her breath as she rose and came back to him.

Gone was the tortured emotion he hid. With each plunge came a new man, the one she knew before life was cruel to his heart. He braced a hand on the headboard and held her gaze as he left her and pushed home. She wrapped her legs around his hips, and pulled him deeper, wanting him harder, faster, but he was intent on her pleasure, on satisfying her when she knew he was ready to explode.

The wet slide of him pulsed with savage desire. Their pace quickened. The bed shook, their climax rushing ahead of them.

Cain wanted to slow down but it was impossible. He thirsted, his need to claim her, if only this way, was rooted in his being. Not in sex.

His hips pistoned, her body a slick glove pulling pleasure from him. She splayed her hands on his chest, taunting him with words, with her hands.

She hid nothing from him, open and bare, and for a moment, they watched him disappear into her. He met her gaze, loving that she was not timid, that she was herself in all aspects. Her boldness was part of her, her need to find freedom in everything, and Cain clutched her close to his heart, hoping to know it, share it. Even when he knew he would not.

Their gazes locked, the searing heat destroying his reservations about himself, her, his life.

"This will never be enough," he said. "Never."

"I know. I know."

And he lowered onto her, cupping her buttocks and rolling to his back with her locked to him.

She rose up, smiling, knowing she had the power and he gave it to her.

On a mound of pillows, Cain enjoyed the splendor of her, leaning up to capture her nipple. Her hips shot forward, her body sliding slickly onto his. She gripped his shoulders, holding his gaze, her quick breaths, her tender pleas to join her were enough to destroy him. He was there, sheer will keeping the explosion back and he dribbled his hands down her body and touched the bead of her sex with infinite care. She slammed down onto him and found rapture.

The eruption tore through them with bone-racking power. The pound of bodies tore passion from its cage and Cain gripped her, grinding her to him and she answered the push, equal in her pleasure, her need, her demand.

He cried out her name.

She cupped his face, and thrust, experiencing his pleasure, watched it darken his eyes, turn them liquid wild, releasing all he kept banked from the world.

Feminine muscles tightened, and his shattering pulse made him buck. She held on, suspended and fused with him, and they clutched for long breathless moments, riding the wave of their pleasure.

Phoebe collapsed on him, breathing hard, and Cain held her, silent, his chest aching with emotions he didn't want to examine. He kissed her hair, her cheek, and when she lifted her head to look at him, there was a tear in her eye.

"Phoebe?"

"I knew it would be like this, you know."

He stared for a moment, thinking of lies he might tell, ways to keep his heart out of this, but right now, he couldn't. "Yeah, I think, so did I."

She laid her head down and sighed, and Cain felt at once free and chained tighter to his past.

Nine

Cain stood on the balcony outside the master suite, staring at the moon glistening on the river. The view was spectacular, despite the shifting storm clouds threatening to unleash again. Yet a gale raged inside him and he glanced back at the bed.

The air-conditioning stirred the drapes, revealing the tiny beauty sprawled in his bed. The last few hours bloomed in his mind with the power to leave him hungry for more of her.

What have I done?

Cain didn't regret the last hours; the passion between them was unlike anything he'd experienced before with any woman.

But then, he knew it would be.

It was the reason he'd avoided her since that first kiss under the stairs. She consumed him, and he felt almost obsessed with having her again. Always. He could spend a lifetime with her, and he'd never have enough of her sweet, vibrant energy.

But morning would bring reality, he thought, and when she stirred on the sheets, he was reluctant to speak to her.

To end it.

He forced himself to move toward her, tugging the sash of his robe. She rolled to her back, her bare body seductively draped in sheets.

"I'm hungry. Feed me."

He chuckled to himself and settled on the edge of the bed. She sat up and scooted close, her slender arms sliding around his neck. She kissed him, the heat gathering and stealing Cain's will. With a groan, he deepened the kiss and drew her across his lap, running his hand upward from her thigh till he cupped her bare breast. He rolled her nipple under his thumb, feeling it peak deliciously for him.

She arched into his touch, gasping for air. "I'm *really* hungry."

"So am I."

He pushed her to her back, his warm mouth laving over her breast, drawing on her nipple. She curled toward him, as if all her nerves were locked between his lips.

"Cain, Cain." Frantically, she searched the bedsheets for a condom packet.

His hand slipped between her thighs, fingers sliding and teasing. "You're so beautiful when you're like this." She was spread wide and uninhibited, letting him see every curve, feel every sensation he created in her.

"Now," was all she said, tearing at his sash. She enfolded him, sheathing him as he moved between her thighs.

"Phoebe." He hadn't meant for it to go this far.

He thrust, burying himself in her, and she arched passionately, then jerked back till he left her completely. He plunged again. And again.

And she coaxed him faster, her hands taunting his restraint, and braced above her, Cain withdrew and answered the rushing passion.

They were savage, flesh meeting flesh and melting into one stream of heat and desire. He was afraid he'd hurt her yet she answered him, wild and erotic. The clash pushed them across the bed till she was gripping the headboard and begging him to let go. He gripped her hips bringing her to him, a passionate command quickly taking them over the edge of passion and into a spine-tingling climax.

His gaze never left hers. Her eyes expressed her desire, and something more. Something he'd longed to see in a woman—in Phoebe.

It slayed him.

Because even as they collapsed onto the bed, Cain knew he couldn't have her. Not the way he wanted. Completely. Phoebe would want the same from him, and he could not give it.

Ever.

Sheltering the feelings in his heart was far better than seeing loathing in her eyes.

Cain stood at the foot of the bed, staring down at her as he buttoned his shirt. She'd slept all night without waking. Probably for the first time since Kreeg had ruined her life. While it pleased him, Cain knew they'd made a mistake.

He'd made the mistake.

He should have shown more willpower, he should have kept his distance. But with her, he had no will and he'd only himself to blame.

But Phoebe would be hurt. He hated himself for it already, yet she'd expect him to leave Nine Oaks and return to the life he had before Lily died.

He wouldn't. In that, nothing had changed.

His chest tightened, a knot locking around his heart. When she rolled to her side and smiled at him, Cain savored it for a moment, memorizing the look of pure contentment on her face.

"Good morning." She rose to her knees, naked and rosy and the temptation to have her again nearly stole his breath. He would never have enough of her and without asking, he knew she'd want more than he could give.

"You're dressed already?"

"I have work to do."

"Could I interest you in taking another day off?" On her knees, she reached, her fingertips dipping beneath his belt and tugging him closer.

"Phoebe, last night—"

"Was great."

"It was magnificent, however—"

Frowning, Phoebe let go and eased back, a horrible feeling skating over her spine. "However what?" She could feel the blow coming before it struck.

"I think this was a mistake."

Tension leaped into her and she snatched up the sheet, pulling it with her as she left the bed. "How can you say that?"

"Passion isn't everything."

"It's a damn good start and who says that's all there is? Don't you know how I feel about you?"

Please don't say more, he thought. *Please don't.*

"It wouldn't matter."

"Oh really? Why?"

"I won't leave Nine Oaks, Phoebe, and I know you're expecting me to now."

Angry heat flamed her face. "Don't tell me what I'm thinking or what I want, and yes, I do want you to leave here, but for your sake, not mine! Good God, you are so dense sometimes." She threw the sheet around her like a toga. "I want you to come back to the real world, Cain, for you. You're not happy and you won't be till you face what's out there." She gestured to the balcony. "And making love with you has nothing to do with it. You've hidden long enough. I know Lily did something to make you this way, and right now, I hate her for it."

Cain said nothing.

Phoebe felt it, that door slamming, the emotional shield closing him off from her.

And it hurt.

God, it hurt.

Her heart burned, her eyes seared and she blinked. "Damn you, Cain. It doesn't need to be like this."

Her tears destroyed him, each one cutting him to ribbons down to his soul. Cain wanted things to be different, wished to God that he'd followed his heart nine years ago and not his head. But right now, his head was clear. Staring into her teary eyes, he knew—his heart was breaking.

She moved toward the door.

"Phoebe."

"Go to hell, Cain." She stepped out the door and shut it behind herself.

I don't need to go to hell, Cain thought, staring at the empty room. *I'm in it.*

And he'd made it himself.

Phoebe hurried toward her rooms, covering her mouth, and wanting to scream *why!* Inside her room, she shut the door and fell back against it. The tears came, hard and mean, and she crumpled to the floor in a heap, and let them fall. She cried for the man Cain once was, for the one she'd glimpsed this week, and last night, for the passion they'd shared and never would share again.

He couldn't see a future, refused to see anything beyond the walls of Nine Oaks. Drawing him out had changed nothing and Phoebe told herself she had to face the fact that the past few days were merely a vacation from reality.

He's still in a damn cave, she thought.

Cain heard the chink of china and looked up as Benson deposited the tray on his desk with more force than necessary.

"Will there be anything else, sir?"

Cain frowned at his bitter tone. "No, Benson. Thank you." Yet Benson didn't move, staring down at him as if looking down his nose in disgust. "Have you something to say?" Cain asked.

"Yes, sir."

"And?"

"You're an ass, sir."

Cain's brows shot up.

"You have allowed that witch Lily to ruin your life yet again, and now you are also letting her ruin Miss Phoebe's."

"You've seen her?" Cain hadn't seen Phoebe in two days. They'd avoided each other when Cain wanted nothing more than to go to her. But he had nothing to say.

"Yes, I have. At present she is in the gym, sir, beating the stuffing out of a punching bag."

Cain scowled darkly. "Anything else, Benson, since you seem to be airing your feelings today?"

"Not anything I'd want repeated in civilized company, *sir.*" Benson spun around and left, shutting the door hard.

Cain threw down his pen and mashed a hand over his face. Great. He left his offices and headed to the gym where, as Benson said, she was going to town on a punching bag.

The instant he drew near, she stopped, met his gaze, then went back to pounding.

"Phoebe."

"I'd stand clear if I were you."

"I took advantage of you, and I'm sor—"

She stilled, glaring at him and cut him off with, "If you try to apologize for making love to me, I'm going to break something *very* expensive. And we took advantage of each other. And you know what?" She walked up to him breathing hard, sweating, and he wondered if he should duck. "I loved it. Every second of it. And I don't regret it."

"Neither do I!"

"Then why are you apologizing?" The pain and hurt in her eyes stung him again. He was right in doing this, he knew. She would not stay here, locked away, and he'd never expect her to. Cain could face Phoebe, but not the world beyond Nine Oaks. Not the crimes he'd committed.

"I've hurt you."

"You're hurting yourself and you're lying to yourself. Big, strong, rich and powerful Cain Blackmon, and you let some ghost haunt you?"

"And you're letting Kreeg haunt you," he threw back.

"Kreeg is not stopping me from enjoying life. He's stopping me from a good night's sleep." She lifted her gloved hand to her mouth and used her teeth to free the knots. Cain came to her, holding the glove and helping her.

"You're wasting your life."

"It's mine to waste."

She lifted her gaze to his. "And what about me, Cain? Do I mean nothing to you?"

His eyes flared. "You mean everything to me."

Somwhere in her heart, a spark lit. "Then tell me about Lily, about the rotting boat on the shore."

Cain went still as glass, his gaze riveted to her, but not seeing her. "No."

"Why?"

"No!" He turned and left.

Phoebe sagged and threw the gloves across the room and snatched up a towel, wiping her face. She'd had free access to everything except the boats. Lily had died in a boating accident.

Refusing to let this go, she left the gym, listening for the sound of his voice, his footsteps. She found him on the back veranda, his hands on the stone rail, his shoulders stiff. His head was low, as if a great weight pushed it down.

"I understand your need to shut out the world, Cain. I did that. But now it's time to get back in and fight."

"Leave it alone, Phoebe. Please."

"Don't leave me, Cain," she said softly. He lifted

his gaze to hers. "You left me nine years ago. Don't do it again." Tears choked her throat, fracturing her voice.

She loved him. In that splintered moment, she knew it without a doubt.

"Phoebe, I can't. You don't know what I've done."

"Then tell me and let's work past it."

His ugly past pressured him to cut the ties and go back to the way things were before she entered his life again. He didn't want to. God, he wanted her to stay, to be a part of his life, just as she was a part of his heart.

She was the breath that moved each day along, he thought.

"Cain, talk to me."

"It's no use, Phoebe." She'd despise him and be gone anyway, he thought. "I can't give you what you want. I won't leave here and I won't ask you to stay.

"And if you did? What do you think I'd say?"

"It would be cruel to you, sweetheart." He passed a hand over her hair, cupped her jaw. "You're so vibrant and alive."

"And you were last night, too."

His lip twitched, and Cain gazed into her soulful eyes, and wanted to end his seclusion. "I will not leave here."

Her expression fell and she stepped back. "Then I will."

"What?"

"I'm leaving. In the morning."

"It's your choice." The heart-wrenching pain in his chest made his words soft, and as she turned away, Cain knew he was watching his one chance at something wonderful slip through his fingers.

She won't be here every day, a voice said. Cain wondered how he'd survive. How he'd breathe without her near.

Phoebe hung up the phone, old fear skating through her. She hugged herself, walking through the house without any direction. Beyond the walls a storm raged in tandem with her feelings.

"Who was on the phone?"

She stopped, refusing to look at Cain. "No one."

"Phoebe."

"Leave it alone. I don't need your help."

"I want to help." He reached for her, touching her shoulder and she flinched and whipped around to glare at him.

And Cain saw fear. He frowned. "Phoebe, tell me what's wrong? What's happened?"

"That was my lawyer. Or rather the one you hired. The trial starts tomorrow."

"That's good then. It will be over soon."

"He'll get off and it will never be over!"

She rushed away from him, leaving him standing in the foyer, watching her race up the stairs. Cain spun on his heels and went to his offices, dialing the lawyers. Phoebe refused to testify.

If she didn't, then Kreeg walked.

She'd spend her life looking over her shoulder in fear and want to hide from the world. *She'd become him.* He couldn't let that happen and he hurried to her suite, opening the doors without knocking.

"You have to testify."

"No, I don't."

"Phoebe, he committed a crime against you, you have to put him away."

"The evidence speaks for itself."

"But your testimony could clinch it."

"I can't," she cried.

Cain's heart softened, and he went to her, kneeling beside the chair, and forcing her to look at him.

"You're scared."

"I can't look at him, I can't. He hurt me, he touched me. And I know he'll have the best lawyers and money, and get off. I'm nobody."

"No, you're not. You can do this."

She shook her head, and Cain saw her recovery in the last weeks crumbling. "You can't hide from it. You'll never be safe if you don't put him away." He swallowed hard. "And then you'll turn into me."

She met his gaze. "That's not so bad."

"Yes, it is." His expression darkened. "And I won't allow it."

"And just how will you do that?"

"I'll go with you."

Her eyes flared wide. "What?"

Cain took a deep breath before he said, "I'll escort you to the trial and stay right beside you."

She was silent for a moment as his words hit her. He'd leave Nine Oaks? He'd break a five-year seclusion for her? "Do you realize what your appearance in public will do? It will cause more stir than the trial."

"Then attention will be on me and not you, right?"

"Why? Why would you do this?"

"I want you to feel safe again, Phoebe, and if you don't go and tell the jury what he did to you, then he could walk away and do the same thing to another woman." Or to her again, he thought, but knew he'd never let that happen.

"Cain." Tears slid down her cheek.

"I'll be with you, baby. I swear, I'll protect you."

She fell into his arms, clinging tightly, touched beyond thought, beyond breathing. Over her shoulder Cain squeezed his eyes shut, realizing he wanted Phoebe's happiness more than he did his own.

Ten

When Cain Blackmon stepped back into the real world, he did it with style, Phoebe thought. A chopper had landed on the Nine Oaks front lawn, and flew them to the airport where they boarded a Gulfstream jet and headed toward California for the trial.

"You're gawking," he said with a gentle smile.

She kept looking around the lush cabin. "You've never used this, have you?"

"Suzannah does, and my other employees. But no, I haven't."

But he was using it for her.

The impact of what he was doing hit her all over

again. He left five years of seclusion behind to be with her now. To shield her. And if she loved him before, she loved him more today. He met her gaze, a tiny frown knitting his brow and she wondered if he knew she'd fallen in love with him.

"I hate flying by the way."

"You've done admirably well considering we're landing."

The instant they were out of the jet, they were besieged.

"Word's out you're here," she said and he simply smiled tenderly down at her and guided her to the limousine. She saw another side of him, a man who commanded the world around him, and expected to be obeyed. Cameras flashed, people shouted, and yet she felt safe and guarded in a mad crowd of onlookers. Cain said nothing, refusing to respond to a single question even when they were offensive and cruel. His arm around her was a comforting shelter as he escorted her into the courthouse and to her lawyers.

She stilled when she saw Kreeg enter, and that smug smile of his fell when his gaze landed on Cain. He went pale and turned to his attorneys, whispering furiously.

Phoebe looked up at Cain. His expression was murderous as he stared at Kreeg. She nudged him and when he met her gaze, the look evaporated, replaced by a smile.

Bending to kiss her cheek, he whispered, "Be brave. I'm right here. He can't touch you anymore."

The trial proceeded, evidence produced and debated. The lawyers Cain hired were magnificent, and the private detective shed light on Kreeg's past. This wasn't the first time he'd tormented a woman, and a parade of victims on the stand confirmed it. Phoebe's stomach clenched when she had to take the stand, yet she kept her gaze on Cain. He was her anchor, and she gathered strength from him, his encouraging smile, and when Kreeg's lawyers tried to destroy her, they failed.

Then the jury was sequestered. Cain had taken a suite in a nearby hotel and posted guards around the clock to keep the press and the curious away. Watching him take control of the situation, Phoebe didn't say much. She was grateful for his strength.

"Phoebe, you should rest."

She looked up from her perch on the sofa. "I want it to be over."

"It will be." He looked at his watch.

"What's taking so long? It's been a while," she said.

"No, it hasn't. They are deciding a man's future. I'm just wondering where dinner is."

That made her smile, and the corners of his mouth lifted in tandem. He came to sit down beside her.

"Thank you," she said.

"You're welcome."

"It wasn't so hard, was it?"

He thought for a second. "I didn't seclude myself because of the press and nosy people, Phoebe. I secluded myself because I didn't want to be near anyone and inflict my moods on them."

"Well, I've seen some of those moods. They aren't so bad."

He eyed her, knowing the truth.

"Well, you've been wonderful to me," she said.

He smirked to himself. "Yes well, you're hard to resist and difficult to keep away."

"Are you saying I'm pushy?"

"Oh hell, yes."

She laughed and Cain grinned. "Admit it, you've had fun," she said.

"Nah, you'll get an ego."

She gave him a playful shove and unwound her body from the tight curl in the corner of the sofa. "You know the ugly parts of my life, Cain. When will you tell me yours?"

Cain leaned forward and clasped his hands, staring at them. "Phoebe, please understand." Cain could feel the battle boiling inside him, sudden and harsh at the first thought of his crime. The power of guilt was an ugly creature and it had badgered him for years.

"Cain, please."

He didn't answer, and Phoebe could see the emotion simmering under his expression.

"I can't understand any of it, if I don't know the truth."

He rounded on her, his expression contorted in guilt. "You want the truth? Are you sure?"

"Yes, I do."

"I killed my wife, Phoebe. Is that truth enough?"

She reared back. "What? No, that can't be true."

"I let her go out on a boat when I knew she wasn't skilled enough to sail!" He started to stand.

Phoebe pushed him back down. "Whoa, wait a second." She touched his face, making him look at her and his dark, tortured stare broke her heart. "Take a breath."

He did, pushing his fingers through his hair and knowing it was now or never. Cain realized he was simply postponing the inevitable, but he didn't want to lose her now.

"I told you I married her because she carried my child. I didn't love her and I never claimed to love her. She was a weekend in my life that ruined both our lives."

"But she loved you, didn't she?"

"Yes. God, it killed me to see it in her eyes all the time. When she lost the child, I tried to make it work.

But we were strangers in the same house. She wanted me to love her and I couldn't." He looked at Phoebe. "I tried, but it wasn't there." *Not like it is for you*, he thought, and looked away. "And after a couple of months, she knew it never would be. Her feelings turned to hate and anger, and we fought over everything. I talked to my lawyer about filing for divorce. I meant to tell her that night, but she learned it by eavesdropping. We had a terrible fight, said things to each other that were cruel."

"How did she die on the boat?"

"After the fight, she went outside. I knew she was on the property from the cameras and staff. I thought she'd cool off and we could at least part like adults, be civil. She went off like that a lot when we'd argue, but she was gone a long time. So I went to look for her. She was in the boat, just sitting in it. It was tied to the dock and she shouted at me to leave her alone."

Cain rubbed his mouth, then clasped his hands again. He'd never let himself think of that night for long, but now it unfolded in his mind.

"I didn't think she'd take the boat out. She wasn't a skilled sailor, and she knew it!"

"Was there a storm or something? The river is wide, but it's pretty calm."

"No, not at first. The sun was setting and it started to rain, but nothing bad. When she didn't come back near sundown, I went looking again. That's when I realized she'd taken the boat out." He glanced at her. "It wasn't the first time she did something like that to get my attention. So I called the sea rescue, and went looking for her in the speedboat. But even the sea rescue couldn't spot the boat with floodlights. She just vanished." He flopped back into the cushions. "I'd hoped she drew in downriver somewhere south."

"She didn't."

He shook his head. "The rain worsened. I didn't come in, just drifted up and down the shore. I stayed out there all night and in the morning, I found the boat. Then her."

Phoebe could only imagine what he'd felt at that moment, and knew without asking he'd carried that tortured reminder with him ever since.

"Cain, she was skilled enough to bring it in, wasn't she?"

"I don't know." He pushed off the sofa and paced. "No, I know she wasn't. I let her go out on that boat and she died."

"Oh my God. You blame yourself for her death?"

His gaze slammed into hers. "I killed her! I could have stopped her, carried her back into the house, anything to keep her from sailing. I destroyed her, Phoebe. I couldn't love her and it destroyed her."

"Wait a minute, Lily was a grown woman, and she knew her skill level." She stood before him, gripping his arms, wanting him to hear her so badly. "*She* knew she couldn't sail and yet she did. In a storm. It was all intentional. She took that boat out to kill herself!"

Cain shook his head. "Don't you think I want to believe that? She said, 'I'll see you later, I'll come in a minute.' She didn't mean to…"

"Die?"

"Yes. What did the coroner say?"

"No injuries, a drowning."

"She could swim?"

"Yes."

"Then she didn't want to."

"I should have forced her inside. I should have made her come back."

"You should have loved her, isn't that what you're saying?"

He crumpled before her eyes, his shoulders drooping, his head bowing.

"Oh, Cain." She brushed her mouth over his, her throat going tight. "Oh honey, you can't force love when it's not there."

He lifted his gaze to her.

"There's no crime in not loving her. There is when you let it keep *you* from loving."

His features tightened, and he bent, calling her name. Before their lips touched, the phone rang.

Cain straightened, and went to answer it.

Phoebe hugged herself, watching his expression. He gave nothing away as he hung up. "The jury is in," he said. "Let's go."

Cain whisked her away from the courthouse so fast she didn't have time to think about anything but that she was free, and Kreeg was behind bars for a very long time.

On the plane Cain didn't talk, and barely looked at her. It hurt that he wouldn't look at her, yet Phoebe left him to his thoughts. She could see his torment, as if he was reliving his wife's death. When the plane touched down, he looked up as if just realizing he'd been silent for so long. He apologized and within an hour, she was walking back into Nine Oaks.

On the stairs, she looked down at him. "Cain."

"I'll see you in the morning."

Phoebe's heart broke. He didn't have to say it. He was closing himself off. Nothing she'd said had made a difference, and he wasn't letting her share his burden. Now he was letting her go.

"I can't stay here anymore."

He jerked a look up at her. "Yes, you can go home now. You're safe."

"Oh Cain. This is my home." His features went taut. "Don't you know? You have my heart." Her voice broke. "My very soul. And that will never change, but I can't stay with a man who is too trapped in useless guilt to see a future."

His features tightened. "Phoebe, please."

"No, Cain, it doesn't have to be this way. Open your eyes! You didn't do anything wrong! Except give a ghost power over you."

His eyes narrowed, and yet Phoebe simply sighed and turned away. She loved him. She'd always loved him, she realized. And now, she would lose him to a woman who'd been dead for five years.

She came to him like soft fragrance on the breeze, stirring his senses, shifting the air surrounding him.

Cain felt her touch before he heard her whisper his name. He shifted on the bed and saw an image that would stay with him for a lifetime—Phoebe, naked and ethereal, sliding onto his bed and into his arms.

Cain didn't think, didn't question, and when she tipped her head back, meeting his gaze, touching his face, she gave no answers. Then he kissed her, a deep slow kiss of love and passion. The fast heat and demand they'd felt before was tamed. Now the need to show and revere overtook him. In the back of his mind, Cain knew this would be the last time he touched Phoebe.

His patience showed in his touch, in the way he stirred her body. Phoebe took what she wanted for herself, sliding down his body to pleasure him like no other. Cain groaned and yanked her up to him, a look full of sensual promise lighting her heart. He tasted her body, claimed it as he had never done before, with complete possession, taking part of her soul with every kiss.

His hands played over her skin, memorizing her shape, his mouth drawing on her nipples, teeth scraping erotically over the swells of her breasts and lower. Then he spread her wide, and gripped her hips, lifting her to his mouth.

He laved at her center, making her cry out softly, making her squirm for more. Her beauty enthralled him, burned into his mind and still, he tasted her, toyed with her pleasure. It was his, he owned it, he wanted no man to do this to her. Ever. She was his, he thought. No matter what he felt or said, Phoebe was his.

And he showed her, bringing her to peak after peak, skillfully letting her dangle on the edge, then releasing her and covering her body with his.

She spread herself for him and Cain slid smoothly inside her warm wet center. The heat of her nearly undid him and he moved slowly, his tempo measured, her desire blossoming. He wanted to savor each sensation, the womanly muscles gripping and flexing on him, the short gasps tumbling from her lips. He pushed and withdrew, watching her eyes flare, her heart in her beautiful face.

Cain's throat locked and he could barely breathe, knowing this was the last time, and knowing he would die without her in his life.

He groaned her name as he kissed her, quickening, and she clung to him, her limbs wrapped tightly. The spiral of heat climbed as their bodies took control in a powerful rush to find the summit together.

Then it came, a swell of throbbing skin and heated kisses. His tongue plunged into her mouth as his body thrust hard into her. She whispered his name, he called hers and threw his head back as the tight pulse of their climax exploded and fused between them.

The moment suspended, heartbeats matched, passion spreading out like ribbons to tie them together. Cain felt everything with an odd clarity and when he looked down at her, she was smiling, her teary eyes so somber and heartbreaking. Cain felt his heart shatter.

"Don't leave," he said, dragging her to his side. "Don't."

She said nothing, stroking his face, his hair, and then cradling him to her breast.

Cain felt emotion grab him, its powerful surge pulling him in, and he wanted it, desperate to latch on tight. But something else tugged at him, the old feelings, old pain, and it wasn't till he was drifting off to sleep that he realized the chance of his life beckoned, and his ties to his past were only tattered fringes in his mind.

Cain stood several yards from the shore and tossed a match on the ruined sailboat. The dry, old wood flamed quickly and he sat on the ground, watching it burn to ashes.

He let himself be burdened by guilt. When he woke alone this morning, the scent of Phoebe lingered, reminding him what he was losing for the sake of a ghost.

It wasn't so much her words that changed him, it was realizing he hadn't thought of Lily in weeks, not in the way he had in the past. Now she was an old memory he tried to keep alive for all the wrong reasons.

He'd made a mistake by trying to love someone he couldn't. He bore the burden of giving Lily hope when he should have ended their relationship quickly. He would not shoulder the blame any longer.

Not at the cost of his love for Phoebe.

I'm done here, he thought.

Free. Down to his soul.

The wood popped and hissed as Cain let out a deep breath. He'd known he would come to this place, this moment, someday, but it took Phoebe's resilience to make him step this close to his past. She gave him the strength, his love for her overshadowing Lily.

Ashes spiraled toward the sky and he smiled. With it, went his past. His guilt.

Then he heard the sound of an engine and twisted to look toward the house. In the distance, he could see figures near the garages—Benson, Willis, Mr. Dobbs.

And Phoebe.

Cain jumped to his feet, glanced at the dying embers, then ran toward the house.

She was leaving.

Phoebe hugged Benson and tried to hide her tears as she walked to her Jeep. The others departed quickly, and she was opening the door when she heard her name and turned. First she saw the trail of smoke spiraling toward the sky, then Cain walking briskly toward her.

Instantly she noticed something different about him.

"I've never seen you dress like that." His worn jeans molded his body, the T-shirt snug over his wide chest, but it was the ease of his stride, the softness in his moves that caught her in the chest.

"I thought it was time I left some things behind, and buried them forever."

Phoebe's heartbeat skipped and stuttered. "What things?"

He advanced, his steps determined. "The ogre, the guilt. I needed room for other feelings."

"Oh, really?"

He grinned. "God, I love it when you get that sass in your look."

Phoebe's breath caught as he walked right up to her and cradled her face in his cool hands.

"Don't leave me."

Tears blurred his image. "I can't stay here locked away with you."

"Then don't. Open more doors with me." She started to speak, but he kept talking. "Shh, listen to me. I've been an idiot." Her lips quivered at that. "I let myself be trapped, I made my own life more miserable, and yet, you stuck around, you dragged me out of that dark place. Don't give up on us now. After all we've been through, please don't."

She covered his hands. "Oh, Cain."

He swallowed, gazing deeply into her green eyes. "I need you so much I can't breathe without you. You're my life. I love you, Phoebe DeLongpree, *I love you.*"

"Cain." Her breath caught and a tear fell. "I love you, too. I think I have for years."

He smiled, his own eyes burning as he thanked God for her. The other half of his soul. "Stay with me. Make a life with me. Have babies with me." He brushed his mouth to hers. "Marry me, Phoebe. Marry me, please."

She didn't hesitate. "Yes, yes."

"Ahh," he said. "Thank God." He captured her mouth, lifting her off her feet and crushing her in his arms. He peppered her face in kisses and she begged for more, laughing. They tumbled to the grass, the dogs rushing to leap and bound over them and Cain flopped to his back, Phoebe in his arms. She stared down at him, her fingers trailing lightly across his brow.

"I love you," he said, his gaze sketching her face, the sunlight glittering in her hair.

A happy tear trickled down her cheek. "Took you long enough."

He laughed and squeezed her and smiled, and with her nestled at his side on the sun-kissed grass, peace settled over them, wrapping them in a bright future.

Cain kissed the top of her head, and could almost feel his ancestors staring down at them, pleased that Nine Oaks was alive with hope again, that laughter would fill its rooms and shower endless Southern nights with a love that would span centuries.

* * * * *

A sneaky peek at next month...

Desire

PASSIONATE AND DRAMATIC LOVE STORIES

2 stories in each book - only **£5.30!**

My wish list for next month's titles...

In stores from 20th January 2012:

☐ Caught in the Billionaire's Embrace – Elizabeth Bevarly

& The Tycoon's Temporary Baby – Emily McKay

☐ The Proposal – Brenda Jackson

& To Tempt a Sheikh – Olivia Gates

☐ Reunited...with Child – Katherine Garbera

& One Month with the Magnate – Michelle Celmer

☐ A Lone Star Love Affair – Sara Orwig

& Falling for the Princess – Sandra Hyatt

Available at WHSmith, Tesco, Asda, Eason, Amazon and Apple

Just can't wait?

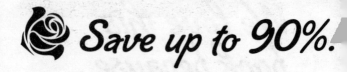

Special Offers

Every month we put together collections and longer reads written by your favourite authors.

Here are some of next month's highlights— and don't miss our fabulous discount online!

On sale
20th January

On sale
20th January

On sale
3rd February

On sale
3rd February

Save 20% on all Special Releases

Have Your Say

You've just finished your book.
So what did you think?

We'd love to hear your thoughts on our
'Have your say' online panel
www.millsandboon.co.uk/haveyoursa

- ❦ Easy to use
- ❦ Short questionnaire
- ❦ Chance to win Mills & Boon®
  goodies

*Visit us
Online*

Tell us what you thought of this book now at
www.millsandboon.co.uk/haveyoursay

YOUR

Mills & Boon® Online

Discover more romance at
www.millsandboon.co.uk

- 🌹 **FREE** online reads
- 🌹 **Books** up to one month before shops
- 🌹 **Browse our books** before you buy

...and much more!

For exclusive competitions and instant updates:

 Like us on **facebook.com/romancehq**

 Follow us on **twitter.com/millsandboonuk**

 Join us on **community.millsandboon.co.uk**

 Visit us online

Sign up for our FREE eNewsletter at
www.millsandboon.co.uk

WEB/M&B/RTL4